Silver Mo

HAVE A COLLECTION
OF 60 GREAT NOVELS
OF
EROTIC DOMINATION

If you like one you will probably like the rest

A NEW TITLE EVERY MONTH

Silver Moon Readers Service
c/o DS Sales Ltd.
PO Box 1100 London N21 2WQ

Distributed to the trade throughout North America by
LPC Group, 1436 West Randolph Street, Chicago, IL 60607
(800) 826-4330

Caged ! first published 2000, copyright Dr. Gerald Rochelle
The right of Dr. Gerald Rochelleto be identified as the author of this book has been asserted in accordance with
Section 77 and 78 of the Copyrights and Patents Act 1988

CAGED !
by
Dr Gerald Rochelle

CHAPTER 1

Deborah had only been working at Theron Exports, a company trading in phosphates from North Africa, for a fortnight and still she had not found very much to do. It was run by Arabs and there were always strangely dressed and unusual looking people coming and going.

There was only one other woman who worked there, Chrissie. Deborah had met her in a club when she had first come to London, alone after the death of her parents and with no other relatives to turn to, hoping to start a new life. It was Chrissie who had got her the job.

Chrissie, like Deborah, was very attractive. They were both slightly built but Chrissie was a little taller than Deborah. Both had long, dark hair but Chrissie's was an intense black and fell around her face in heavy tangles whereas Deborah's was more brown, straighter and was cut slightly shorter. Chrissie had a large mouth with full lips and, when she laughed, her white teeth flashed. When they went out together in the evenings they helped each other with their make up and sometimes Chrissie lent Deborah a skimpy dress which clung to her smooth skin when she danced. They joked about the dress being loose as Deborah's breasts were smaller than Chrissie's. Deborah liked Chrissie, she was the only friend she had, and she looked forward to seeing her each day in the office.

Apart from her boss, Mr Kamil, Deborah had not got to know any of the other staff and when Chrissie had rung to say that she would not be in today Deborah felt lonely and disappointed.

As she scribbled aimlessly on her note pad, she heard some men in the adjoining office talking in heavily accented voices and she pushed herself back on her chair so that she could listen.

"Then they lowered this cage down. A woman was crouching inside it, she was beautiful: long, black hair, small breasts and firm buttocks. She was tied by the wrists, really

5

tight, and the rope was attached to the bars at the top of the cage. She looked desperate and she pleaded for them to ... "

Deborah leaned back further, craning her neck and letting her long hair fall down loosely onto her shoulders.

"In the end, they undid the cage door but she wouldn't come out. A man prodded her with a short whip but she refused to move. She clung onto the rope around her wrists trying to get it loose then she leapt forward and grabbed the bars of the cage like an animal ... "

Deborah felt herself beginning to sweat as she turned her head and moved it closer to the door.

"'Get out bitch!', the man with the whip shouted but still she crouched in the cage. He reached in and she went to bite him and, when he grabbed her white panties, she yanked herself back and they ripped at the waist. You should have seen them hanging down in tatters from her hips. Her cunt was shaved and the material of her panties was caught in her naked crack."

"What happened next?"

"The man with the whip went around the back of the cage and prodded her in the back and finally he drove her out. Then he stood in front of her and forced her onto her knees. 'Suck this bitch!', he shouted as he forced his cock into her gaping mouth.

Deborah felt the veins in her temples throbbing and her heart pounding in her chest as she craned her neck back to listen.

"Then they couldn't stop her from sucking. A couple of others dragged her away and tied her up really tight, then they dragged her around the room shouting at her, 'On your knees bitch! On your knees!', but every time she tried to get up she was knocked down again and they dragged her around more."

Deborah pushed her hands down towards her knees and felt how wet and clammy they were. She squeezed her palms against the insides of her knees and pressed her legs tightly together.

"Then they bent her over this bench, ripped her panties off completely and stuffed them into her mouth. She tried to scream but they wouldn't let her. Every time she opened her mouth they stuffed the white panties in further. Her face went really red as she gulped and fought for breath then Saab came in. Oh yes, she looked amazing, yes, she was dressed in red as usual and she went straight over to the woman and gave her such a beating. Sweat poured from Saab's forehead as she whipped the cane down on the woman's buttocks then she said... ..."

As Deborah strained back, her legs tensed and her knees opened enough for her hands to move upwards. She felt her sweaty palms against the insides of her thighs and, as they moved up to the tops of her smooth, white stockings, she felt the warm softness of her thin, white panties against the backs of her thumbs.

"Then Saab straddled the woman. 'Lick it bitch before your next punishment', she said. The woman reached her face up and they pulled the panties from her mouth. She didn't hesitate, she just stuck her tongue straight in. As she licked Saab between the legs, Saab brought the cane down on the woman's back. The woman screamed like an animal but Saab wouldn't stop until she was satisfied. Then Saab said, 'Bring them in now', and they opened the door and ... "

Deborah pressed her thumbs back and squeezed them against the furrow that ran along the gusset of her white panties. She lifted them away slightly and allowed the soft flesh to part along its crease. As she felt the warmth between her legs, she hung her head back further, straining the muscles of her stomach and causing the furrow of flesh to open even more.

She felt a flush spreading across her face as she thought of the woman in the cage. She pictured her being prodded and whipped and forced to suck, then she thought of her licking the mysterious woman who commanded her obe-

7

dience and demanded her service. Deborah pulled her thumbs higher as she imagined the mysterious woman barking her commands and her heart started pounding wildly as she wondered what it would be like to be enslaved and what other ordeals the caged woman had been forced to suffer.

Deborah wanted to hear more and strained back to listen but all she could hear was her own name being shouted repeatedly. It was as if the men were now talking about her, as if she was the woman in the cage, clinging to the bars and shrinking back as she was prodded and whipped.

"Deborah! Deborah!"

She could see herself reaching her face up between the woman's thighs and extending her tongue towards the beckoning channel of flesh.

"Deborah! Deborah!"

She pulled the gusset of her panties aside and plunged her fingers into the wet crease of her cunt. She felt its moisture running down onto her knuckles as she imagined licking her tongue out and probing it between the fleshy slit that was splayed out before her.

"Deborah! Deborah!"

She felt her tongue reaching out and she tasted the tang of moisture as its tip finally touched the swollen edges of the waiting cunt.

"Deborah! Deborah! Come in here!"

Deborah's eyes rolled back as she felt the insides of her thighs pressing against the backs of her hands then suddenly, she shook herself and looked around wide-eyed and startled.

"Deborah! Deborah!"

It was her boss, Mr Kamil, calling from his office.

"Deborah! Get in here and be quick about it!"

Startled, Deborah pulled her hands from between her thighs. Her white panties were pulled down exposing some of her pubic hair and one of the suspender clips that hung from her white suspender belt had come undone. With shaking

8

hands, she pulled her panties back up and clipped the top of her stocking back into the clasp. She licked her dry lips, jumped up off her chair and smoothed her dress down at the front. Her face was red and flushed and her hair was in a mess. She tried to tidy it as she entered the office but when Mr Kamil looked at her she knew she still looked flustered and dishevelled.

Mr Kamil brushed back a length of black, greasy hair that hung across his forehead.

"Deborah, at last. What have you been doing? You look a mess. Sit down, sit down and tidy yourself up."

Deborah pulled the hem of her dress down over the fronts of her thighs and sat on the hard chair across from Mr Kamil. She felt him looking at her knees and she squeezed them together tightly so that he could not see between them. She did not like the way Mr Kamil looked at her and sometimes, when he had helped her on with her coat, he had run his hands across her breasts and squeezed them before she had moved away.

A tall woman in dark glasses and a long, red overcoat sat beside him. Her long-fingered hands rested casually on the arms of the chair, her fingers dangling like claws over the edges and a thin, gold bangle falling loosely around one of her of her slender wrists. Her black hair was cut short and her lips were neatly emphasised with bright red lipstick. Mr Kamil did not introduce her but when she turned to him and whispered something he responded immediately.

"You've been listening to the men in the office again have you?"

Deborah felt embarrassed at his question and disconcerted by the presence of the silent woman.

"I couldn't help hearing. The door was open and they were talking loudly."

"That is very naughty of you, listening in to other people's conversations."

Deborah rested the palms of her hands on her knees

then started to pick at her fingernails distractedly. She was thinking about the woman in the cage again and was not really taking in what he said.

Mr Kamil stood up and leant his arm on the back of Deborah's chair. She smelled his aftershave and felt the heat from his hips as he pressed them against the back of her neck.

"Perhaps you would like to tell us what they were saying?"

He pressed the front of his hips harder and she felt sweat breaking out on her skin. She squirmed forward to try and move away and, as she did, she felt her hair sticking to the material of his trousers and she eased back.

"No, it's alright really, I didn't hear much anyway."

He pressed harder against her.

"Perhaps you could tell us what you did hear then."

This was no longer a question, it was more an order and she felt frightened by the sudden change in his tone. She fidgeted on the chair, still feeling hot and flustered and still unable to stop thinking about what she had heard the men in the adjoining office talking about.

"Yes, I'm sure we would both like to know what you heard and what it made you think." He turned to the woman in dark glasses and she slowly nodded her head. "Yes, we would definitely like to know."

Deborah felt her face going red and she bit her thumb nail nervously.

"Please, Mr Kamil, I don't think - "

He leant harder against her and rested his hands on her shoulders, gripping his fingers into her shoulder blades and tightening them. She tried to pull herself away but her pressed his fingers even harder.

"Please, you're hurting me, please - "

"'You're hurting me'," he mimicked. "Tell us what you heard and stop snivelling."

Deborah's eyes widened as she felt his fingers digging deeply into her shoulders and she felt afraid as his tone of voice became even more angry and impatient.

"Come on! Tell us!"

She began to think again of the men's conversation about the woman in the cage. Had it been a film or a story of some kind or, and she went cold as she thought of it, had it been real? As she pictured the scene she felt the flush of heat returning and, in an effort to distract herself, she bit down harder onto her thumb nail.

"And take your hand away from your face bitch!"

Mr Kamil grabbed her wrist and pulled her thumb out of her mouth. The tall woman sniggered and peered over the top of her dark glasses to get a better look.

Deborah turned to Mr Kamil, flustered and confused and increasingly frightened.

"Please, can I go - "

"No, you can't go. Now, tell us what you heard!"

He loosened his grip on her shoulders and ran his hands down her arms. Before she knew what he was doing he had taken hold of her wrists and lifted her arms wide. She felt her breasts tightening inside her bra as her arms were stretched, and she struggled against him and tried to get up, but he clasped her wrists together above her head and held them tight.

"Now, go on."

She could not believe what was happening. Her mind was racing with the images of the woman in the story and she was trembling uncontrollably as she realised that she was being held captive.

"They were talking about a woman in a cage, that's all. Now please can I go - "

"That's not all," he pulled her arms higher and the material of her thin dress pulled tightly against her breasts. "Now what else?"

She could do nothing but tell him.

"They said how she was crouching inside with a rope tied around her wrists. This man prodded her with a whip to try and get her out. She was too frightened to come out though

11

and the man had to prod her from behind to get her to move."

"Go on, and then?"

"Please, please let me go. I'll tell you but please let me go."

He slackened his grip slightly.

"And then?"

"The man ripped her white panties."

Mr Kamil held her wrists with one hand and ran the other down across her breasts and onto the tops of her thighs.

"Why did he do that?"

"Because when he tried to grab her she went to bite him."

"She was a bitch then wasn't she? She should have been punished then shouldn't she?"

Deborah did not reply.

"Shouldn't she!"

"Yes, yes, I suppose so - "

"Show me how she went to bite him."

Deborah turned to the side, opened her mouth and bared her teeth.

"Go on, show me."

She leant forward then suddenly tried to bite his arm.

"Bitch! How dare you! You need teaching a lesson like the woman in the cage."

He thrust his hand down between her thighs and grasped the hem of her short dress. He lifted it and rolled it back exposing the tops of her stockings. She pulled her knees together as he pulled it higher and revealed her white panties.

"Try again bitch and I'll show you what you get."

She did not know what to do, she felt confused and helpless. She must do what he said then perhaps he would release her and she could go. She went to bite his arm again, more ferociously this time and he thrust his hand between her legs and grabbed the gusset of her panties. She tried to bite him again and he pulled at the panties until they tore and exposed her dark pubic hair and the smooth flesh that lay be-

12

neath it.

"What then bitch?"

"He dragged her out and said, 'suck this'."

"Yes, and what did the bitch do? Was she obedient?"

"Yes, she took it in to her mouth."

"What? What did she take into her mouth?"

"His, his - "

"Go on bitch, his, his what?"

"His cock. She took his cock into her mouth and sucked it."

He let go of her wrists, twisted around and stood in front of her.

"Get it out bitch and show me."

Deborah hesitated and looked down at her stocking tops and bare thighs, her torn panties and her exposed pubic hair.

"Show me I said!"

She reached forward and pulled down the zip of his trousers.

"Get it out and show me!"

She ran her trembling fingers inside the zip and felt his throbbing cock pressed hard against the material of his trousers. She wrapped her fingers around it and felt the veins pulsating along its still thickening length. With her other hand, she opened the zip wide and eased his cock out. She squeezed it hard and pointed the engorged glans at her face.

Suddenly, she realised what she was doing and could not believe it. She let go of his cock, jumped up and ran to the door.

"I can't, I can't, please, please let me go ... "

As she grabbed the handle of the door, it opened and two of the men from the office came in.

Mr Kamil shouted angrily.

"Get back here bitch! On your knees! On your knees and suck this!"

The image of the woman in the cage flooded back

into her mind again. How she had fallen to her knees and sucked the man's cock and how they had forced her to crawl around and suck them all until there was no more to suck. Deborah shrank back against the door terrified.

"On your knees bitch!"

It was as though the story was coming alive and, like the woman in the cage, she did not dare disobey. As she realised what she must do, she felt a hot flush spreading within her stomach and a wetness running across the fleshy folds of her cunt. She turned, went to the middle of the room and stood before Mr Kamil.

"On your knees bitch and suck this!"

Obediently, she knelt down in front of him and reached her face forward. As she got closer to the stiff cock, she felt its heat and she opened her mouth. She slid her lips around the engorged glans and tightened them at its back before running them down the shaft until she felt its throbbing end pressing against the back of her throat.

She opened her eyes and stared at the mat of hairs that curled around its base before slipping herself back and watching the shaft come from her mouth, shining with spit and beating hard from the pressure of her sucking lips. She ran her mouth down again then began rhythmically pulling her mouth up and down it. She felt his cock hardening even more and the throbbing glans swelling in her mouth as the pressure of his spunk built up inside. She felt it running up its length and sucked it as deeply as she could as the hot semen exploded from its end and shot down her eager, gulping throat.

She released it from her lips and licked its end until there was nothing left to come.

"Now suck this one bitch!"

One of the men from the office was standing in front of her with his hard cock thrust towards her.

"And this one."

The other man who had come in pulled his trousers down and stood beside the first man.

"Suck them both bitch!"

Still with spunk dripping from her lips, Deborah reached her hands forward and took the two cocks in her hands. She pulled them together and drew them slowly into her mouth. They were both thick and hard and her lips were forced wide as they entered. She ran her tongue between them and licked their veiny skin before sucking them in and taking them as far back as she could.

Deborah sucked at the cocks frantically, pulling them back into her mouth and pressing them harder against the back of her throat every time. She gagged as they went too far but she welcomed the heaving tightness in her throat that forced her tongue upwards and increased the pressure against their throbbing weight. She pressed her tongue against the swelling ribs that pulsated along the base of each of their stiff cocks. She felt the pulsating increase as their spunk began to flow and, when she tasted it against the back of her tongue, she squeezed them hard in her hands and sucked frantically as their hot spunk burst out in strong, pulsating torrents. She tightened her mouth around them as much as she could and swallowed it all in heavy, ravenous gulps.

She fell back, wide-eyed and trembling but now eager for more.

"Stay on your knees bitch! You're not finished yet!"

Some of the other men from the office had come in and one by one she was made to suck them all. Each one finished fully in her mouth and every time she swallowed it all down, letting the creamy hot liquid run slowly along the sides of her throat and not being satisfied until she had taken every drop.

Suddenly, she was grabbed, hauled over to a desk and thrust down face-forward onto its cold, leather-covered surface. Two of the men held her by the wrists and stretched her arms out wide so that she could not get free. Mr Kamil grabbed hold of her torn panties and pulled them down. They tangled in her pubic hair as he ripped them off and she shrieked

15

out in pain. He ignored her cries and held her bottom still with one hand while he pulled the panties down over her feet with the other.

The woman in the red coat got up and walked over. Everyone went silent and Deborah's screams got louder as she was overwhelmed with fear by her sudden captivity.

"Stuff them in her mouth and keep the bitch quiet."

Mr Kamil grabbed Deborah's hair and pulled her head back. She looked at him appealingly as he stuffed the white panties deeply into her mouth then clamped his hand across her face to stop her spitting them out.

The woman in the dark glasses held out her hand and one of the men stepped forward and placed a short, leather whip into it. She flexed it back and ran her hands lovingly along its length. She prodded its end against Deborah's back, poking it into the material of her thin dress and lifting it up in puckers.

"Strip her!"

One of the men reached forward, grabbed Deborah's dress by the neck and ripped it down to just above her suspender belt. Except for her white bra strap, her back was exposed and her naked buttocks squirmed as she fought for breath and tried hopelessly to wriggle free.

The tall woman poked the end of the whip underneath the clip of Deborah's bra strap.

"Undo that thing."

A man reached forward, undid the bra strap and it fell free at the sides.

The woman paced around Deborah, staring inquisitively at her frightened face as she rubbed her hands across Deborah's smooth back.

"You are a pretty one aren't you? Yes, a very pretty one. And you seem to like having your mouth filled. Don't you?"

Deborah shook her head but Mr Kamil's grip was too tight for her to break free. She pulled at her wrists but they were held fast and she could not move them either. She kicked out her legs in desperation but before she knew what was happening she felt a stinging blow across her back as the whip came down.

Whack!

She stretched out her body in agony and shock, shaking her head from side to side as the pain cut into her skin and sent a smarting fire deep inside her.

Whack!

The whip fell even harder and, as the pain burned through her, she stretched out tautly. She struggled and pulled against her captors but she was unable to break free and unable to scream.

Whack! Whack! Whack!

The whip came down across her bare back remorselessly, each blow laying a thin red mark across her smooth skin. She wriggled and pulled in desperation but the whip kept slashing down.

Whack! Whack! Whack!

Every time it fell across her back she tightened more and her whole body felt on fire.

Whack! Whack! Whack!

She felt her eyes filling with tears and, as she was overcome with the pain and felt herself falling into unconsciousness, she bit hard onto the panties that plugged her dribbling mouth.

Finally the punishment ended and the woman stood back. She prowled around Deborah, running her fingers along the red lines that were raised across Deborah's skin.

"Would you like to lick me bitch?"

Mr Kamil pulled Deborah's head back more and she stared up into the woman's face. Her spit-smeared panties hung from her open mouth.

The woman folded her arms and sneered down at Deborah.

"I don't think so bitch." The woman turned to Mr

Kamil. "Yes, she will do. I think Theron will reward me well for this one. You know what he can be like but I think he will be pleased. Yes, send her to me in the usual way. Oh, and tell that mongrel Gross to keep his hands off her. Theron says that if he misbehaves again it will be the last time."

"Yes, Saab, yes."

"Now, my friend is waiting and we have arrangements of our own to make."

"A word Saab. Jabari has been in touch with me again. He keeps pestering me - "

"You fool Kamil. I told you to have nothing more to do with him. Theron sees him as a threat and that makes him angry and you know what he's like when he gets angry."

Saab threw down the whip and left the room. Mr Kamil ushered the others out, pulled the white panties from Deborah's mouth and lifted her onto a chair. He walked over to the window and watched Saab as she got into the back of a large car. He saw a woman's hand stretch out and touch Saab's face. For a moment, he saw the flash of the woman's white teeth before Saab pressed her mouth against the woman's full lips and, in a sudden passion, drove her fingers up into the tangle of black hair that fell about the woman's face.

He turned back to Deborah.

"Now, you'll stay here for the night until I can arrange for you to be transported."

He left and locked the door behind him.

Deborah sat alone in the office. She could hardly believe what had happened and she trembled with shame and embarrassment. She tried to pull her torn dress together but it was hopeless and, when she reached around to her back, she felt the painful cuts of the whip still burning on her skin. Her ripped panties lay on the desk and she picked them up. They were wet from her spit and stuck to her stockings as she pulled them up. When she drew them against her cunt the moist material stuck to her flesh. Her stomach filled with anxiety as

18

she thought of the way she had been humiliated and the surge of nervousness increased as she thought of how she had reacted.

She played absently with a silver identity bracelet on her wrist. It was a gift from her parents and had her name and old address engraved on the inside. She realised how alone she was, she had no one to turn to except Chrissie. The thought that she might never again see her only friend caused tears to well up in her eyes and she hung her head and fidgeted nervously on the leather covered chair.

She wriggled her bottom and felt the thin material of the damp and torn panties pulling up against the soft folds of flesh between her legs. She lifted herself slightly and pulled it away and, as it peeled back, she felt a warm moistness holding it between the soft furrow of her cunt. She felt the delicate skin tingling as the thin material clung to it and she felt a warm and growing wetness spreading across its swelling edges. She felt shocked and ashamed and dropped herself back onto the seat in despair, but she was unable to stop her fingers working eagerly between the soft petals of her swollen, receptive cunt, and unable to draw them away again until she had recovered from a slow, pulsating orgasm.

CHAPTER 2

Deborah was woken by the clanking of keys as the office door was unlocked. She jumped up and pulled her thin dress around her to try and cover herself. When she saw Mr Kamil at the door, she felt suddenly relieved. She imagined that he had come to release her, that it had all been a terrible game that had got out of control and Mr Kamil had come to apologise and ask her to forget it.

Deborah looked up at him and smiled, hoping that he would realise that she was prepared to forget what had happened, but he did not smile back and, when he shouted at her angrily, she shrank back with renewed fear.

"Come on bitch, get up. "You're going on a little trip. I hope you don't get sea sick!" He laughed and beckoned to a figure who was hanging back in the shadows. "Here is your escort. Gross! Show yourself!"

Gross stepped into the light that shone through the open door. He was short and bent, his head was large and shaven and his arms were long and dangled loosely at his sides. His large white eyes bulged out from his jet black face and, as he leered at Deborah, his yellowed teeth showed their sharp, broken edges. He reached forward to touch Deborah but Mr Kamil smacked his hand viciously.

"Don't touch! You must not touch her. Mistress Saab says she must not be touched! Especially not by you!"

Gross cringed at the sound of Saab's name and started mumbling nervously.

"Mistress Saab, must not touch, no, must not touch, must not touch ... "

"No, you must not touch, remember that. Now, introduce yourself properly."

He came forward again, still muttering, and bowed his head slowly.

"Must not touch, must not touch - "

"I said introduce yourself you idiot."

20

"Me Gross, must not touch."

Mr Kamil laughed and tossed back the strand of black hair from his forehead.

"Gross! Shackle her."

Gross leaned towards Deborah and held up a heavy chain with large, iron shackles attached to each end. Deborah shrank back against the wall in fear.

"Please Mr Kamil, I'm sorry about what happened, please - "

"Shackle her and be quick about it!"

Gross held the chain in front of Deborah but she pressed herself hard against the wall and squeezed her hands behind her back. He cocked his head from side to side and rattled the chain at her, inviting her to put her wrists into the open shackles.

"Gross must not touch. Saab says Gross must not touch." He flashed his eyes around the room. "Saab may be watching Gross. No, no, Gross must not touch."

Deborah pushed herself tightly against the wall but Mr Kamil grabbed her shoulders and yanked her forward. He held her wrists and, as she struggled to break free, he dropped them into the heavy shackles and clamped them shut. They snapped together pinching her skin, the one on her right wrist squeezing her identity bracelet tightly inside the iron band and causing her to cry out in pain.

Mr Kamil ignored her distress and shouted to Gross.

"Now take her, the van is waiting at the back."

Gross gathered up the length of chain and pulled Deborah to the door. The shackles dug into her wrists and she shrieked as he jerked the chain to get her through the door.

"Please, where are you taking me? Please, please let me go."

Gross took no notice and hurried down the passage, dragging Deborah behind him and yanking at the chain when she lagged behind or stumbled because she could not see her way.

21

Outside, a large, windowless van waited in the road. Its back doors were open and Gross leapt inside, pulling at the chain and dragging Deborah up behind him like a frightened animal. She cowered in a corner and he squatted down beside her, his large white eyes flashing as he looked fearfully around. Someone came and slammed the doors shut and the back of the van was plunged into darkness.

They drove for hours but Deborah stayed crouched in the corner too terrified to speak or move. Every so often she felt Gross's breath on her face as he pulled himself nearer to her but, as soon as she felt the heat from his cheeks and twisted away, he also pulled back muttering and anxious.

"Gross must not touch. Did once before with other girl. Gross touched and Gross was punished by master. Gross was punished very much. Gross will not let master down again." He cocked his head to one side, dipping it into his shrugging shoulder. "Gross say don't worry. Gross will care for pretty girl. Pretty girl is safe with Gross."

Suddenly the van stopped and the doors were flung open. Deborah blinked in the glare of bright lights but before she could focus on anything Gross jumped out of the back and dragged her roughly behind. He pulled her along, stopping occasionally and yanking the chain hard as if to punish her for something.

As they approached a large warehouse, he got more agitated and started muttering and grumbling to himself.

"Me Gross, me escort, must not touch, Gross in charge - "

Deborah yanked against the chain and tried to pull herself away but she screamed out as he dragged her back powerfully.

"Pretty girl must not escape. Gross is escort. Gross in charge."

She hung her head hopelessly as he pulled her into the large building and stood waiting in the darkness with his long arms dangling by his sides. The heavy chain that hung loosely from Deborah's shackled wrists led back into one of his hands and lay draped across his bent fingers.

A door opened at the opposite end of the building and two muscular, black men walked towards them.

"What have you got for us Gross?"

Gross looked down at the floor.

"Gross must not touch. Saab says Gross must not touch."

One of the men pushed Gross aside and stood in front of Deborah.

"You've brought a very pretty one this time Gross." He ran the back of his hand across the side of Deborah's face and down the front of her torn dress. "Very pretty indeed."

"Must not touch! Must not touch!"

"Quiet Gross!"

The man leered at Deborah and she turned her face away. He grabbed it, squeezing her cheeks between his thumb and forefinger, and pulled it back.

"Beautiful mouth as well."

He leant forward and pressed his thick lips against her mouth. She tried to pull away but he held her firmly as he kissed her. She closed her mouth and clenched her teeth together.

"But not very friendly. Come on my pretty thing, just a kiss for your new friend Wesley."

He pressed his face at her again but Deborah tightened her lips and managed to turn her head away.

"Not very friendly at all and not very obedient either, eh Winston?"

The other man laughed.

"Gross! Pull her onto her knees, I think she needs a lesson in obedience."

Gross looked at Wesley and tilted his head to the side questioningly.

"Pull her onto her knees you idiot!"

Gross looked at Deborah, her eyes wide with fear as

23

she pressed the side of her face against the wall. He opened his mouth in a grin, exposing his yellow teeth then suddenly he snatched the chain viciously. As Deborah lost her balance and fell forwards onto her knees, Gross yanked the chain again, pulling her arms out at full stretch and throwing her face-forward onto the floor.

"Hold her there Gross!"

Gross leapt forward and jumped on the chain, pinioning her wrists to the ground. She yelled out in pain as the shackles twisted around her wrists and she pulled at them frantically in an effort to break free. Gross squatted down with all his weight on the chain and grinned as Deborah pulled and wriggled hopelessly.

Wesley picked up a length of rope and bent down to Deborah.

"Stop wriggling bitch!"

Deborah pulled at the chain desperately and threw herself from side to side in fear and panic.

Wesley bent down, put his face close to hers and spoke quietly.

"You are a disobedient little bitch aren't you? See this?" He held up a thick, hemp rope in front of her. "I am going to give this to Winston and then I'm going to see if you can follow some simple instructions."

Wesley handed the rope to Winston. He held it up in the centre, folded it in half and let the two frayed ends dangle down from his outstretched hand. Wesley bent down lower and placed his hands on the floor in front of Deborah.

"Now bitch, I am going to tell Gross to release you and I want you to crawl forward when I say. Do you understand?"

Deborah stared at him for a moment then started pulling frantically at the shackles again.

"Gross! Let her go!"

Gross stepped off the chain and Deborah stopped moving.

"Now come towards me little bitch. Come on, come on."

Deborah snatched her hands backwards, spun around and tried to get to her feet but stopped when Wesley stood up in front of her and smirked.

"That's too bad bitch. You see, if you are disobedient I tell Winston to punish you. Like this, Winston! Give her, let me see, perhaps to start with, just a single lash!"

Deborah did not hear what he said, she could only think of escape but, as she struggled to get up and break free, Winston brought the two frayed strands of the rope down across her back and she froze. She was consumed with a mixture of surprise, pain and terror.

Lash!

She yelled out as the ropes cut into her skin and she fell back to the floor gasping breathlessly.

Wesley bent down to her again.

"Now little bitch, let's try again. On your knees!"

She looked at him for a moment then jumped up and made a dash for the wall.

Wesley laughed as she held her shackled wrists across her chest and shrank close to the wall.

"Bring her back Winston. Bring her back here and we'll start again."

Winston grabbed her arm and pulled her, still struggling, back to Wesley.

Wesley turned to Gross.

"Gross! Pull her down again and this time keep hold of her."

Gross grinned then grabbed the chain and yanked it forward. Deborah fell onto her knees and when Gross pulled the chain again she fell down painfully onto her elbows.

"Now bitch! Come towards me on your knees. Let

Deborah looked at him. She could not believe what was happening. The way he spoke to her made her feel like an animal - like a dog - and, as he commanded her again, she felt herself

25

dropping her jaw and exposing her teeth.

"Come on little bitch. Come on."

She lifted one of her hands from the ground and the chain clanked as the shackle dug into her wrist. She knew she would be punished if she did not move but she could not find it in herself to obey him so easily. She looked to the wall again and thought of jumping up and running to it but she was unsure and too frightened to make a decision.

"Too slow bitch! Winston! Give her two lashes this time.

Lash! Lash!

The rope ends fell across her buttocks, burning her skin then folding around her hips and cutting into the crease of flesh at the top of her thigh. She shrieked in pain and twisted away.

Wesley held out his hand towards her and rubbed his fingers and thumb together as though he was offering her a tit bit of food.

"Now come little bitch, do what your master says, come forward when he instructs you."

Deborah got up on her knees again. As she lifted her hips, her torn dress pulled up around her waist exposing her smooth bare thighs above the tops of her stockings and her ripped, white panties as they pulled tightly between the crease of her buttocks. She felt the gathered material tightening between the fleshy edges of her cunt and, as she lifted her hips higher, she felt it pressing against the tip of her clitoris.

"Come on, come on little bitch."

Deborah lifted her outspread hand from the ground and held it up hesitantly, the heavy shackle hung loosely from her wrist and the trailing chain curled weightily on the floor.

"Come on little bitch, come on."

She dropped her jaw again and felt a trickle of spit running from the corner of her mouth. Her buttocks were still stinging and she could hear Winston dropping the ropes across his hand in expectation of punishing her more. Her panties pulled tightly between the tops of her thighs as she swayed from side to side and she felt the heat from her fleshy outer labia as they pressed against the filmy gusset.

Something inside her, something she could not understand, was driving her to move forward yet, at the same time, her fear was telling her to run. She knew that if she did not obey him she would get more punishment and, when she thought of the ropes lashing down again on her buttocks, her stomach filled with waves of nervousness. But as the fear of the stinging lashes spread from her stomach into her chest she felt her nipples hardening and the heat between her legs increasing. She dropped her hand to the floor purposefully, putting it back in the same position as before, then she raised her hips higher, exposed her teeth and stared at Wesley defiantly.

"Not ready yet eh bitch? Winston! Give her three lashes this time! And make them hard ones! This bitch will not give in easily."

Winston drew the halved rope back high above his head then brought its flailing ends down hard.

Lash!

The rope lashed across her buttocks and she squeezed them together tightly but kept them raised as high as she could.

Lash!

The halved rope curled around her hips and cut into her skin but still she did not move.

Lash!

Again it came down viciously, this time snatching at the material of her torn panties and pulling it painfully against the soft outer flesh of her cunt.

"Ready yet?"

Still Deborah did not move. She felt transfixed. She opened her mouth wider, allowing the trickle of spit to run freely from the corner of her lips. She watched it dribble down in a long sticky strand until it reached the floor. She licked her tongue out and tasted its cool sweetness and she raised

27

her buttocks higher.

"So you want more do you?"

She stared at him fixedly, still licking her tongue eagerly around the dribbling strand of spit and sucking it back noisily into her gaping mouth.

"Give her more and this time don't stop until she does what she's told!"

A strange wave of excitement ran through her as she realised that he knew what she wanted. She wanted to be his slave, she wanted to obey him and crawl on her hands and knees when he instructed her, but she could not serve him, not yet, not until she had been overcome with the punishing pain of the rope.

Winston drew the halved rope back and Deborah tightened her bottom and shoulders in readiness. She wanted to move forward, she wanted to obey him so much, but she needed to be forced to do it and she had not felt enough pain yet to make her do his bidding.

Lash! Lash! Lash!

The ends of rope cut across her buttocks and lashed her bare thighs causing red lines that contrasted vividly against her pale flesh and the whiteness of her panties and stocking tops. The pain tore through her, searing her skin and sending agonizing shocks through her tightened limbs but still it was not enough.

Lash! Lash! Lash!

The ends of the rope pulled at the tight suspenders that pulled against her stocking tops and she felt her suspender belt digging into her hips. She dropped her shoulders lower, falling onto her elbows, but still she kept her bottom as high as she could and still she wanted more.

Lash! Lash! Lash!

The rope ends tangled around the tops of her legs and pulled at the edges of her panties as they were drawn back. She yelled in agony as her torn panties twisted into her pubic hair and pulled against her flesh. She felt herself writhing uncontrollably, but still she needed to present herself for more, still she had not felt enough pain to be driven to obey. She stretched her arms forward until her chin nearly touched the floor as she strained her bottom even higher.

Lash! Lash! Lash!

The heat of the pain spread though her whole body in waves. Her face was reddened by the strain of holding herself up for the lashing ropes and her nipples stood out hard and aching against the material of her bra that still hung loosely from its shoulder straps. She felt the burning of her skin where the lashing rope scourged it but she felt herself burning even where it did not touch and, as she screamed out her suffering, she was consumed by its overpowering heat.

She twisted her hips and writhed her buttocks but now she knew she could take no more. Her cunt was hot and she could feel her distended flesh pulsating against the tight-pulled gusset of her panties and, like a bursting dam, she felt a rush of uncontrollable excitement surging through her stomach as her will to resist was broken. Another lash and she would be ready, another flailing stroke from the rope and she would be able to obey. Just one more stinging lash and she could crawl towards him as he commanded. Just one more lash and she would be able to stand no more pain, then, when she was overcome by the torment of the rope she would at last be able to relinquish herself to delightful servitude.

Lash!

That was all she could stand. At last the suffering had released her!

She drew her breath in deeply, tensed her muscles and reared backwards on her knees. She lifted the heavy shackles that bound her wrists together above her head then, releasing her breath in a noisy, spluttering growl, she fell forward, crouching again on all-fours and ready to serve.

Shaking with the pain and sweating from the heat in her cunt she lifted her hand and moved it forward. This time she did not hesitate but dropped it straight down in front of her, showing him that she was under his control and that she was doing only what he ordered.

"Good! Come on more little bitch."

Wesley moved back, still holding his hand towards her and enticing her with his rubbing fingers, and she moved herself towards him, feeling the strength of his mastery and the delight of her own humiliation. The pain had driven her to act and the action was so delicious, so much the will of her master, that it transcended the agony she felt across her flesh. Now she felt her cunt moistening with delectable desire. She felt its warm edges swelling and rubbing against each other as she crawled forward again. She felt the luscious thrill of her orgasm boiling up inside her every time he ordered her to move and she felt its fiery heat spilling into her cunt as she followed his commands. She wanted to race forward in a frenzy so that she could release it. She wanted to throw herself on her back before him and open her legs so that he could see her swollen cunt pulsating with her climax, but now she was his slave and she knew she must wait until he allowed her to let it go.

"Come on little bitch, come on."

He drew her forward slowly and she responded to his every command. He made her turn and stop and wait then start again until finally he led to her towards the wall, made her face it and left her there.

"Now bitch wait until I give you further orders."

She knelt on all-fours in front of the wall, staring ahead, trembling with excitement and only able to hold back her orgasm because he had not told her to finish. She wished she could ask him to order her to finish but she knew she must wait until he decided the time was right. She lifted her hand and ran it down the front of her stomach, hoping she could find some relief by delving her fingers into her aching cunt but, as the shackles clanked around her wrists, she looked back in fear and, when her master stared at her reprovingly, she dropped her hand back to the floor and waited without moving.

Gross went over to her and crouched by her side, cocking his head and pawing at her without touching her. Wesley shouted and, as his voice echoed around the cavernous warehouse and Deborah heard what he said, her heart leapt with fresh excitement.

"Come here bitch!"

Her stomach churned with excitement as she turned and began crawling across the floor, lifting her hands slowly and placing them down carefully as the chain clanked between her wrists. She felt the tension of her suspenders as they pulled against her stocking tops and she dribbled uncontrollably as the gusset of her panties stroked the engorged labia of her distended cunt.

"Here!"

Wesley pointed to the opposite corner of the huge building and Deborah made her way towards it without hesitation. Her cunt was hot and wet and she could feel the thin material of her panties sticking to its swollen edges. The pressure against her throbbing flesh sent shivers into her hard clitoris. It tingled deeply, as if begging to be relieved of the strain of the pent up orgasm, but she knew she would have to wait. She sensed her master's control so strongly that she knew the boiling forces within her would remain suppressed until she was told.

"Come here and stop!"

He pointed at something shrouded by a heavy, green tarpaulin.

She approached it and looked up at him so that she would stop exactly where he said.

"Here bitch!"

She moved to where he was pointing then stopped and waited. The stinging pain from the lashing rope was subsiding and she lifted her hips higher to show him she was ready for more, but she dropped them back as she realised that now anything she did without his orders was disobedience.

Winston grabbed a rope on the edge of the tarpaulin and pulled it down to the floor exposing a large cage with a heavily barred, iron door. Deborah stared at it and her heart started pounding with a fresh mixture of fear and excitement.

Images of the woman in the cage started flooding back into her mind. She pictured the terrified woman clinging to the bars and the fear in her eyes as she was prodded and whipped by her tormentors. She thought of how she had resisted coming out and how she had been prodded with canes until, in the end, she was forced into the open and made to suck the men who were taunting her.

"Don't look frightened little bitch. You will quickly learn that the cage will be your only place of rest."

Deborah did not understand what he meant and without thinking, without doing what he told her, she shrank back from the thick, iron bars.

"Come here!"

She scuttled towards him, hoping he had not seen her act without his orders.

"Sit back on your knees."

She raised herself obediently, parted her knees slightly and rested her bottom onto her calves.

"Now, raise your wrists."

Deborah lifted the heavy shackles and chain above her head. The thin material of her dress twisted in the links and pulled up exposing her torn white panties and suspender belt, her bare waist and the bottom edge of her white bra. The chain looped down and hung beneath her chin and, when he told her to raise her arms higher, it pulled hard against her throat until she could lift it no more.

"And open your mouth."

She dropped her jaw and parted her trembling lips but it caused the tension of the chain at her throat to increase and she choked.

"Wide!"

32

Fighting against her need to cough, she forced her mouth wider until he nodded.

"Now wait."

Wesley walked over to the cage and opened the door. Deborah felt the strain of the heavy shackles on her wrists and tightened her shoulders to keep them as high as he expected. Her neck muscles started to feel cramped as her arms seemed to get heavier and, as the chain between her shackles pulled up even more against her throat, she began to close her mouth.

"Keep your mouth open bitch!"

She breathed in deeply and pushed the shackles high. The chain pulled tightly against her throat but she opened her mouth as wide as she could and waited.

Winston pulled on a heavy block that hung from a pulley attached high on a round supporting post that led up into the roof. It clanked down noisily as the free end ran through a loop in the opposite wall. He clipped the chain between Deborah's shackles into a hook on the block then waved to Gross who was holding the other end.

"Haul her up Gross!"

Gross pulled on the chain and Deborah felt a sudden upward strain on her arms as the tightening chain pulled her wrists together with a smack. The chain between her shackles snatched against her throat and her head was thrown backwards. Gross pulled again and the tensioned chain threw her against the steel pole, knocking the breath from her and forcing her to gasp frantically. For a moment, her elbows bent around the pole but, when Gross heaved on the chain again, her arms were stretched up high and her feet were pulled off the ground. She could hardly breathe as she swung on the chain, spinning dizzily and banging jarringly against the post.

"Now clear off Gross. We don't need you any more."

Gross looked unwilling to leave Deborah and, as he turned reluctantly to go, he cocked his head to one side and took a long, strangely compassionate look at her before swinging around and disappearing into the darkness.

"Now, pull her panties down Winston!"

Winston reached up and grabbed the torn waistband of her white panties. The flimsy material rucked up between her buttocks and pinched her skin and she twisted herself in a hopeless effort to release it. He yanked at them again and the creased up panties pinched the soft edges of her outer labia and caught in her pubic hair. She squirmed and shrieked in pain as the hairs pulled at her soft flesh.

"Pull them down! I want to see her bottom."

Winston yanked the panties hard and, with some of her pubic hairs twisted up in the material, they came down to just above her knees. The soft folds of her labia were burning with pain and she tried to pull her legs up to protect herself but the strain on her arms was too great, and she could do nothing else except hang there limp and exposed.

Wesley stood behind her, reached up and stroked his hands across her exposed buttocks, circling around them as he followed the line of her suspender belt, then running his fingers deeply between the crease of her taut bottom. He pushed his hands back to back, squeezed them between the tops of her thighs and pressed them apart. He pushed his face between her buttocks and she felt his wet tongue reaching out between them. He licked the tip of his tongue against the hard, muscular ring of her anus and probed at its centre. He lapped at it hungrily, wetting it with his spit and delving further each time he touched it.

As Wesley probed his tongue inside her anus, he forced her forward against the round, steel pole. She felt its coldness against the tops of her thighs and, as he pressed her harder, she felt the front of her naked crack squeezing against the unforgiving metal.

His tongue went deeper and she lifted her legs and squeezed them around the pole. She felt the heat of her cunt against its coldness and she opened her legs wider. As her hot flesh touched the cold metal, she felt the blood throbbing in

34

her outer labia and she opened her legs even more. She wrapped herself onto the pole and allowed the rhythmic probing in her anus to lift and rub her against it, each movement opening the swelling folds of her cunt even more and pressing her ever engorging clitoris harder against the cold, steel pole.

She dropped her head back further and saw the cage and, as his tongue thrust as far as it could and his fleshy lips squeezed around the ring of her anus, her head filled again with the images of the woman in the story. But this time Deborah imagined it was her in the cage and the more she looked at the bars and saw herself clinging to them in fear the more she squashed herself against the pole and the more she opened herself up for the delving tongue in her anus.

She wrapped her legs around the steel pole and squeezed her open crack against it. She rubbed her hard clitoris against it more rapidly and felt the full weight of her body on her wrists but, as she felt the stinging heat of her orgasm flooding within her, she also felt the darkening mist of unconsciousness and she dropped against the pole unknowingly jerking and twitching as he continued to lick her as deeply as he could.

CHAPTER 3

Deborah opened her eyes wide. For a moment she did not know where she was, she almost felt she had been dreaming but, as she stared around the huge warehouse, she realised that everything that was happening to her was frighteningly real.

She closed her eyes and thought of Chrissie. She remembered the time in the club when they had first met. Deborah had been so nervous about going, she knew no one, had hardly got any money and was staying in a hostel. Chrissie had been drinking and flopped down on a chair next to her, exhausted from dancing. She looked beautiful, sweat glistening on her face and her long, black hair sticking to her cheeks and across her mouth. When she had reached across the table between them Deborah had noticed how Chrissie's breasts squeezed together in a tight cleavage above the neat edge of her low-cut, white top. They had started to talk and Chrissie had said she could get her a job at the office where she worked. The next day she had gone for an interview with Mr Kamil, got the job and an advance on her salary and by the weekend, again with Chrissie's help, had found a small room to rent. Deborah pictured Chrissie's face and wished so much that she could see her again.

She was still shackled by the wrists but had been let down from the chain and was curled up at the foot of the metal pole with her panties around her knees. Gross emerged from the darkness, crouched down by her side and cocked his head to one side.

"Gross in charge. Pretty girl, but must not touch. No, Gross must not touch or Saab will be angry with Gross."

"Please, can you help me, please, I must escape from here. This is all a terrible, terrible mistake."

Gross cocked his head to the other side then closed the heavy lids of his bulging eyes tightly together and laughed.

"Cannot escape. Gross in charge. Gross is guarding pretty girl. No, cannot escape."

"Please, please help me ... "

Gross laughed again and pawed his hands towards her. She reached out to him and he shrank back fearfully.

"Must not touch! Must not touch!"

A door opened and Winston strode over.

"Awake at last eh? What a pity you missed all the fun last night. You as well Gross. Poor Gross, never has any fun."

Gross muttered and pushed his hands under his legs.

"Gross must not touch. No, must not touch - "

"Shut up Gross!"

Deborah sat up and straight away felt how sore her bottom was. Her anus ached and when she looked down she saw angry red stripes criss-crossing her breasts. She rubbed them but flinched as her fingers touched her burning skin, then she realised her bra had gone and her dress had been torn completely open at the front. She pushed her hand down to her pubic hair and it felt sticky and matted. A fresh wave of panic spread over her.

"What have you done to me? You must let me go. You have no right to ... "

Winston laughed and swung around to Gross.

"Gross! She is to be shipped out later tonight. Take her and clean her up."

Deborah pulled her panties up as well as she could and her face flushed red with embarrassment. She opened her mouth to speak and winced as she felt her sore lips. Gross yanked on the chain that ran between the heavy shackles on her wrists, hauled her to her feet and dragged her away. She stumbled as he pulled her into a small washroom.

"Clean up pretty girl. Gross in charge."

He leant clumsily against the basin and turned on the taps then yanked the chain between her wrists and pulled her towards it. He stared at her as she dipped her hands in the water and began splashing it over her arms and face.

"Clean up all over. Gross in charge."

He watched her closely as she splashed water across her breasts and down the front of her stomach.

"Clean up all over. Panties down. Gross in charge."

"No, it's alright really, that's enough - "

"All over! Panties down!"

He yanked the chain hard and the shackles dug painfully into her wrists. She cried out as he held up the chain, threatening to pull at it again.

"Panties down! Panties down!"

She took hold of the waistband of her torn panties

37

and slipped them down over her thighs.

"Panties down. Further!"

He tugged at the chain again and she pulled them down to her knees.

He watched her closely, tipping his head from side to side, as she splashed water around her pubic hair and washed away the stickiness that clung to it. She cupped her hands, filled them with water, and bathed her cunt, gently washing the folds of her outer labia and drawing her fingers slowly between the soft furrow of her flesh. She rubbed her wet hands between the crease of her buttocks and around her sore anus, then, when she had finished, she dried herself carefully with a small, dirty towel. All the time, Gross pawed his hands towards her, tracing his fingers around the outline of her breasts and pulling them back jerkily whenever he felt they got too close.

"Now in here."

He pushed open the door of a small cubicle, crouched down behind the toilet and dragged her backwards onto the seat. She sat there nervous and embarrassed with Gross staring between her legs until finally she managed to urinate. Her face flushed red as he drew closer and watched the last trickles dripping from her. She wiped her cunt with a paper tissue and reached down to pull up her torn panties. She held the tattered material between her fingers and a wave of despair spread over her. Even though she wanted to cover herself with them, she could not bear them any more. She wriggled them down over her ankles and stuffed them behind the toilet pedestal before Gross grabbed her wrists and dragged her back into the warehouse.

Winston was holding a heavily knuckled, rattan cane and, as he eyed her up and down, he prodded her in the side with its tip.

"Good, now on your knees again to meet our guests."

He poked her with the cane and she twisted away and turned her back to him. She wanted to beg him to let her go but before she could collect her thoughts he prodded her again more sharply.

"I said on you knees bitch!"

He lifted the hem of her flimsy dress with the end of the cane and hung it onto her shoulder. Her suspender belt was pulled closely against her firm buttocks and the white suspenders were drawn tightly down across her thighs and clasped to the tops of her stockings. He smiled broadly and brought the cane down hard against her bare buttocks.

Whack!

The pain stung her deeply and she cried out and fell forward as anxiety welled up in her stomach.

"I said on your knees bitch!"

Whack!

The cane fell across her back and she yelled out again. She tried to run away but Gross yanked the chain and she stumbled over and fell to the floor. She felt her heart pounding and crawled forward on her stomach as she tried hopelessly to get away from him, then she saw the cage in front of her and stopped.

Winston stood in front of her and placed his feet on either side of her hands. He stared down at her as she trembled and shook with fear.

"Still frightened of the cage eh? That will not last long. You will beg me to put you in the cage before long. Do you hear bitch? You will beg to be locked in the cage and when you do, yes when you do beg - and I promise you that is what you will do - you can only hope that I will let you in!"

He lifted the cane back threateningly and she cowered beneath it. She knew she could not escape and slowly got up onto her knees.

"Now wait there for our guests."

Deborah crouched on all-fours staring down at the ground. Gross knelt beside her, occasionally pulling at her chain and muttering. He reached out and moved his hand above her upturned buttocks then jumped back fearfully as the door burst open.

Two black men strode in dragging a young woman behind them. She was wearing a short red skirt, flesh-coloured stockings and an open necked, white blouse. Her long, black hair was in disarray and the mascara around her eyes was smudged and smeared across her cheeks. The men pushed her up against the wall and shouted to Winston and Wesley who greeted them keenly.

"Mingo, Clay, who have you got here?"

"Some tart we found in the street. Thought she might like to join the party."

Deborah kept her eyes fixed firmly on the floor, not daring to look up in case she was punished again.

Winston grabbed the young woman under the chin.

"What's your name tart?" She pulled back, too afraid to speak. "I said what's your name?"

Her voice was frail and trembling.

"Please Sir, my name's Chrissie."

Deborah's heart started pounding wildly as she heard the familiar voice. She looked up fearfully and saw Chrissie's frightened face as Winston lifted her chin and stared menacingly into her dark, wide eyes. Without thinking, Deborah lurched forward but Gross yanked her back and she looked down again, too scared to say anything and too frightened to move.

Winston pressed his face close to Chrissie's.

"Well, at least you know how to address me."

He laughed and let her go but she grabbed him by the arm and pulled him back.

"Please Sir, please let me go. I promise I won't say anything, please - "

"Let go tart!"

She clung to his arm but he prised her away and pushed her roughly back against the wall.

"Bend her over boys, I think little Chrissie needs a lesson in obedience!"

40

Mingo and Clay grabbed her arms and bent her forward. Winston lifted the hem of her short skirt and revealed the backs of her bare thighs outlined by her white suspenders and the edges of her tightly pulled white panties.

"Please let me go, please - "

"Shut up tart!"

Winston un-clipped the suspenders from her stockings and reached his hand up to the waistband of her white panties. He grabbed the flimsy material and peeled it down slowly, revealing her firm buttocks and the dark crease between them. She tensed herself and struggled to get free but they held her too tightly and squeezed their hands around her arms until she gave up.

"Bend her over more boys. Let's see her cunt."

Mingo put his hand on the back of her head and forced it down until it almost touched her knees. Her legs opened slightly and the soft edges of her cunt squeezed out between them.

"More!"

Mingo bent her head between her knees until the tangle of black pubic hair at the front of her pink slit could be seen between her tightly stretched buttocks.

Deborah trembled with fear as Winston handed the cane to Wesley then slowly unbuckled his heavy leather belt and removed it from his trousers. He stretched it between his hands then pressed it against Chrissie's upturned bottom. She tightened as she felt the leather against her skin and he pressed it harder until its edges were firmly against the folds of her protruding outer labia.

"Hold her tight boys! Let's see how much she can take!"

He held the belt by the buckle, drew it back behind his head then brought it down against her buttocks.

Whack!

Chrissie screamed as the belt smacked against her skin and she pulled against the men's restraining arms in panic.

Whack!

The leather belt smacked down again, hitting her buttocks flatly and leaving a wide red stripe across her taut skin. She screamed again, louder than before, and thrust her hands backwards to try and cover herself.

"Hold her arms!"

Whack!

The belt came down again and another wide, red stripe appeared on her tight-stretched skin. She howled loudly and, overcome by the pain and desperate to escape the punishment, she threw herself to one side.

Whack!

The belt curled between her legs and fell fully across her squeezed-out labia. She screeched at the top of her voice and, in a frenzy, twisted herself away from the men's grasping hands and ran towards the door.

Winston laughed as Mingo and Clay dragged her back.

"Please Sir, please, I will do anything, but please, no more, I can't - "

"Bend her over again, and this time keep hold of her!"

They bent her forward again and, as she screamed like a tortured animal, Winston beat her relentlessly.

Whack! Whack! Whack!

She screeched and shouted for mercy as spit sprayed from her gaping mouth, but he did not stop until she was exhausted and could scream no more.

"Tie her ankles and pull her up on the chain. Let's see if she's learnt her lesson."

Clay found some ropes nearby and started winding them tightly around Chrissie's ankles. Gradually, as she recovered, she started to struggle again but Mingo wrapped his elbow around her waist and lifted her off the ground.

Deborah crouched on all-fours and watched the desperate girl as her eyes blazed wide with fear. Deborah edged forward slightly and, as Gross tugged her back, she saw that

42

Winston had noticed her moving. He smiled at her menacingly and she dropped back but still kept watching.

Clay knotted the ropes around Chrissie's ankles then bound them into the block that hung from the long chain in the ceiling. Mingo lct her go and she fell on her back, twisting and rolling from side to side with her feet held just off the ground by the hanging chain.

"Gross! Haul her up!"

Gross hesitated for a moment, unsure about leaving Deborah, then he jumped up and lurched over to the opposite end of the chain and began hauling it through the pulley. Chrissie was pulled up by the ankles until she was suspended with her head clear of the ground.

"That's enough!"

Gross tied off the chain and rushed back to Deborah's side.

Chrissie's eyes were wide with terror as she hung upside down on the spinning chain with her short skirt tangled up at her waist and her blouse twisted around her neck.

Winston pulled back the belt again and brought it down across her rotating body.

Whack!

It lashed across her back then wrapped itself around her hips, tightening up and stopping her spinning. She tried to cry out but her attempts turned to coughing and choking and spit dribbled from her mouth as Winston unwound the belt, drew it back and lashed it down again.

Whack!

The belt slashed across her exposed breasts and wrapped itself around her back. She spun wildly and her face reddened as her hair stuck to her spit-smeared face.

Whack!

The belt lashed down and caught her breasts again but this time it wound tightly around her neck before she spun back under its tension and was released. A long dribble of spit ran from her mouth until it reached the floor.

43

Whack! Whack! Whack!

He beat her remorselessly, each time allowing the belt to wind around her and stop her spinning before pulling it free and starting her again like a top.

Deborah eased further forward. She felt herself tingling all over and, as she moved, she felt the redness in her neck spreading down across her breasts and burning around the base of her hardening nipples. She squeezed her legs together and felt the heat in her labia and, when she squeezed her buttocks, she felt the edges of her cunt swelling and throbbing against the insides of her thighs. As she watched Chrissie's spinning body, Deborah lifted her buttocks higher and opened her legs so that the edges of her cunt were fully exposed.

Winston threw down the belt and started undoing his trousers.

"Now, suck this tart!"

He peeled them down and pulled out his cock. It was hard and black and, as Deborah stared at it, she could see the raised and throbbing veins along the full length of its stiff shaft.

Winston grabbed Chrissie by the hips and stopped her spinning. He pulled her close to him and placed the engorged tip of his cock against her spit-smeared mouth.

"I said suck it tart!"

Her eyes were wide and she struggled giddily to focus as he pressed his cock between her lips then reached down and grabbed the back of her upturned head.

"Don't just lick it. Suck it! Right in!"

He pressed the back of her head and Deborah watched as the shaft of his cock slid deeply into Chrissie's mouth. She choked as it met the back of her throat and she twisted her face away. He pressed it in again but again she choked as her throat gagged and made her heave.

"Suck it tart!"

Chrissie choked again, wriggling and twisting and fighting against him in desperation, but he would not release

44

her.

"Give her some of the cane. Perhaps that will make her more obedient."

Winston held her cheeks and pinched her mouth around his engorged glans as Mingo brought the cane down across her buttocks.

Whack!

She tightened her body in pain and Winston thrust his massive shaft into her mouth but she choked and pulled back as sticky streams of spit dribbled from her mouth and ran down onto the floor.

Whack!

He thrust it in again but still she could not take it.

Whack! Whack! Whack!

Mingo beat her buttocks with the stiff cane, causing thin red stripes to appear across her taut skin but no matter how hard Winston thrust his cock into her mouth she could not keep it in. She tried to plead for mercy but, as the cane kept flailing her, she gradually grew weaker and hung more limply from the swinging chain.

Deborah raised her buttocks higher then starting creeping forward. Gross yanked at the chain between her wrists but this time she pulled against him. He tugged hard to hold her back but she knelt up, snatched her wrists to the side and broke free. He tried to grab her but she twisted past him and crawled across the floor until she was crouching at Winston's feet.

Winston looked down at her and grinned as Gross grabbed hold of the chain and tried to pull her back.

"Gross! Leave her!"

Gross let the chain fall to the ground and crouched down on the ground.

"Could you do better bitch?"

Deborah looked up at him and opened her mouth wide.

"I said could you do better bitch?"

She looked up at his glistening, black cock and felt a fresh surge of heat in her cunt. She lifted her bottom high and felt her swelling labia pulsating and, when she pressed her buttocks together, she felt the moisture that ran between them sticking to her pubic hair. She licked her tongue along her lower lip and tasted the spit that was running over it, then she held her tongue out and let a long strand of spit dribble from its end.

"Tell me bitch. How would you suck it?"

She raised her face towards his stiff cock and felt its heat. Beyond him she could see Chrissie hanging upside down and beyond her, at the end of the warehouse, the cage. Its glistening bars shone into her eyes and she flinched as again she imagined the woman in the story. She pictured her being forced from its sanctuary and she felt a wave of heat in her hips as she saw again the images of her suffering.

"Deep," she said softly and, as she spoke, she experienced a gushing heat that surged from her hips deeply into the flesh of her throbbing cunt. She felt her outer labia swelling and opening and she sensed her inner petals forcing out against them.

"Deep," she said again and the thrilling surge of excitement throbbed through her body again, burning into her aching thighs and sending shivers into her engorging clitoris.

"Deep," and she raised her buttocks to allow the fleshy edges of her cunt to expand and, as they opened fully, she felt the hardening thrust of her clitoris as it poked out from the front of her dampening crack.

"Deep, deep, deep," each time she said the word her cunt got wetter and, as she lifted her buttocks even higher, she thought of the cane and the punishment it could give. She stared at the cage, fixated by the hard, steel bars, and waited for his command.

"Suck it then bitch!"

But she did not move, she could not. She knew that even though she was under his control she could not obey him yet. She dropped her head and started to lick the floor, dripping spit from her tongue then licking it up and rubbing it around her mouth and cheeks. She lifted her bottom higher.

"Suck it bitch!"

His orders thrilled her even more and his anger made her lap the floor like a hungry animal. Her cunt was wetter and she felt its moisture trickling along the dilated crack of flesh and onto her tangled pubic hair. She waited, staring at the cage then glancing at the rattan cane that hung from Mingo's hand.

"Thrash her Mingo. Thrash her until she does what she is ordered!"

She lifted her buttocks as high as she could and squared her elbows against the floor, licking her tongue out onto the ground and waiting for the blows that would allow her to obey.

Whack!

She flattened her face against the ground and licked at it eagerly.

Whack!

Her spit tasted sweet and warm and she fed on it as the cane fell again.

Whack!

The blow stung her buttocks deeply but she only raised them higher, licking at the floor and looking up longingly at the bars of the distant cage.

Whack! Whack! Whack!

The pain cut deeply inside her and caused the burning heat in her cunt to boil. She felt the dripping wetness running around her throbbing clitoris and the sticky strands of her own moisture dribbling from her pubic hair and running against the insides of her thighs.

Whack! Whack! Whack!

She felt her knees buckling and she fell forward but still she had not felt enough pain. She opened her mouth wide and pulled her lips across the spit-drenched floor.

47

Whack! Whack! Whack!

Her head was reeling as the blows of the cane knocked her flat against the floor. Her arms stretched forward and she clawed at the ground to try and pull herself up again.

Whack! Whack! Whack!

Each time the cane crashed down across her red-striped flesh it forced her hips flat against the ground. The front of her slit splayed open exposing her engorged clitoris to the hard floor and she felt giddy with the agonizing punishment as it flooded through her throbbing veins. She was ready now. She wanted his orders, she wanted to be told to act, but he was making her suffer more before releasing her into the pleasure she craved.

Whack! Whack! Whack!

She gasped breathlessly and twisted on her side but still the thrashing cane did not stop. She glanced at the cage but all she could see was a blur then, somewhere in the back of her mind, she heard her orders.

"Now bitch, suck it deep!"

She struggled onto her knees, unsure whether she was still being beaten or not and took the stiff, black cock into her mouth.

"Suck it bitch! All the way down!"

She felt the throbbing glans against her sore lips and folded them behind its wide flange. The skin behind it was smooth but, as she took it in further, she felt the raised veins that pulsated down its length. She cupped her tongue beneath it and licked the thickened flesh then ran her mouth down it, hungry for its base, ravenous for its throbbing veins and thirsty for its spunk.

The hot glans pressed into the back of her mouth and, for a moment, she felt her throat gagging as if it should be resisted, but she sucked it deeper and when it touched the back of her throat again she felt herself opening to receive it. The pressure of the throbbing end forced her throat wide and, as she imagined its length and thought of its hairy base against her lips, she swallowed hard and it went down.

She could not breathe but she held it there, deeply inside, until she felt it thickening along its length and running with spunk. The beating surge opened her mouth even wider, then pressed against her tongue then finally, as his throbbing glans swelled against the sides of her throat, his spunk shot from its dilating end and she swallowed it hungrily until there was no more left.

He pulled back and she gasped for air, sucking in deep breaths and gulping wildly. She opened her eyes and there was another cock in front of her face. It was Clay's. He held it out in his hand, it was thick and long, even longer than Winston's and, as she continued to gasp for breath, he pressed its massive end against her dripping lips.

She reached up her hands, raising the weight of the shackles and chain around her wrists, and wrapped her fingers around it. It throbbed heavily as she drew its black end into her mouth. She ran her hands down it as she took it in, feeling every pulsating vein along its length, then she took a deep breath and forced it to the back of her throat. She squeezed the base and took it deeper until her hands were forced wide by her mouth and it was all inside. She held his heavy balls and pressed her fingers against his anus, feeling the rush of his spunk and drawing it out with her gulping breathless convulsions. As it splashed down her throat, she felt dizzy and faint and when he pulled it out she could hardly get her breath back, but the taste of spunk in her mouth made her desperate for more and she looked up appealing for her mouth to be filled again.

As she drew the next one into her throat then swallowed onto it and pulled it down, she felt her sopping cunt dilating and throbbing, she sensed the rush of her own orgasm and, as it boiled within her, she sucked the cock down in a frenzy.

As the spunk splashed into her throat, she felt the seizure of her exploding climax gripping her body and she took the next one in without another breath. She held onto it and sucked at it with the gulping spasms in her throat as her own orgasm burst and flooded through her, throwing her into a rigid convulsion that left her gasping for air, jerking uncontrollably and yelling for more.

"Can you take more bitch?"

"Yes! Yes! Deep! Deep! More! More! ... "

She yelled in a frenzy, screaming at the top of her voice as though she was possessed. Her own words rang in her ears until they filled her mind. Suddenly she stopped, as she realised what was happening to her and what she was saying. She looked around and saw where she was, it was as if she had woken from a dream and she felt confused and muddled. She looked at the shackles and tasted the semen in her throat and was seized with panic. Fear flooded through her and she started screaming and shouting hysterically.

"No! No! Please, please let me go! Please let me go! Let me go! Let me go!" She twisted sideways and started rolling around on the floor in a panic-stricken frenzy. "I'm frightened, I'm frightened, please, please, I - "

"Shut up bitch! Tie her ankles and make it tight! Gross! Pull her up! As high as you can! We've only just started with you bitch."

Deborah crawled across the floor towards the cage. She reached out for it, hoping to feel the cold steel of its bars, but Winston blocked her way.

"Please, please," she begged, "please put me in the cage - "

Her cries were stifled as she felt the tightening of a rope around her ankles. She struggled to get free but it was hopeless. She watched Chrissie, spent and barely conscious, being let down and hauled away by the ankles. She tried to call out to her but could no longer make any sound then, as Chrissie was pulled into the darkness and thrown down against the wall, Deborah felt a sudden, painful jerk as the rope tightened and she was hauled across to the swinging chain. They lifted her legs and tied the rope to the chain then, as it clanked noisily through the wooden pulley block, she was yanked up until she was clear of the ground. She spun giddily as the men crowded around her and she fixed her eyes on the hard bars of the cage in the hope that when they had done with her they would let her rest inside its sanctuary.

CHAPTER 4

Deborah lay on the grating floor of the cage. The heavy tarpaulin had been slung over it but she could see light coming through tears in the sides. She felt cold and shivery and, because she had been unable to stop herself thinking about what had happened in the warehouse, she had not slept. She felt so ashamed and humiliated but that was not all. Even thinking about how she had been degraded caused a confusing mixture of fear and craving to well up inside her. She could not hold back the strange surges of desire to be enslaved, and that frightened her, but worse than that was how she had felt the overpowering and terrifying need to be disobedient in order to suffer the levels of pain she craved. It was like a madness! She had to have the pain before she could be released into the pleasures of servitude, and she wanted both so much. She did not understand it but she knew she could not resist it and she shivered all over as the images of her suffering again filled her mind.

After they had finished with her in the warehouse they had thrown her into the cage. She had huddled against the bars shivering and sobbing. A few hours later she had heard voices and had shouted out and pleaded to be released but she had been ignored as the heavy cage had been moved out of the warehouse. She had stared between the bars of the floor and watched in disbelief as the cage was swung up on a crane and dropped onto the deck of a ship.

The clanking of chains, the whirring of machinery and the smell of oil had made her shiver and when she heard the ship's siren and felt the vibrations of its engine her terror had overtaken her. She had cried loudly as she felt the rolling motion of the ship as slowly it made its way out to sea. She had wiped her eyes with the back of her hand and rubbed the spit from her chin and even though she could see the trembling of her fingers it still all seemed too much to believe. But, as the ship went further out into the darkness of the open sea and the sounds became isolated from the noises of the land she knew it was all real.

She dozed fitfully then woke up suddenly, confused and afraid and thinking of Chrissie. What had happened to her? Was she alright? She could hardly bear the thought of her friend, her only friend, being mistreated so cruelly. She tried to imagine that it was all a terrible nightmare and that she would wake up to Chrissie's broad smile and the excitement of an evening out together. She screwed up her eyes until she pictured Chrissie's flashing teeth and long black hair then, holding her breath and keeping the image firmly fixed in her mind she opened her eyes wide. Her heart sank as she looked around in the blackness of the covered cage and the impression of Chrissie faded from her now blinking and tear-filled eyes. She felt embarrassed and foolish; she was utterly alone.

She jumped up as the tarpaulin was ripped away and the iron door of her cage was opened. She squinted her eyes and lifted her face into warm rain. She opened her mouth and let it drip onto her lips and, as a warm wind blew across her face, she felt the stinging saltiness of sea air against her soft skin. For a moment she felt free and excited then, as she went to wipe her wet forehead, she felt the weight of the shackles around her wrists and her stomach filled with renewed anxiety. Her fears were fully awakened as Gross pulled on the chain between her shackled wrists and she fell backwards against the grating floor.

"Food," he muttered. "Come get food."

He hauled her out of the cage and down a metal gangway. She had to drop her head low to get underneath the rusty, white painted pipes and cables that were entwined around the narrow passage, and, as she ducked and stumbled down the steps, she felt the throbbing drone of the ship's engines beneath her stocking-covered feet and the sickening movement as the ship rolled slowly on the open sea.

"Where are you taking me? What's happening? Please, tell me where I am being taken?"

"Gross must not say. Gross must not say."

He pulled her past a large, open tank of water and into a narrow galley. A tangle of pipes ran along the ceiling and a stainless steel cooking range took up the whole of one side. It was hot and steamy and crammed with steel saucepans and cooking utensils. He dragged her to a small table where there was a plate of food and pulled her down onto a seat.

"Eat."

He crouched down opposite her and looked around the small galley furtively.

"No Saab here. No Saab to see Gross."

He pressed his tongue out and squeezed his lips onto it, then, still looking around to check that no one was watching, he reached forward under the table. He splayed his stumpy fingers between Deborah's knees and edged them apart. She felt a warm draught of steamy air between her thighs. Gross's fingers pressed her knees wider and she felt the soft, naked edges of her cunt peeling apart. He forced her thighs further apart and the warm, moist air caressed the inner edges of her soft labia as they opened under the pressure. He moved his fingers to the tops of her stockings then onto the moist, naked flesh that lay above them.

As Gross's fingers crept higher, he pressed her knees further apart with his elbow. She felt the painful pressure of the outsides of her thighs against the hem of her short dress.

53

She pulled herself further back in the seat, hoping he would give up and draw away but, as she moved back, he pressed his fingers further. Her knees parted even more and the pressure of the hem of her skirt against her skin increased.

She felt his fingertips touching the creases at the tops of her thighs, pressing into them and causing her labia to part even wider. She eased back more on her seat but he ran his thick fingers to the top of her crack and splayed her outer labia wide. The warm, moist air touched the exposed edges of her inner labia and she felt wetness running down between her flesh and settling against her dilating anus. He pressed his finger against her clitoris and her labia opened even more. She felt his broad fingertip sinking between them and she squirmed against it to try and pull away. She could not move back any further and, as he pushed his finger deeper inside her wet cunt, she felt herself beginning to drive herself forward and draw it in.

Suddenly there was the clattering of footsteps on the gangway and Winston appeared.

"What are you doing Gross?"

Gross pulled his hand back and hung his head.

"Trying to get a feel eh? That's very bad Gross, very bad. I don't know what Saab would think about that."

Gross looked up under his eyes and started mumbling to himself fearfully.

Winston pushed himself behind Deborah. He squeezed her shoulders and she tensed up as his powerful hands pressed down on her. He extended them around her throat then ran them down the front of her torn dress until he reached her breasts. He cupped his hands around them and lifted them slightly. Gross stared at them as Winston lifted them in his hands, squeezing them tightly and pressing his thumb and forefinger around her nipples.

"Like to look as well eh Gross?"

Deborah's face flushed red with embarrassment as Winston opened the front of her dress and exposed her breasts to Gross.

Gross leant forward inquisitively as Winston released his grip and pulled Deborah backwards on the chair, dragging her away from the table so that her legs were exposed.

He reached his hands down between her legs, running them along the tops of her thighs until he reached her knees. He pulled them wide and, as her legs parted under the pressure, her dress rode up to the tops of her thighs, exposing the tops of her stockings and the glistening wet flesh of her dilated cunt.

Deborah pushed her hands down to try and release his grip but he was too strong. She grabbed his wrists but he twisted them away and dragged her to her feet. He took hold of the shackles, pulled them as wide as the chain would allow and latched each one to a stainless steel hook that was fixed to a round, metal bar running across the ceiling. He pulled her dress up around her waist, exposing her completely to Gross's piercing stare.

"Gross like. Gross like pretty girl."

"Nice soft cunt eh Gross? Want to get another feel eh?"

Deborah tightened her bottom and tried to push Winston away but he yanked at the thin material of her suspender belt and pulled it painfully against her hips. He grabbed the material and pulled it away from her hips, twisting it painfully until it dug deeply into her skin. She tried desperately to squirm away but he was too strong and she could not stop him.

Gross leaned forward and stared as Winston forced her knees wide apart with his spare hand. Still twisting the material of her suspender belt, he grabbed hold of her pubic hair, pulling it upwards and exposing the moist flesh of her soft cunt.

"Beautiful soft cunt eh Gross? But not much to see is there? I think she needs a shave."

He let go of her suspender belt and it snapped back

against her writhing hips.

Deborah started twisting on her shackles and kicked out at Winston.

"Let me go! Let me go!"

She kept yelling and screaming to be released as he twisted up some plastic bags and tied them around her ankles. He pulled her legs as wide as they would go and secured the bags to another steel bar that ran just above floor level in front of the stainless steel range.

She felt so exposed, stretched out on the metal bars and unable to protect or cover herself. She started swallowing and gulping as a panic began to spread through her. It built up inside them suddenly she started screaming. She could not stop herself. It was as though all the things that had happened to her were flooding back into her mind and throwing her into a desperate frenzy. She tossed her head from side to side in blind panic.

"Let me go! Let me go! Let me - "

"Shut up bitch!"

"Let me go! Let me go! Let me - "

Winston grabbed a long stainless steel spoon and thrust it sideways across her mouth. It clanked against her teeth and squeezed the sides of her mouth wide, stifling her cries and sending fresh shivers of fear through her trembling body. He took two more plastic bags, twisted them up and tied them around the ends of the spoon. He pulled the free ends around the back of her head and, tangling them in her hair, he secured them in a tight knot behind her head.

Her eyes blazed wide with terror as he grabbed a sharp knife and rested its cold tip against the top of her crack. She gazed down in horror and gasped for breath as she tried to pull herself away from the shiny blade. But it was hopeless, she could hardly move and she screwed her eyes up, not daring to watch, as she felt the sharp tip of the knife first pressing against her exposed flesh then being twisted amongst her pubic hair.

56

He twisted the tip of the knife around her pubic hair, tugging them and sending shivers of pain through her flesh as they were pulled. As he entwined them around the sharp metal she tightened her buttocks but this only exposed her cunt more fully and made him twist the blade harder. He lifted the knife higher and turned it so that the flat edge of the blade lay fully across her cunt. She felt its sharp metal surface digging into her tender flesh and she froze, not daring to move as he continued to twist the tip amongst her pubic hair. She felt the pressure increasing then she felt it released as the sharp tip severed the entwined hairs around its edges. He pressed the blade harder against her flesh and, still with her eyes closed, she held her breath as he pulled her hair out between his fingertips and sliced through it slowly.

"Give me that washing up liquid Gross!"

Gross did not take his eyes from Deborah's exposed cunt as he handed the plastic bottle to Winston.

Winston laughed as he squirted the liquid onto her pubic hair.

"I hope the blade is sharp enough!"

He rubbed the liquid in and it foamed up and dribbled down her thighs. He pushed his fingers between her legs and rubbed the bubbles around the edges of her cunt, parting the fleshy furrow and running his finger along its inside.

His fingers were warm and slid easily against her soft outer labia and she felt an anxious thrill as they slipped in further, parting the swelling inner leaves and glancing against the tip of her swelling clitoris.

Winston wet the blade under a running tap and placed it against the top edge of her pubic hair. Deborah shook her head and the steel spoon bit into the edges of her mouth but she stopped as she felt the blade being drawn down slowly across her trembling skin. She froze as she felt the sharp blade slicing through the hair. He drew it away, washed the blade and continued, slicing the black mat away bit by bit until she was completely shaved at the front. She felt a coolness against her skin as her nakedness was exposed to the air and she drew in breath, relieved that he had stopped.

As Gross cocked his head from side to side, Winston pressed the blade between her legs and carefully cut away the hairs that clung to the edges of her cunt. He kept washing the blade then taking it back to her skin, slicing through each hair as close to its base as possible. He rubbed more soapy foam onto her and worked carefully until he was satisfied that she was completely shaved.

Winston filled a metal container with water and sloshed it over her, wiping away any bubbles and feeling around her cunt for any stray hairs. When he found one, he pulled it out by the root causing her to tense and bite down on the steel spoon in pain.

She felt degraded by the shaving but she felt her naked labia still swelling and she knew her hardening clitoris was poking from between the pink edges of her uncovered slit. She bit onto the steel spoon to try and distract herself but the pain only increased the hotness that she felt running inside her naked flesh. She pulled at her wrists and ankles but the unyielding tension started a flood of heat running within her tightly pulled hips. It was as though any effort she made increased her pain and this only fed her uncontrollable desire for pleasure. She dropped back hopelessly.

Winston filled the container again and emptied it over her head. She threw her head from side to side as the water dragged her hair heavily over her face before flowing over her breasts and dripping down her stomach. He filled it again and she gasped as water ran between the tight-pulled spoon and her outstretched mouth. She tried to escape it, squirming against her bonds wildly, but she could not avoid it as it poured over her naked cunt and dripped down the insides of her splayed-out thighs.

"I think she likes the water eh Gross?"

He doused her again, throwing the water fully into her face and making her choke.

58

"Untie her Gross, she needs a proper wash."

Gross knelt down and unravelled the twisted up plastic bags from the bars, all the time being careful not to touch her and pulling his hands back sharply if her got too close. For a moment she stayed frozen, her arms high and her legs wide with the plastic bags still tied tightly to her ankles and wrists, then suddenly she slumped forward onto her knees, biting onto the hard, steel spoon and gasping for breath.

Winston grabbed her by the hair and hauled her out of the galley. He dragged her back along a rusty gangway and stopped at the tank of water. He threw her down on her back and she fell heavily on the open iron grating that formed a platform in front of it. He bound her wrists together in front of her by winding the bags tightly around them. He took their trailing ends, pulled them behind her back and knotted them securely then tied her ankles together and rolled her over.

Her eyes were wide with fear and she panted frantically, water still running from her mouth and her hair sticking in black strands across her reddened cheeks. The chain from the shackles hung down in a heavy loop from her bound hands which were pressed hard against the base of her stomach under the strain of the plastic bags tied behind her back. She wanted to plead for mercy but it was impossible and, when he grabbed each end of the long, steel spoon that stuck out from the sides of her mouth and dragged her up by it, her body filled with a painful nausea of hopeless dread.

He yanked her to her feet, thrust her against the edge of the open water tank and tried to push her in. Her legs caught on the side and she managed to keep upright but he pushed her harder and she plunged backwards into it.

The water surged up around her in a wave and splashed across her face. Winston held tightly onto the spoon, forcing her mouth wide, and water flooded in, running straight to the back of her throat and making her cough and choke. Her eyes widened even more as water and spit frothed from her mouth and she pulled wildly with her shoulders to try and get her hands free.

He lifted her up with the spoon, holding her head above the water as it sloshed around her breasts. She drew her legs up to try and get some purchase against the side of the steel tank and, as she pushed them wide, the heavy chain between her shackles sank between her legs. She felt its weight pulling her down and she tried to grab it, thrusting her hands between the tops of her thighs and stretching out her fingers frantically to try and reach it. For a moment, as she splashed and flailed in the water, she felt the naked edges of her cunt against the backs of her hands, then she was thrown into blind confusion as he pushed down on the spoon and thrust her beneath the surface.

The echoing noise of exploding bubbles burst into her drumming ears. She kicked her feet against the side of the tank and heard the chain clanking dully against its metal edges but she could do nothing to break free. She opened her mouth as wide as she could and tried to break herself free from the metal spoon but it filled with water straight away and she swallowed it down in involuntary, stinging gulps.

He lifted her back up and she struggled to get her breath back. Water ran from her mouth and the burning in her throat made her heave. She thought she was going to be sick and she bit hard onto the spoon and pulled her wrists against her bonds until the nausea passed.

As her body tensed with the strain, she stretched her fingers out as far as she could and they pressed against the insides of her writhing thighs. As she bit harder, she tensed her chest and curled her fingers back until they reached the naked edges of her shaved cunt. She bit harder, thrust her thumbs into the front of the fleshy furrow and pinched onto it with her fingers, squeezing her outer labia as tightly as she could and sending an absorbing pain deeply into her hips.

She hardly felt the pressure of the spoon as he lifted her higher above the surface of the water. She pinched her fingers deeply into the soft flesh of her labia and gasped noisily with the ever-increasing pain. She panted fast, spitting water from her mouth and trying to cry out for mercy yet, all the time, pinching her swelling flesh harder and driving the delightful pain deeper.

She felt the pressure of the metal spoon against her grinding teeth and clamped her mouth around it as her confused mind threw her into an uncontrolled mixture of panic and desire. She wanted him to let her go, to release her and set her free but, at the same time, she wanted lifting on the spoon so that she could dig her fingertips deeper into the soft flesh of her cunt. She wanted him to haul her up like an animal on a hook and she wanted to feel the desperation of her captivity and she wanted to be consumed by the flames of desire that were lit by the brutal self-punishment of her ever-delving fingernails.

Her fingers dug deeper into her burning flesh and she splayed the swollen folds back so that the cold water flooded against them. She bit hard onto the spoon that stretched her cheeks and stared forward wildly as the water frothed and bubbled around her breasts. She tightened her grip on her swelling flesh. She pinched her nails in deeply and pulled at the engorged edges, opening her cunt and exposing its inner warmth to the cold shock of the water. She pulled more and felt, not only the pain of her pinching nails and the ecstasy of being held up by the spoon in her mouth, but the shocking delight of the cold water as it forced itself into the entrance of her vagina.

He lifted her higher and she felt the water running from the ends of her hard nipples and she tossed her head back throwing her wet, tangled hair away from her face as if to tell him to lift her higher. She felt almost the full weight of her body hanging on the spoon and, as the heavy shackles pulled against her arms and the water splashed around her hips, opened her legs more, splayed the edges of her naked cunt as wide as she could as she pinched the stretched-out flesh with all her strength.

With her eyes wide open and holding her breath, she let go of her labia and thrust her finger deeply inside her vagina. Water ran up into its warm entrance and she felt the tip of her clitoris pressing against the palm of her hand.

He pulled her up even higher until her splayed-out cunt was just below the foaming surface of the water. She bit harder onto the spoon and held a quickly snatched breath. She opened her legs as wide as she could and pressed her knees against the sides of the tank. She pushed a finger into the warm entrance to her anus. It closed tightly around her knuckle but she pushed it in until she could get it no further. Her eyes opened wider as she thrust into herself deeply, burying one finger into her vagina and the other as deeply as she could into her anus.

She wanted him to pull harder on the spoon. She wanted to feel the tension and strain as she braced her legs against the tank and she wanted to feel the grating of the spoon between her clenched teeth. She wanted to feel the splashing water against her exposed flesh and she wanted him to hold her there until she finished. She wanted to feel the rhythm of the frothing water and the empty heaving of her desperate breaths and she wanted to feel the control that he had over her and the strain against her legs as she was taken over by the spasms of her orgasm.

He lifted her some more and she drew a deep breath through her nostrils, biting down onto the spoon and pushing her fingers even deeper. She looked down into the water, watching it as it foamed between her legs and splashed up against her straining stomach. She reached her head down against the pressure of the spoon and with one final effort stuffed her fingers even deeper into her cunt and anus. A wave of heat coursed threw her as she felt her orgasm building up. Her fingers felt on fire as she felt the anxiety of her pent up desires being released. She braced her knees as hard as she could against the sides of the tank and bit harder on the spoon but suddenly, as she felt the frenzy of her climax straining in her chest and throbbing in her throat, he pulled her out over the side of the tank and threw her onto the wet deck.

She struggled to keep her fingers tightly inside her vagina and anus but, as she fell heavily, her legs were knocked apart and her hands were dragged away by the weight of the shackles and chain. Frantically she thrust her hands back between her legs, desperate to release her orgasm, but Winston grabbed hold of her shoulders and turned her over.

"On your knees bitch! On your knees!"

She lay flat out on her front, still scrabbling to get her fingers back to her cunt and anus. She managed to reach her cunt and probed at it in a frenzy.

"I said on you knees bitch!"

He looped his arm under her hips and lifted her buttocks. She thrust her other hand between her legs and clawed her fingers desperately towards her dilated anus.

"Want your arse filling eh bitch?"

He knelt down behind her and parted her buttocks. Her hand was still trying to reach its goal but he slapped it away. She froze for a moment then thrust her hand back, straining her fingers out desperately. He smacked it away again and this time pressed his own finger against her pulsating anus.

She felt the probing tip of his finger and instantly sank back against it. The muscular ring of her anus welcomed it as he pushed it in and she raised her buttocks higher to get it as far as it would go.

He pushed it in and lifted her higher on it while her own finger delved deeply into her throbbing cunt. She drew it out and grasped her clitoris, squeezing it hard and sending shivering spasms of heat into her hips. She bit onto the spoon in her mouth but it did not give her enough pain and suddenly she pulled away from him and scuttled back to the side of the tank. She crouched with her back against it, her legs wide open at the knees and her finger and thumb pulling wildly at her hard and swollen clitoris. She stared at him defiantly, urging him to force her to obey.

"Bitch!"

Winston picked up a broad, steel spatula.

"On your knees bitch! Do what you're told!"

She sensed his anger and, still refusing to move, she pulled harder at her clitoris, pinching it and digging her nails into its hard and throbbing flesh.

He raised the spatula threateningly but she just dropped her knees further apart.

"On your knees bitch!"

She held her clitoris out of the front of her slit then slowly reached forward with the fingers of her other hand and pressed one of them firmly against her exposed anus.

He took a step towards her and raised the spatula again but she did not flinch or shy back, she only pressed her finger into the circular muscle and delved it in until it would go no further.

He stared at her for a second then suddenly kicked out at her. As she fell on her side, he smacked the spatula down across her exposed buttocks.

Smack!

She reeled sideways but still kept her finger deeply in her anus. It contracted tightly and an extra surge of excitement shot through her.

Smack!

The hard spatula cut across her taut skin and a shock of pain sent a wave of heat through her hips. The pain contracted her anus again and she thrust her finger up and down frantically against the constricting muscle.

Smack! Smack! Smack!

She felt the power of his punishment as the blows rained down on her bottom. Yet still she felt defiant, she knew she was giving him a reason to discipline her and it added a strange but necessary meaning to her pain. The thought started a welling heat of what she knew would be a massive orgasm and she turned and stared back at him insolently.

Smack! Smack! Smack!

The pain was terrible as the steel spatula flailed across her skin but still it was not enough, still she needed more and she turned again and stared at him in wanton contempt.

Smack! Smack! Smack!

She felt her blood boiling with the surge of her orgasm. She probed her anus deeply and pulled wildly on her clitoris, revelling in the pain and relishing the ferocity of her punishment.

"Gross! Bring her onto the deck! The bitch needs more discipline!"

She dropped her knees back even more to try and show him she was ready. She did not need any more. She had received enough punishment. No, she did not want to be taken for more. It was enough. She needed to finish. But, as Gross pulled at the heavy chain and she was dragged forward, she realised that it was Winston who was in control, that she had been deceiving herself with a game that she thought was for her benefit. Her stomach was seized with anxiety and she pulled back, but, as Gross yanked the chain hard and she felt the surge of pain in her wrists, she knew that this was not a game.

Gross dragged her out onto the deck. She only had a second to look around and see where she was before Winston brought the metal spatula down across her buttocks again.

Smack! Smack! Smack!

She bit onto the spoon in her mouth as she was gripped with pure, stinging pain.

Winston shouted to the others who were pulling back the hatch of a gaping hold on the ship's deck.

"Come on boys! Our little bitch needs bringing to heel!"

They ran over, Wesley trailing a long rope in his hands and Mingo and Clay hurriedly unbuckling their belts.

"She seems to think she can do what she wants. She needs a lesson in obedience that's for sure. Gross! Untie her!"

Gross pulled the twisted up plastic bags from her

ankles and wrists and, as soon as she was free, she crawled fearfully to the bottom of a gangway and cowered against it.

"Crawl bitch! Crawl when your master commands you!"

She pressed herself against the rusty metal afraid to move.

"Give her a few lashes Wesley!"

Wesley brought the rope down across her back.

Lash! Lash! Lash!

It burned into her skin and she tried to scuttle away.

Lash! Lash! Lash!

"Crawl bitch! Here!"

She looked at Winston and tried to move towards him but Wesley flailed her again in a frenzy.

Lash! Lash! Lash!

"Here bitch! Here!"

Racked with pain, she crawled forward and stopped in front of him.

"I want to see you crawling around the deck. Everywhere you go, you crawl and if you don't satisfy us you will get a beating. Do you hear that bitch? You only do what we say!"

Deborah dribbled spit from her mouth and it ran over the spoon before dripping down onto the floor. Her body was soaked and the lashing rope had left her skin stinging and red. She felt hopeless and wretched and could only nod her head in futile submission.

"Good! Now start crawling and we will make sure you do what we ask."

They drove her down the gangway and onto a lower deck. She sensed the rolling of the ship and heard the clanking of winches. Her nostrils were filled with the scent of oily fumes and, as she was driven past heavy open gratings, her skin was scorched by hot blasts of air from noisy fans. Her knees were sore but every time she stopped the rope was lashed across her back and she was forced on.

Lash! Lash! Lash!

It was relentless, and, as she became more exhausted, she could only crawl slowly so Wesley tied the rope around her neck and dragged her on. In the end, even though he yanked the rope violently, she collapsed and could not move at all. She lay on her front exhausted. Mingo beat her with his leather belt, flailing her with it until finally, she managed to summon the strength to get back to her knees and carry on.

It became dark but still they drove her around the deck, thrashing her to make her go faster and thrashing her again when she stopped. Mingo straddled her and tried to ride her but she did not have the strength to support him. She fell flat on her front and they turned her over and held her down and flailed her with their belts while he wanked over her face. With his spunk running down the side of her outstretched cheeks, they forced her back onto her knees and he tried to ride her again. Again she collapsed and they rolled her onto her back again and the other three wanked over her, spurting their spunk over her face and hair and rubbing it over her breasts.

She tried to plead for mercy but only frothy spit came from her mouth. She wanted to beg them to fuck her and make her suck their cocks and wank them and drink their spunk, anything as long as they would stop her torture. She wanted to be locked up in the cage so that she could be shut away from the terror they were inflicting on her, but she could do nothing except crawl when they told her and take their beating when she failed to please.

She fainted when they made her crawl along a narrow metal gangway and they threw water over her to bring her around. Mingo wanted to tie her by the ankles and hang her over the side of the ship but Winston said he had had enough. Wesley pulled her on the rope to the centre of the deck where they had opened the hatch. He pushed her to the rusty rim, held her there for a moment as she swayed giddily above the dark abyss, then he released the rope around her neck and pushed her down into the gaping hold.

Her nostrils filled with dust as her wet and semen-covered body landed on a huge pile of musty grain. She rolled down the side, barely conscious and unaware of where she was, as the images of her ordeal flashed like a nightmare through her mind. She crashed against the steel-plate side of the hold and lay there stunned.

Slowly, she came to her senses and looked around. She shivered all over as she stared into the darkness then she jumped around in panic as a soft hand reached out behind her and stroked her shoulder. It was Chrissie!

Chrissie reached up and undid the plastic bags that held the spoon across Deborah's mouth but when it was free Deborah would not let it go.

"Let me take it," said Chrissie softly.

Deborah pulled back in fear, clenching her teeth tightly to the hard steel spoon before gradually releasing it and falling back against the rusty walls of the grain filled hold.

"What's going on? What's going to happen to us? Where are they taking us? Oh, Chrissie, I'm so afraid."

Chrissie wrapped her arms around her and pulled her close.

"I don't know," she whispered, "I just don't know, but at least we are together."

"Oh Chrissie, are you alright? I've been so worried about you. I'm so afraid."

Chrissie stroked Deborah's face and wiped away the hot tears that trickled down her flushed cheeks.

"Calm down Deborah. We can help each other. I'm sure we'll get a chance to escape. Yes, I'm sure we will. Calm down."

Deborah started crying uncontrollably and pulled herself as close to Chrissie as she could, pressing her face against Chrissie's naked breasts and feeling the pounding of

Chrissie's heart against her tear-stained cheeks.

CHAPTER 5

Deborah and Chrissie were still sleeping deeply when they were woken by Winston and Wesley as they climbed down a long ladder into the cavernous hold. Their clanking footsteps echoed around the deep, steel-walled chamber. They jumped off the bottom of the ladder onto the steel-plated floor. Winston threw a heavy switch that hung from a rusty gantry and some dim, yellow lights flashed on and glowed amid circling clouds of dust. The two men strode over to Deborah and Chrissie between huge piles of grain that stretched back like pyramids into the darkness beyond the lights.

"Wake up bitches! You've got work to do!"

Deborah jumped up, naked except for her torn white stockings and suspender belt.

"Where are you taking us? You must let us go. Please
_ "

Winston kicked out at her and knocked her backwards into the pile of loose grain.

"You'll find out soon enough. Now, come over here, on your knees! And stop whining!" He turned to Chrissie who was wiping her smudged eyes. "You as well tart!"

Both of them crouched on all-fours and crawled over to him.

"Pretty pair eh Wesley?"

Wesley laughed as he dragged over a metal cart with long handles and two wheels.

"Yes, pretty little ponies."

He fetched another cart and wheeled it alongside Deborah. She raised her head to see what he was doing but Winston kicked out at her again and she flinched and looked down at the floor.

Wesley pulled one of the carts behind Deborah and lashed some thin, leather leashes to the handles.

"Back up here little pony," he ordered.

Deborah looked around but he shouted angrily.

"I said back up, not look around! Do what I say!"

Looking ahead fearfully, she started to move backwards slowly as he gave her more instructions.

"To your left, slowly, back up more ... "

She felt his domination and followed his orders blindly. It was as though she was an animal in his service, she could only respond to his will and when he told her to stop she did so instantly.

Wesley led the leather leashes on the handles under her hips. He knotted them then pulled them tightly between her legs, folded them onto the small of her back then secured them to another leash that he stretched between the two handles. As he tugged on the straps, she felt the smooth leather pulling between the soft folds of her shaved cunt and, when he twisted the last knot tight, the leather pinched the edges of her naked labia and made her cry out.

"Quiet while you have your bridle fitted!"

Wesley yanked her head back and held a leather bridle in front of her face. It had several shiny straps, one broader than the rest, and two shiny rings with a steel bar stretched between them.

"Open your mouth pony."

Deborah's eyes widened as she opened her still sore mouth.

"Open your mouth wide."

She dropped her jaw and spit dribbled over her bottom lip and ran to the ground in a long, sticky thread.

Wesley drew the bridle across her face. The thicker strap stretched across her forehead and tightened at the back of her head as he pulled the metal bit between her teeth. He yanked the thin straps on the bridle rings and buckled them together at the back of her neck.

70

"Walk forward!"

She edged forward and the straps around her waist cut into her skin as she took up the weight of the cart. It was heavy but she braced herself and clenched her teeth around the metal bit until finally it began to move.

"Too slow! I can see you need some encouragement little pony. Wesley! Fetch me the driving whip!"

Wesley handed him a long leather whip. It had a stiff, braided handle that tapered to a frayed and broken end. He pulled it back and cracked it behind his head.

Deborah tried again, bending her elbows and straining to move forward but it was not enough and, as she took a deep breath and tensed her muscles for another effort, she felt the stinging blow of the whip fall across her harnessed buttocks.

Crack!

The frayed end cut across her skin and, as he snapped it back, it cracked and burned her with a deep, penetrating pain.

"Get moving pony!"

Deborah fought against the pain, crouching lower and pulling as hard as she could, but her knees were sore and the cart was heavy and she knew she was not moving it fast enough for him.

Crack!

The whip cracked across her buttocks again and she tensed them together and twisted to the side in agony.

"Get going bitch!"

Crack!

She bit hard onto the metal across her mouth and moved forward.

"Stop!"

She dropped down on her elbows, panting and gasping as spit dribbled from her mouth.

"Now harness our other pony!"

Wesley made Chrissie back up between the shafts of

71

the other cart but when he pulled the straps between her legs she twisted away in panic.

"Get back here tart! Get back into your harness!"

She stared at him for a moment, her face filled with fear, then made a dash for the bottom of the pile of grain. He chased after her and grabbed her by the hair. She tried to pull away, spinning around desperately but he held on and her hair spun up tightly until she could no longer move. He dragged her back to the cart, let go of her hair then wrapped his arm beneath her hips and lifted her off the ground, holding her buttocks high as she kicked and fought against his powerful grip.

"Give her a few lashes, perhaps that will make her more obedient."

Winston laid the whip against her wriggling buttocks then drew it back. He held it there as she wriggled and screamed frantically, then he changed his mind and threw it down.

"I think a spanking would be better for a disobedient tart like this. I want to save the whip for when she is harnessed and working."

Wesley smiled and hoisted her buttocks higher. Winston smoothed his large, black hand across her bottom, feeling her taut skin and running his fingers between the tight crack.

"Are you ready to be harnessed tart?"

She struggled and screamed and threw her arms about frantically. He smiled, pulled his hand back and brought it down fiercely.

Smack!

She screeched as his hand smacked down and she flailed her legs out, kicking and struggling against Wesley's powerful grip.

Smack!

She screamed again and stretched her legs back as the pain surged through her body.

Smack!

Every time his hand smacked down she screamed louder and stretched her legs out more.

Smack! Smack! Smack!

She kept screaming but gradually her legs relaxed and she dropped her feet to the floor, bending her buttocks more tightly and opening her thighs.

Smack!

This time she only moaned and her thighs fell wide apart.

Snack!

His hand smacked against the exposed flesh of her cunt.

Smack!

She hardly made a sound and her buttocks opened more as if she was willing him to smack her cunt.

Smack!

He smacked her fully across her fleshy cunt and this time he did not pull his hand back. He kept it there and probed his fingers around her swollen outer labia then pressed them into the fleshy furrow. She raised her buttocks higher as he plunged his finger into her vagina and she dropped her head to the floor as he bent down and started licking around her dilating anus.

Deborah watched as he licked her deeply and she lifted her own buttocks higher as if imagining it was her being probed by his long tongue. Suddenly, he broke away as if bored.

"Now harness the tart!"

Wesley dragged her across to the cart and pushed her backwards between the handles. Her hair hung down across her dirty face as he tied her in and Deborah saw the glistening wetness between her upturned buttocks as he pulled the strap tightly between her legs

Winston cracked the whip across Deborah's buttocks.

Crack!

"Now my little pony, back up here for your first load."

Crack! Crack! Crack!

The whip burned her flesh as she struggled to back the cart. Her knees were so sore and the strap between her legs cut deeply between the furrow of her cunt as she tried to push backwards.

"Stop!"

She stopped obediently.

"This grain has to be moved from here, to over there."

He pointed across the dark hold.

"And you two little ponies will move it!"

Wesley took a smooth handled shovel and loaded grain into her cart, filling it to the brim.

Crack!

"Now pull pony! Pull!"

Deborah dropped her shoulders and pulled with all her strength. The cart would hardly move to start with but, as she strained and dropped her shoulders lower, she managed to get the wheels turning.

Winston followed her across the hold, snatching the whip back and cracking it across her buttocks whenever she slowed down and kicking at her of she steered herself from a straight line. When he ordered her to stop she was exhausted and her elbows collapsed throwing her face-forward onto the dusty ground. The musty smell of grain filled her nostrils and she choked as she panted and gasped for breath and dribbled around the metal bit that cut into her mouth.

"Stand on hind legs pony and unload your cart!"

She struggled to get back onto all-fours.

"On hind legs!"

She tried to stand but the straps around her waist twisted in the shafts of the cart and tightened, pinching the skin of her hips and grabbing at the edges of her cunt.

"On your hind legs pony!"

The pain in her labia sent shivers through her body as she struggled to her feet. The thin, leather straps pulled at them and pinched the naked flesh but she clenched her teeth onto the bit and managed to get up. As she stood up, the grain tipped from the back of the cart and she fell backwards as the weight was released. The straps pulled at her more tightly and she opened her legs to ease it but it was so great that, for a moment, she did not dare move.

"Back for another load pony!"

As she got down on all-fours again, the straps untwisted and the pain eased. As Winston drove her back to the pile of grain, she passed Chrissie as Wesley whipped her bottom with a rope to keep her going. Her dirty face looked pained and tired and her dark, blackened eyes stared forward anxiously. She dropped on her elbows from fatigue and, as Wesley thrashed her and she tried to drag herself forward again, her hard nipples scraped across the rusty, steel floor.

They were made to work for hours, if Deborah slacked or moved too slowly she was punished with the cracking whip and when Chrissie dropped onto her elbows she was thrashed with the rope.

Every time Deborah had to stand to empty her cart the pain from the twisting strap between her legs grew stronger as it tightened and pinched her naked flesh but, as she strained against it, she felt again the strange desire for more. As the sensation spread across her, she found herself labouring harder and pulling the cart quicker so that she could feel the sweet pain of the twisting strap. Each time she tipped the cart back she stood up straighter and squeezed herself more keenly against the entwining strap and, when she felt it cutting into her, she opened her legs a little more and let it dig deeper.

They were tied up to a steel stanchion and two buckets of water were put in front of them. Deborah managed to squeeze her tongue past the bit and lap at the water but Chrissie just stayed on all-fours looking ahead vacantly. Deborah pushed herself against Chrissie but she did not respond. A rush of panic flooded through her as she nudged herself insistently against Chrissie's unresponsive body. When the buckets were taken away they were put back to work.

As Deborah strained to pull the cart, she felt as if she was a pony, driven by a cruel master to labour relentlessly. She imagined herself harnessed to the cart every day and driven out by the cracking whip. Each time she reared back to empty the cart she imagined herself prancing in front of her master and each time she felt the twisting straps against the swollen edges of her cunt, she imagined it being filled by a stallion that her master had selected for her. Her mind was saturated with images of being thrust from behind with a huge cock and she felt her cunt warming and, when she stood back to empty her cart, she felt wetness dribbling from it, running out over the pinching straps and trickling down the insides of her aching thighs.

Suddenly, Wesley started shouting angrily.

"This one's not working hard enough! I think she needs a dousing!"

He picked up one of the buckets of water and threw it over Chrissie's face. The water drenched her hair and it hung down in wet tangles across her dirty, dripping face.

Deborah looked into her eyes and saw only hopelessness and despair.

"That's not enough. She needs waking up properly."

He threw more water over her then unharnessed her, pushed her down on her back and spread her legs wide.

Winston whipped Deborah and kept her hauling the heavy cart as Wesley held Chrissie's legs up high and forced his thick, black cock into her cunt. He held her legs up by her ankles and thrust at her until, as she cried out loudly, he pushed it as deeply inside her as he could and finished. He pulled his cock out and made her suck it until it became stiff again, then he turned her over, held her buttocks apart, and drove it into her anus. He wrapped his arms beneath her hips and lifted her up so that he could get it as deep as possible and, when he was ready to finish, he pulled it out and splashed his spunk over her back and into her hair. When he let her go she fell onto her side, groaning and breathless with her knees bent up to her chest.

Winston threw his whip down and stood over Deborah.

"Follow me little pony and watch."

He strode over towards Chrissie and Deborah crawled behind him, dragging the cart and squeezing her buttocks against the pinching strap between her legs.

He grabbed Chrissie by the hair and pulled her up.

"On your knees pony! On your knees!

She struggled onto all-fours and, still holding her long, wet hair, he straddled her and wedged his legs against her hips.

He turned to Deborah.

"What do you think of my little pony? Do you want to watch her fucked by a stallion?"

Deborah bit onto the metal bar in her mouth and edged forward. The weight of the cart pulled the straps tightly around her waist and, as she moved her legs to crawl forward, the leather thong pinched into her outer labia.

"Come closer little pony. Come and see what the stallion has got to offer her."

She moved again and clenched her teeth tightly against the unforgiving bit, biting onto it and stroking her wet tongue against it. Winston directed her until she was at right angles to Chrissie and, when he got her close enough for her face to touch his leg, he made her stop. She spread her shackled wrists wide as he undid his trousers and pulled out his hard, black cock.

Her eyes widened as he pulled his hands along its length and the throbbing glans swelled as he squeezed the shaft. When he drew his hands down and pressed at the base it pulsated along its full length and, as he wrapped his fingers around his heavy balls, she saw the raised veins pounding as his cock continued to grow.

"Are you ready little pony? Are you ready to see what

it's like to be fucked by something this big?"

Deborah wanted to lick her tongue out to it. She wanted to drool over it and slaver her lips along its length then she wanted to hold it in her hands and feel its throbbing veins. She squeezed her buttocks together and felt the strap tighten but it was not enough. A burning heat was boiling up in her cunt and the pinching of the strap was not enough to allow it to be released.

"Are you ready little pony?"

She knew she wanted to see him driving his cock into Chrissie and thrusting her until he strained to release his surging spunk. But there was something missing and she pulled against the harness restlessly squirming her buttocks and lifting her hips higher. She shook her head slowly from side to side, trying to show him she was not ready, hoping her lack of compliance would infuriate him and he would take the whip to her and beat her until she was driven by the pain to release her climax.

"Watch," he shouted. "Watch!"

Again she shook her head and this time turned away indolently, looking down to the ground and trembling all over with expectation as she sensed his anger and frustration.

"I said watch!"

She could hardly bear not to look but she knew she must disobey. She wanted so much to show him how she could be his slave but she knew she had to resist him first in order to be punished into compliance.

His anger increased.

"I said watch bitch! Watch!"

She pushed her head lower and felt the heat in her cunt burning against the strap that pinched its edges and she thought of his throbbing cock and the slashing whip and the humiliation of the heavy harness and they all blended into a desperate need for pain.

"Wesley! Take the whip to her! Show her what she gets if she does not obey her master!"

Her heart leapt and started pounding frantically in her chest as she heard the words of her master and she clenched her teeth against the metal bit as she heard Wesley bringing the whip over. Her cunt got hotter and her nipples ached as they hardened and throbbed. She felt a flush of shame and fear running down her neck and spit seeped from her mouth in long, sticky strands. She sucked them back up and felt their coolness across the hard bit between her teeth and she raised her buttocks higher then, at last, looked up at him before the whip even fell.

"Wesley! Force her to watch what a pony fucks like. Show her what she gets for disobedience."

She stared at his huge cock and shook her bridle from side to side, frothing spit over her bit and splashing it onto the ground. She heard Wesley lifting the whip behind his head and she raised her buttocks to receive it.

Whack!

He brought it down hard and it struck her fully across her upturned buttocks. Frothing spit shot from her mouth and she fell forward in her harness as Winston lifted Chrissie's buttocks higher and placed the throbbing tip of his cock between their crack.

Whack!

The whip came down again and Deborah clenched her teeth on the bit and squeezed her buttocks together tightly as the pain burned deeply into her flesh.

Whack!

She stared wide-eyed as she watched Winston's cock pushing into Chrissie's exposed cunt.

"Watch pony! This is what it's like to be fucked by a stallion. Look at its length, its stiffness, and see how the stallion rides her and drives his cock into her cunt. See how he mates her and forces her to submit to his fucking."

Whack!

The whip bit deeply into her again but her mind was filled by pictures conjured up by his words and the scene before her. She could smell the sweet mustiness of Chrissie's cunt and, as she watched Winston's cock forcing up inside her, she could see him only as a wild, rearing stallion and Chrissie as a frightened, whinnying mare.

Whack!

Deborah pulled on her harness and shook her head from side to side. The tension of the strap between her legs opened the folds of her cunt and she felt its heat burning around the exposed entrance to her vagina. She wanted the stallion's cock driving into her. She wanted to feel like a mare shackled to a post as he pinioned her with his massive, black cock. She raised her bottom high, exposing herself for more of the whip. She needed the pain to release her and let her live the images which were flooding into her mind.

She waited for the blow of the whip and lifted her buttocks even higher but it did not come. She felt a surge of anxiety as the pictures in her mind became confused and she forced her buttocks up, willing the burning crack of the whip to come down remorselessly on her waiting flesh, but still it did not come. She squirmed herself against the pinching strap and forced open her wet labia, wishing that his cock was penetrating her and forcing forwards in her tightly bound leather harness.

She tossed her head from side to side then suddenly, she felt a hardness against her dilated cunt and the images in her mind flooded back as she watched the black cock thrusting wildly into Chrissie's cunt. Deborah opened her buttocks and pressed back against the strap between her legs, letting it peel back her labia so that the hard shaft could enter her. She was shocked at its coldness and tightened up as her labia folded around it. It was hard and strangely smooth and, as she glanced back, she saw Wesley holding the handle of a shovel and driving it into her cunt.

Wesley pressed the rounded handle of the shovel further in. She felt its unforgiving hardness and she raised herself onto it, imagining the stallion riding her and lifting her on its massive cock. She watched Chrissie fall face-forward onto the ground as Winston's cock drove in up to its base and she pushed back at the handle and felt it penetrating deeply inside. It touched the top of her vagina and she reared her head back in joyful pain, slobbering spit from her mouth and breathing wildly through her flared out nostrils.

She wanted to scream as the handle pulled back, dragging at her flesh and sending tremors of delight through her hips, and she wanted to snort and whinny and show him what she was thinking, but she could do nothing but submit. He pushed it back hard and forced it deeper and she felt the uncontrollable heat of her orgasm building inside. It flushed across her spit-smeared face, down her straining neck and across her throbbing nipples. She felt it draining moisture from her innards and she felt the wetness from her cunt running down the piercing shaft and along the insides of her straining thighs. She raised herself on it, fixed her eyes on Winston's thrusting cock and, as he pulled it out and she saw it pulsating with a surge of spunk, she drove herself back for a last time and finished in a massive, quivering convulsion.

Wesley kept thrusting her with the wooden handle as she watched the spunk splashing from Winston's throbbing cock and, each time he drove it in, she jerked and shook as another spasm burned through her. As the last drops of spunk dripped from Winston's cock, and he bent forward and rubbed it into Chrissie's hair, a final seizure overtook Deborah and she fell forward in her harness, heaving and gasping and frothing at the mouth. She rubbed her face into the dusty floor and panted through her nostrils, her buttocks still held high by the harness at her waist and the handle still thrusting up her cunt.

Finally, she felt the handle being pulled out and, still in a daze, watched as Wesley held it behind Chrissie.

"Now let's see if this little pony can do as well."

Deborah looked over to Chrissie. She was barely conscious and, as Wesley prised the edges of her cunt wide and stuffed the glistening end of the handle into it, Deborah's stomach filled with fear. Chrissie stared impassively towards her and reared back as the wooden handle squeezed between her distended labia, then she stiffened and screamed out as it penetrated her vagina in one heavy thrust.

Deborah crawled forward. She wanted to offer herself again. She wanted to feel the thrust of the handle inside her and she wanted to feel the pain of the twisting strap around her swollen labia. She craved the hot sting of the whip across her bottom and the smacking hand that made her shriek so eagerly with pain. She wanted to see Winston's cock and she wanted to be forced to imagine him as a rampant stallion fucking an unwilling and stubborn mare. She wanted to be driven forward by the pain and she wanted to feel the humiliation of punishment and degradation. She wanted so much but, as she moved, she felt herself becoming dizzy and she collapsed exhausted and fell at Winston's feet. She shivered uncontrollably as spit flowed from her mouth, then, unable to keep the images in her mind, and struggling to lift the weight of the chain and shackles at her wrists, she held up her hands in loose fists, as if she was clinging to the bars of the cage.

"You want to rest eh? Want to be back in your cage eh? Then you know what you must do."

He picked up a thick piece of tarred rope that hung nearby and, as he flexed it and smoothed out the tattered ends, she lifted herself onto her knees and raised her buttocks as high as she could.

CHAPTER 6

Deborah was thrown across the cage as it lurched to one side. She grabbed hold of the bars, falling from side to side and trying desperately to steady herself. She peered through the rips in the tarpaulin and, as her eyes slowly adjusted to the brightness of the North African sun, she saw the deck of the ship spinning below her as the cage was hoisted across to a dock. She clung to the bars until, with a sickening thud, the cage crashed heavily to the quayside.

The heat from the ground rose up into the covered cage, trapping itself beneath the tarpaulin, stifling her and making her feel faint and dizzy. She pushed her face against a rip in the heavy tarpaulin so that she could get some air but, when she breathed in, it was as hot and dry as the air around her and she choked as it seared her throat. Heavy, spicy smells filled her nostrils.

She heard the sounds of ships' sirens, the clanking of winches and cranes and the clamorous shouting of men as they worked on the dockside. The sight of land filled her with renewed hope of escape. Perhaps she could attract someone's attention, tell them the situation she was in and get them to go for help? Yes, surely now she could find a way of escaping.

She stared through the gap in the heavy material and saw Winston pulling Gross down a gangway from the ship and onto the dockside. Gross hung his head low as if he was afraid of being hit and, every time Winston pulled on his arm, he shied back and turned his face away.

A large, black car drew up and one of the rear doors opened. A woman's leg, dangling from the slit in a long, red skirt, hung from the open door but no one got out. Winston dragged Gross to the door and Deborah heard shouting then she saw the flash of a shiny, gold bangle as the woman's hand struck Gross hard across the face. He fell back, holding his hands across his cheek but Winston pulled him up and the woman struck him again viciously.

Gross fell back and crouched down by the side of the open door with his hands clasped together. The door closed and, as the car started to move off, the rear window was let down and Deborah saw Saab adjusting her dark glasses and smoothing her black hair behind her ears. Deborah squinted and saw the figure of a woman with long, black hair beside Saab. It was dark inside the car and Deborah could not see the woman's face. Saab turned and kissed the woman fully on the lips and plunged her fingers deeply into the tangle of black hair that fell loosely around her shoulders.

Deborah felt a surge of anxiety in her stomach and looked away nervously. Suddenly, she fell sideways as the cage was lifted again. Arabs milled around, shouting and arguing and tugging on ropes until finally it was secured to the back of an open lorry. Winston pushed Gross up onto the lorry and he crouched down by the side of the covered cage.

"Now, you'd better behave yourself. You heard what she said. You've had your last chance. Mess with the goods again and you'll pay dearly. Got that? And don't let her out of your sight, or else ... "

Gross cowered against the ripped tarpaulin but, as his shoulder touched it, he pulled away and looked around anxiously.

"Gross must not touch again. Never. No, Gross must never touch little slave again. Gross must obey Saab or he will be punished."

As the lorry drove off, Deborah felt the oppressive heat burning down on the tarpaulin and her nostrils filled again with the scented smells of spices and herbs. Every so often, as the lorry bumped over potholed roads, clouds of dust billowed around the cage and she choked as it flooded in around her and stuck to her skin.

The lorry stopped at a congested junction of narrow streets and straight away men started lifting the edge of the tarpaulin and peering in at Deborah. Some of them jumped up onto the back of the lorry and poked their hands between the bars.

Gross jumped up and tried to stop them.

"Must not touch! Must not touch!"

He rushed at them wildly but the men ignored him as more of them scrambled around the cage and ripped the tarpaulin away.

Gross pulled at them in a frenzy but they pushed

84

him back and clamoured around the cage as Deborah shrunk back against the bars in fear. Some of them reached in and started pinching at her arms and legs.

"Must not touch! Must not touch!"

Gross panicked, rushed between the men and yanked the cage door open. He grabbed the chain between Deborah's shackles, pulled her from the cage and, flailing his arms, he pushed the men aside and dragged her out.

"Quickly! Deborah and Gross must get away. Gross must not let Deborah out of sight. Gross must not fail or else ... "

She was terrified as he pulled her between the jostling men. She stumbled over the side of the lorry and he jumped down beside her. He looked around, unsure what to do then, gripping the chain tightly in his hands, he charged blindly into the crowd. He pushed the men aside and pulled her between them. He dragged her behind a wall and she pushed herself against it, panting for breath and looking around anxiously as the men shouted and called to each other angrily.

She looked around dazed then Gross yanked the chain and dragged her into a dark, narrow side street. Arabs pushed and bustled along the narrow alley, carrying heavy bundles, racks of clothing, carpets and pots of sweet-smelling food. As soon as they saw Deborah, naked except for her tattered and torn stockings held by the clasps of her white suspender belt, they turned around and started pointing and shouting indignantly.

As Gross hauled her along, they were jostled and pushed and a small group of Arabs gathered around and pawed at her and touched her breasts. A rowdy crowd began following them and Gross pulled her harder and started running to keep ahead of the shouting men. More appeared ahead and blocked their way and, as they pushed and grabbed at Deborah, Gross was jostled and knocked against her. His eyes widened with panic as the men around them shoved him closer to his terrified charge.

"Gross must not touch! Must not touch!"

He yelled in a high pitched, terror-stricken voice but the crowd pushed closer and he could not keep away from the trembling body of his frightened ward.

"Gross must not touch! Saab will be angry. Gross's last chance!"

He twisted and turned, thrashing his arms around and trying to push the crowd back.

"Keep away! Keep away! Gross must not touch little slave!"

He lunged at them but they pushed closely around him, knocking him to the ground and breaking his grip on the chain between Deborah's shackles. She felt the tension released as Gross fell at her feet and, for a moment, she saw his anguished face before she was hauled away by the shouting crowd and dragged into a dark alley.

Hands pawed all over her, pulling at her hair, feeling her breasts, running up her thighs and probing the crease between her buttocks. Dark faces peered at her and broken-toothed grins leered at her near-naked body as the sea of hands groped all over her. She tried to squirm away but everywhere she turned there were more hands and more ogling faces and the more she struggled the more it excited them and the more they grabbed at her.

Hands clasped across her mouth and she tried desperately to suck air between the dark, sweaty fingers. She felt fingers pinching her nipples and her hair was pulled painfully as she was lifted up and carried into a dark shop. They threw her down on the floor and she fell amongst leather saddles, whips and whole, tanned hides. The men crowded around her and, as she pulled her knees up and clasped her shackled wrists around the fronts of her calves to protect herself, she felt terror-stricken, wretched and alone.

Some of the men poked at her and pulled her hair and then they started chanting in heavily accented French.

86

"Chienne! Chienne!"

She shrunk back, trembling with fear as two of them pulled her legs wide and another thrust his head between her thighs.

"Chienne! Chienne!"

She felt his hot tongue licking against the naked edges of her widespread cunt and she struggled frantically to get away.

"Chienne! Chienne!"

He slurped around her outer labia but, as he thrust the tip of his tongue between them, he was pulled away and another took over. His bearded face scraped against the insides of her thighs as he bit the swollen, wet folds and she shrieked with pain.

"Chienne! Chienne!"

He poked his tongue deeply and stretched his hands up to her breasts, grabbing them roughly in his hands and squeezing her nipples viciously. She fought to escape but more hands pushed down on her shoulders and forced her back.

"Let me go! Please let me go! Please, please ... "

Her cries only made them laugh. The man stretched out her nipples between his thumbs and fingers and, as he drove his unshaven face harder between her legs, he pinched them hard and she yelled in agony.

"Please, let me go. Please, please let me go!"

He delved his tongue in deeper and sucked at her labia, pulling their distended folds into his mouth and biting on them with his broken teeth.

"Help! Help! Please, someone help me!"

The man was pulled away and another one started licking her. This one put his hands beneath her buttocks, lifted her hips high and probed the pointed end of his tongue at the tight muscle of her anus. He pressed it hard and drove it in and she yelled out in panic as she felt it delving deeply inside her.

"Let me go, please ... "

The man was pulled away and another licked her anus. She felt his fingers opening her cunt and then pushing up inside her. She reared up as he pressed them in hard and she felt her cunt widening painfully as he drove them in to the knuckles.

Deborah threw her head from side to side as she felt his hand forcing itself deeply into her cunt. Its width stretched her wide and she felt a surge of nausea spreading into her throat. He pushed again and she felt it going in deeper then, as her cunt throbbed with pain, she felt her stretched labia tightening around his wrist. She screamed in agony but he did not stop until he was dragged away and several of them started licking her again.

She stretched out her arms, hoping to grab hold of something and pull herself free then, clawing desperately, she caught hold of the pommel of a brown leather saddle and pulled with all her strength.

As the men licked her and pulled at her legs, she squirmed towards the saddle, holding the pommel with both hands and dragging herself across the ground towards it.

"Chienne! Chienne!"

She clung onto the saddle as they dragged her back by the ankles and pulled her through the shop and into a narrow, dusty alley. She got up onto her knees and managed to crawl forward but one of them pulled a dust-covered leather strap across her mouth and dragged her back. Two more pulled the saddle from her and threw it over her back, knocking the breath from her and sending her sprawling on the dusty ground.

Her mouth filled with sandy soil and she started choking and tried to squirm away but the leash yanked tightly between her teeth and she was pulled up onto all-fours. They tied the heavy, leather saddle roughly around her waist and dragged her along the dusty alley, taunting her and jeering at her as she struggled to move under its weight.

"Chienne! Chienne!" they kept chanting as they poked at her and kicked out at her as she was dragged past them.

The leash was pulled tighter in her mouth and one of them lifted her buttocks until her legs were straight. She strained to stop herself falling sideways as one of the men straddled her and sat on the saddle. He pressed his weight against it and she buckled under the strain.

"Rampez! Rampez!" he screamed.

She did not know what he meant but she tried to get upright and managed to get her legs straight again.

"Rampez! Rampez!"

The leash was yanked viciously and she was made to crawl forward as the man straddled her back, bending his legs and dropping his weight on her whenever she slowed or stopped.

They drove her along the alley then turned her and drove her back. The crowd of men shouted and taunted her, spitting at her and tugging at her hair as she was ridden past them and kicking out at her if she did not go fast enough.

Her eyes filled with dust and she coughed and choked as they forced her on, different men riding her one after another, pulling her backwards or thrashing her with leather thongs and sticks when they were dissatisfied.

They fought each other to hold the leash between her teeth, pulling at it and snatching her from side to side as they struggled to take control of her. A young man straddled her and dug his knees into her sides as another stood behind her and held her taut buttocks. He opened them and pressed his finger against the rim of her anus. It sent a shock through her and she felt a stinging shiver of heat as he probed it inside. He held it there while they dragged her along the alley again and when he took it out another came and put his finger in.

She crawled along with her legs held stiffly, gasping against the strain of the man on her back and, all the time, with one of the men's fingers pressed deeply into her anus. The pressure of holding her buttocks so high squeezed the

89

insides of her thighs together and she felt the edges of her cunt swelling and the heat of her engorging clitoris burning at the front of her naked slit. Even though she felt terrified and shamed she wanted it filled and she arched her back as much as she could, opening her buttocks wide and exposing the swollen folds of her now wet cunt.

Another finger thrust into her anus then, as the man was pushed aside, she felt his finger replaced by the throbbing end of a cock. She raised her buttocks higher, sensing the strain of the man on her back and pulling hard against the leash. Her suffering was inflaming her and she yearned for more. She gasped and bit into the leash as the cock forced her anus wide and she drove herself back against it to take it in. She felt the throbbing veins along its shaft as it entered and she felt the pulsating tip pressing deeply inside her rectum as he pushed it in as deeply as he could.

She felt the heat of her orgasm building up inside her but she knew she was not ready yet. The humiliation alone was not enough to liberate it. She needed to be forced to let it go. She wanted beating and thrashing until the pain was so great that it burned her climax from her. She coughed and yelled as bubbles of spit foamed from the edges of her gagged mouth as her need for escape was replaced with a desperate yearning for suffering and pain.

"More! More!"

The cock thrust deeply inside her and she bore down on it. She felt it hardening and expanding along its length and, as its spunk flowed along it, she felt its tip swelling against her innards. She drove herself back onto it as its veiny shaft hardened painfully against her anal ring then she felt the wet heat of his spunk as it spurted into her. He thrust her hard as he finished and she lifted her buttocks higher to suck out every drop. But still it was not enough. She needed thrashing and punishing and violating with pain before she could be satisfied.

Another man thrust his cock into her still dripping

anus. It was thicker and longer and she took it in deeply, hoping for the thrashing sting of a whip and the burning pain that would give her satisfaction. He thrust at her wildly until he finished and when he pulled his throbbing cock out his semen dribbled in sticky bubbles down the insides of her straining thighs. She pulled her chin onto her chest to feel the tension of the leash in her mouth and she smelled the tangy sweetness of his semen as her nostrils flared and she gulped and choked.

Her body shook with the pressure inside her and she felt it running through her veins in heavy, pulsating throbs.

"More! More!" she cried desperately but, as she was fucked again and ridden by them all, still she was not able to release her pent up orgasm.

"More! Please more! Whip me! Beat me! Thrash me! Please!"

The heat boiled inside her and her head spun as she screamed and shouted and twisted her body against the thrusting cocks but still it was not enough.

"More! Give me more! I must have more!" she screamed but they only jeered at her, pulling the saddle from her back and rolling her in the dust as they wanked over her face and into her hair.

A young man pulled at her shackles, dragging them forward against her hands and exposing the silver identity bracelet on her wrist. He looked at it inquisitively then stared down at her with pity. She fell back, her body still throbbing with frustrated desire but her mind clearing as she saw the sympathetic look in the man's face. A sudden wave of renewed hope spread across her.

The noise around her abated as the other men backed away. Perhaps, at last, this was someone that would help her? Perhaps, at last, she could escape from her terrible ordeal? She held her wrist up and let the man run the bracelet through his fingers.

"Yes, my name is Deborah. Look, look at the engraving. My name, my address. Please, can you help me?"

At first, he did not seem to understand then he spoke in broken English.

"Deborah ... Address ... Help ... Yes ... Yes ... "

Her heart leapt.

"Take it! Take my bracelet! Get help! Please, get help!"

"Yes ... Deborah ... Get help ... Yes ... Get help ... "

He snatched at the bracelet and it broke free. He looked down at her silently then, holding the bracelet up in his hands and fending off the grasping hands of the others, he ran off shouting.

"Get help ... Deborah ... Get help ... "

Suddenly, there was a commotion and the men started running and shouting in panic. A huge horse charged between them and reared up in a billowing cloud of dust. Deborah looked up through her bleary eyes and saw a hand reaching down towards her. She lifted her arms, raising the heavy chain between her wrists, and was snatched to her feet. Another yank and she was lifted bodily against the sweating side of the horse. She scrambled up in a panic and fell forwards across its heavily maned neck, straddling the front of the hot, leather saddle with her stocking-covered legs and gripping desperately to its greasy bridle.

The horse charged down the dusty alley, knocking the men sprawling. She felt the rider's arm wrapping around her hips and lifting her buttocks onto the pommel of the saddle. She tried to turn around but it was impossible, the man held her bottom high and she could hardly hold onto the horse's mane with her heavily shackled hands. She gripped the muscular shoulders of the galloping horse with her thighs as the man shouted to her.

"You're a fine prize to be sure. I think I'll get a good price for you my little bitch." He stopped his horse at the end of the alley and it reared up on its hind legs. "You have a lot of admirers my little chienne. Are you still in need of their attention?"

Deborah gasped as the horse dropped its front hooves back to the ground. Her trembling body was seething with frustration and, as the man turned the horse, she looked back eagerly at the chasing men.

"I need ... "

"Yes bitch? What do you need?"

"I ... I ... "

She could not speak. Every time she tried she was flung against the huge horse and the breath was knocked from her.

"Tell me bitch! Tell your new master, Jabari!"

"I ... I want ... "

"Tell me bitch!"

Jabari lifted her buttocks higher and she struggled breathlessly to hold on as he pulled them back and dropped her down onto the hard, rounded pommel of the saddle. She felt the pressure of its thickened end against her soft flesh and she tried to lift herself away but she could not keep her balance. She fought with all her strength to grip the horse's shoulders with her straining thighs but the thumping pressure of its galloping hooves pounding on the sandy ground threw her around too much and she fell forcefully back onto the tall, embossed pommel.

Jabari grasped her hips and pushed them down against the unyielding pommel and she felt its wide end forcing apart the soft edges of her cunt. It was thick and hard and, as her cunt distended to its shape, its heavily tooled surface pressed against the entrance to her vagina. She tried to scream but all that came out were gasps of air bursting from her breathless lungs.

"Tell me bitch! Tell me!"

She tightened her chest and screamed.

"I ... I ... I want more ... "

He pressed her hips down harder and the end of the pommel went further into her cunt. She felt the entrance to her vagina opening for it and she gasped and tightened her body as she felt it prising her wide. The horse galloped fiercely and, every time its pounding hooves struck the ground, the jarring pressure passed through its muscles and into her splayed-out cunt. She felt its every movement deep inside her and she was filled with its power. When he pulled her hips down again she did not resist. She wanted more, she wanted it deep and she wanted to feel the pounding of the horse's hooves against her tight-pulled flesh. She tightened her chest again in an effort to control her breathing.

"I want more. They did not give me enough. I could not finish. I needed more ... "

"Needed more what?"

She braced herself and drew in another breath.

"Pain! I needed more pain!"

He thrust her down onto the pommel and she screamed loudly. Its thick end forced deeply inside her vagina and she felt the front of the saddle pressed hard against the splayed-out edges of her cunt. The smooth leather caressed her open labia and she drove herself down onto the pommel in a frenzy. The pounding of the horse sent penetrating shudders through her and she gasped and reared back every time its hooves hit the ground. It was as though the horse itself was fucking her with its heavy, muscular movements yet still she wanted more.

"More! More!"

She felt the rider's hands between her buttocks and his finger pressing against her anus. Every time she was thrown down by the pounding horse his finger went deeper. He pressed it in hard and she felt his knuckle against the outer edges of her distended, muscular ring.

"More! More!"

She felt desperate. The pommel thrust her like a gigantic cock but the finger was not enough.

"More! More!"

She twisted herself higher and he pulled his finger

out. She clung onto the horse's mane and held up her buttocks in front of Jabari, opening them wide and inviting him to fill her anus with more.

"More! More!"

Suddenly, as she was tossed back, she felt the end of his cock pressing against it. She felt its heat and its throbbing glans and she lifted herself higher, grasping the horse's mane and pulling herself up on the thrusting pommel.

"More! More!"

She dropped back and took his cock in. The throbbing glans pushed past the dilating muscle and drove deeply inside. She felt its pulsating shaft and the engorged veins that stood up along its length and she twisted herself down onto it wildly until she had it in up to its base. Tightening her anus around it, she pushed her cunt back onto the pommel and forced herself down, taking them both as deeply as she could.

She clung to the long mane of the horse and pulled her face against his sweating neck. She breathed in its hot scent as its heavy pounding kept driving the pommel ever deeper into her cunt and the cock further into her anus. She wanted to scream out and finish but the heat of her orgasm was still trapped inside. The fucking was not enough. Still she needed pain.

"More! Beat me! Beat me like a disobedient mare! Thrash me like an animal. More! More!"

She bore down onto his cock as hard as she could and waited for her punishment. She tensed her buttocks, desperate for the lashes of his whip and the pain it would bestow. She tightened her muscles against his throbbing cock, craving the searing pain of the whip and the release it would provide. She clenched her teeth and held her breath as spit flew from her mouth. She hung onto the coarse hair of the horse's mane, desperate to feel the vicious lashing of Jabari's whip, hoping he would release her from her torment, then, at last it came.

Whack!

A heavy blow cut across her buttocks. The pain went deep, she released her breath in a gurgling explosion and she drove herself back for more.

Whack!

The searing pain burned deeply inside her and, as waves of heat scorched through her, again she saw herself crawling in the dusty alley being taunted by the men.

Whack!

The muscles of her buttocks tensed in agonizing delight as another blow fell. More pictures were stirred up in her mind. Again, she saw the faces of the jeering men, she heard their taunting and felt their hot spit running down her face. She felt the weight of the saddle they had thrown on her back and their legs clenched tightly around her waist and she felt the heat of their thrusting cocks as they drove them, one after another, deeply into her burning anus.

Whack!

She felt the filthy dust on her face and the humiliation of her nakedness. She sensed how she had abandoned herself like an animal and she slobbered spit from her mouth in gasping, frothing bursts. She felt her hopelessness and degradation and the surges of heat inside her grew stronger, but still she wanted more.

Whack!

Her cunt was filled completely with the pommel and her anus was sore and burning as the cock thrust roughly up and down it. She clung to the horse's mane and saw herself being flailed and racked and branded and pulled on a leash until she passed out. She imagined herself being fucked by hundreds of men, day after day as she lay bound in a dusty arena. She pictured herself tied out by the wrists and ankles between horses who were trained to stretch her wide whenever she had to serve. She saw herself falling unconscious as the ordeal went on and she saw herself being doused with water to bring her around. She saw herself being passed around the watching crowd, being felt and violated and wanked on and bitten and fucked until finally she was taken back to the arena and tied between the horses again.

"More! More!"

Whack! Whack! Whack!

As the blows fell and the images in her mind exploded uncontrollably, she felt the massive surge of her orgasm bursting to escape from the prison inside her. Every pounding of the horse's hooves opened another chink, as its scorching beams radiated from deep inside and sweated out like lava from her burning pores. Her head spun giddily as her muscles tightened and she felt every vein on his thrusting cock and every engrained line on the wide leather pommel as she tightened on them both, held her breath and submitted to a massive, convulsive orgasm.

Whack! Whack! Whack!

He kept beating her but she welcomed the continuing pain. The punishing blows drove her orgasm through every part of her as she stared down at the dusty ground and the frightening pounding of the horse's galloping hooves.

Whack! Whack! Whack!

She did not breathe as her climax ran through her, shocking her body and making her rear and dive involuntarily in overpowering seizures of pleasure and satisfaction. The images continued flashing in her mind and the punishing whip burned deeply as she rode the leather pommel and drove herself back as hard as possible against the stiff cock until, finally, it swelled and spurted spunk deeply inside her throbbing rectum.

CHAPTER 7

Deborah lay shivering amongst some rough, wool blankets in a dark tent. Her shackled wrists were still tied to a stake in the his whip. To start with, he had made her bend over so that he could thrash her buttocks but when she fell sideways, screaming with pain, he had lifted one of her legs and brought the whip down savagely across her distended cunt. Only when she pleaded for mercy had he left and she had curled up and tried to sleep. Now, she was cold and hungry and sore from the beating and ill-treatment she had received. But, as she rubbed her hands against her thighs to try and stop them shaking, she remembered the face of the young man who had taken her bracelet and the memory rekindled fresh hope.

A young Arab boy came in and pointed to a curtain hanging across the back of the tent.

"Allez! Allez!"

Deborah struggled to get up but could not stand because of her tied wrists.

"Please untie me. Please - "

"Allez! Allez!"

He kicked out at her impatiently and she shrank back, extending her fingers in despair and desperate to show him that she could not do as he ordered.

He laughed then untied her and kicked her again viciously.

"Allez! Allez!"

She crawled over to the back of the tent and peered behind the heavy curtain. A slim, young woman was bending over a bowl of water bathing her face. A fat Arab in a multi-colored robe pushed through the other side of the tent, grabbed the young girl by the shoulder and pulled her around. Water ran down her face and when the fat Arab shook her angrily it flew from her nose and forehead in shiny droplets.

Deborah could not stop herself staring at the young woman as water dripped from her chin, ran down her neck and across her chest. Her flimsy dress was soaked at the front and Deborah could see her dark and hardened nipples pressed against the almost transparent material of her flimsy dress. She could see the dark shadow of the young woman's navel and beneath that, only thinly covered by the sticking wet material of her dress, the dark triangle of her pubic hair. She was very attractive, but her pale skin was blotched with purple bruising and her eyes and lips were swollen and red. She looked frightened and helpless and, as she raised her thumbnail to her teeth and started biting at it nervously, Deborah saw tears filling her eyes.

"Come bitch! You're not worth much but it will be better than nothing."

The fat Arab grabbed the girl's bruised arm and she winced in pain as he dragged her outside. Deborah just caught sight of a crowd of men beyond the open flap of the tent and she heard a lot of shouting and cheering then, as the flap dropped shut, it went quiet.

Still crouching on all-fours, Deborah turned back and the young boy had gone. She sat back against the wall of the tent and looked down at her tattered, white stockings. A surge of hopelessness ran through her as she saw how dirty and ripped they were. One of the suspender clips had come undone and she pathetically clipped it back into the soiled top of the stocking. She watched her fingers fumbling with the clasp and, overcome by a deep sense of despair, she sank forward with her head in her hands.

Suddenly, she was startled by a moaning sound coming from the blankets in the corner. She crawled over nervously and pulled them back and her head spun with disbelief. Chrissie lay amongst them, black-eyed and filthy.

"Chrissie! How did you get here? Are you alright?"

Chrissie opened her mouth but flinched and seemed unable to speak.

Deborah bent her face down closer.

"Oh Chrissie, what have they done to you?" Chrissie

tried to smile as Deborah reached forward and brushed the long tangles of black hair away from Chrissie's wet cheeks. "Chrissie, poor Chrissie, what's happening? What are they going to do with us?"

Chrissie opened her mouth again and squeezed up her eyes in pain as she struggled to speak.

"I don't know. I don't know what's happening, and I don't know where I am or how I got here, but I can't stand any more. Deborah, we must escape. I just can't stand it."

"I know we must. Chrissie, I gave a man my identity bracelet. I'm sure he will help us. He looked so concerned, not like the others. Yes, I'm sure he will help. If we can just hang on until we get a chance to escape. I'm sure that if we can get back to the docks we can find help."

Chrissie held out her hand to Deborah but then she saw Chrissie's eyes widen in fear and, as Deborah turned back to see what she was looking at, she saw the fat Arab standing behind her with a thick, leather strap trailing from his hand.

"Come on bitch! You're next."

Deborah shrank back as he approached her but he grabbed hold of the chain between her shackles and yanked her through the curtain into the other room.

"Jabari has left his instructions. I must get as much for you as I can. I hope for your sake you fetch a good price. Jabari is not someone to mess with, as I'm sure you've found out, and I don't want him disappointed. Now, bend down bitch!"

He pushed her forward onto her knees. She struggled to get up but he brought the heavy leather strap down across her back.

Whack!

She screeched out in pain and started to crawl to the side of the tent but she was too slow and he reached out and brought the strap down again.

Whack!

Deborah collapsed face-forward into the sandy

ground. She choked as she gulped for air and tried to squirm away but he kept thrashing her.

Whack! Whack! Whack!

She clawed at the ground but her arms were weak and the shackles at her wrists were so heavy that, in the end, she gave up and lay still.

He tossed the strap down and picked up the bowl of water from the small table.

"Here bitch, clean yourself."

She turned around, dazed and shocked as he emptied the bowl over her. It ran into her eyes and mouth and she choked as it trickled down her throat.

He shouted for the boy to bring more water and when he did the fat Arab told him to douse Deborah down. The boy laughed as he soaked her and when the fat Arab kicked out at her she rolled sideways in the wet, sandy mud.

"Clean yourself I said!"

Deborah tried to rub the water over herself but he kept kicking her and, as the boy threw more water over her, the sand became muddier and she got dirtier. She felt filthy and humiliated as she lay in the wet, muddy sand and looked up at him appealingly but he kept ordering the boy to throw more water over her until she fell back, hopelessly wallowing and distraught.

She was dazzled by the bright sun as the fat Arab dragged her, covered in mud and dripping wet, out of the tent and across to a small wooden stage set up in front of a milling crowd of men. Several vertical wooden posts stood up from the stage and a heavy wooden beam spanned their tops.

The young girl with the black eyes was already tied to one of the posts. Her hands were pulled tightly behind her and bound with leather thongs. A rope was lashed around her legs, holding her ankles and knees securely together. Another rope was wound around her waist and chest, criss-crossing her breasts and pulling her wet dress against her wet, shaking body. A rope was tied across her forehead and secured to the post so tightly that she could not move her head. A piece of white material was pulled across her mouth and spit dribbled from its edges and ran down over her chin. Her bruised eyes were barely open and she stared out into the crowd of men emptily.

The fat Arab hauled Deborah onto the stage and pushed her backwards against one of the wooden posts. She looked around anxiously as the men stared up at her, grinning and pointing and leaning forward as they pawed at her and tried to grab her. The young boy pulled her wrists behind her, tightening the chain between her shackles painfully across the front of her hips. He lashed her wrists together with a thin, leather thong and secured it to the post. He took a long rope and bound it around her ankles, then wound it around her pulling her back tightly against the post. He dangled a thick leather strap in front of her face and, as she tried to pull away, he held it across her mouth. She tried to keep her mouth closed but he forced her teeth apart with his fingers, pulled the strap between them then pushed it back as tightly as he could and tied it behind her head. She twisted and turned but was held fast and she hung her head, gasping for breath and flushing with shame as the crowd of men shouted loudly and tormented her.

The crowd surged forward as the fat Arab dragged Chrissie onto the stage. Like Deborah, she was soaked and covered in wet, sandy mud. Water dripped from the hem of her flimsy dress and she was so weak that she fell onto her knees when the boy tried to tie her to the post. He could not get her to stand so, instead, he yanked a rope around her wrists and the fat Arab lifted him up so that he could secure it to the beam that ran between the posts. Chrissie's head fell sideways as the boy secured it and she hung limply against its tension.

The fat Arab waved a short cane with a broken end above his head and shouted out to the crowd in French. They went quiet and he started speaking in heavily accented English.

"Three beautiful bitches for you today. And I expect the best prices. Do you hear? The very best prices."

They shouted and jeered.

"Every one has something special to offer."

They cheered loudly as he strutted over to the young girl and lifted her spit-smeared chin with the end of the cane.

"Take this one, the bitch called Asia, you can see what a fine beating she takes."

He poked the end of his cane against her erect nipples and the men in the crowd started nudging each other and repeating her name excitedly.

"And this bitch, the one they call Chrissie, you can whip her until you are exhausted and she will still want more."

He brought the cane down across her breasts and she threw her head back in agonized shock then, as her legs gave way, she dropped heavily on the rope. The crowd shouted wildly as the boy punched her in the side until she looked up again.

"And this one, this beauty, the bitch that is called Deborah, she will do anything as long as you make her suffer."

He poked the end of his cane into the front of her shaved crack. She pressed her legs together but it did not stop him and she felt the cane's tattered end opening the flesh of her slit and probing against her exposed clitoris. She could not pull away and, as she tightened the muscles of her thighs, she only squeezed the end of the cane harder against her clitoris and she felt a deep, burning tingle penetrating her hips. She flinched as he snatched it back and strutted over to Asia.

"So, start me off!"

A man in the crowd raised his hand and shouted something. Another jumped up and screamed out his bid and others joined in until the market place erupted in a clamour of noise. The fat Arab encouraged the bidders, poking Asia with his cane or lifting the hem of her thin dress and showing them

103

her dark pubic hair. Slowly, the noise died down until there were only two men bidding. One of them jumped up onto the stage and started pawing at Asia. To start with the fat Arab pushed him back but the man kept shouting.

"Test! Test! Test out girl!"

The fat Arab smiled and turned to the crowd.

"Of course. I like my customers to know what they're buying. Of course you may test her. Boy! Untie her!"

The young boy unwound the ropes and released Asia. She fell to the floor, still with the gag across her mouth and the leather thong securing her wrists at her back. The boy undid the leather thong then kicked her, making her crawl forward until she reached the fat Arab's feet.

The man from the crowd bent down and lifted the hem of her thin, wet dress. Her buttocks were smooth and round and he rubbed his hands across them and looked back at the crowd. He looked up at the fat Arab questioningly.

"Yes, yes, go on, test her as you wish."

The man grinned and pressed his fingers between the crack of Asia's buttocks. She tried to pull away but he wrapped his other arm under her hips and lifted her higher.

Deborah saw the sunlight flash on something around the man's wrist. It was a silver bracelet. She looked at the man and her stomach filled with nervous anxiety. It was her bracelet! It was the man who she had handed it to in the alley! She slumped back against her bonds in despair.

She felt ridiculous and stupid. How could she have been so naive, so pathetically hopeful? How could she have imagined that there was anyone who would help them? How could she have been taken in by her own self-deception? She felt herself trembling as she felt a surge of guilt at having promised Chrissie that there was hope. As the bracelet flashed again in the bright sunlight her face reddened as she flushed with the unquenchable heat of her pitiful embarrassment. How could she explain it to Chrissie? Chrissie depended on her and she had let her down. She felt consumed by her own wretchedness but no matter what was churning through her mind, she could not take her eyes from Asia.

She watched as Asia's buttocks parted and the dark pink of her cunt was exposed. As the man raised her even higher, Deborah saw its delicate, fleshy edges and the tangled mat of pubic hair at its front. The man lifted her off the ground and carried her to the front of the stage. He held her bottom towards the crowd and forced her thighs apart so that they could all see her exposed flesh. She tried to fight against him but she did not have the strength and she struggled weakly as the crowd leered at her.

Deborah felt a sudden, overwhelming flush of heat running down her neck and across her breasts. She eased her head back but, she could not look away from the scene before her and she realised that watching Asia was the reason for her own sudden shock of excitement. The surging thrill ignited in her a confusion of embarrassment and delight and, desperate to cover her reddening face, she dropped her head as far forward as she could. But she could not keep her head down. Something inside compelled her to look at Asia as the man displayed her to the leering crowd. She fought against it and forced her head down again, fixing her eyes on the wooden stage. She felt the rope cutting into her and she pushed herself against it, squirming against it and feeling its unforgiving tension but, as she felt it cutting into her breasts, she reared back and the sight of Asia caused the hot flush of excitement to spread further and deeper.

The man held Asia over the front of the stage and hands pawed and poked at her buttocks. Deborah watched fingers probing between Asia's thighs and she pulled herself tighter against the rope but this time she did not look away. She saw them pulling at Asia's exposed outer labia and probing inside her cunt. She saw fingers pressing against Asia's anus and, when they pushed inside, Deborah felt a massive surge of heat across her body and struggled frantically against her bonds. She wanted to break free but she did not want to escape. She wanted to be lifted and exposed to the men in the crowd. She wanted her buttocks held high and her cunt fingered and opened and she wanted to feel the pressure of fingers against her anus and the hot wave of ecstasy in her hips as they pressed deeply inside. She bit hard onto the gag in her mouth and threw herself from side to side, feeling the tension of the rope around her body and revelling in its unforgiving tautness.

The crowd of men shouted wildly as they took hold of Asia and passed her around, holding her high above their heads and feeling her all over. They fought to get to her, yanking at her flimsy dress and tearing at it until only shreds hung from her shoulders.

Deborah pulled frantically against the rope that held her. She imagined herself being violated by the crowd. She could see herself being held above their heads and she could feel their hands all over her. She could feel the suffocating tightness in her throat as they dragged her down amongst them and pulled her legs wide and exposed her naked cunt. She could picture herself struggling against them, screaming at them to lift her high above their heads again and display her and humiliate her. She pulled wildly at her bonds and, as she threw her head from side to side, spit flew from the sides of her gagged mouth, splashing across her tight-pulled cheeks, running down her chin and splattering on her heaving breasts.

Men in the crowd started shouting and pointing to a man in a heavy, black cloak. The man had his hand held high and, as the noise died down, he shouted out a figure that made everyone gasp.

The fat Arab beamed broadly, looked around vainly for any other bidders and smacked his hands together jubilantly.

"Sold! Sold! And for a handsome price indeed! Now the next one, let's see how much you will pay for the bitch Chrissie!"

He strutted over to Chrissie and threatened her with

106

his cane. She cringed and shrunk back and everyone laughed and jeered. He smacked her calves with the cane and she tried to twist them away but, as she bent her legs, she fell heavily on the rope and her eyes rolled up and Deborah watched her mouth fall open as she hung hopelessly on her bonds.

The fat Arab spun her around and smacked his cane across her buttocks. Her mouth gaped wider but she did not respond and, as he caned her repeatedly, she just spun on the slowly tightening rope.

Deborah struggled frantically, pulling at her wrists and tightening the chain across her hips. She could feel the metal links digging into her skin and she pulled harder and squirmed against them, lifting herself up slightly until they pressed into the front of her shaved slit.

The crowd started chanting and pointing at her.

"Chienne! Chienne! Chienne!"

The fat Arab turned to Deborah and, when he levelled his short cane at her, the crowd started screaming in a frenzy.

"Chienne! Chienne! Chienne!"

He left Chrissie still spinning on the gradually tightening rope and ordered the boy to untie Deborah.

As the rope came free from her ankles and knees, she opened her legs and wrapped her heels backwards around the post, thrusting her naked cunt forward towards the crowd and pushing out her hips to show them its pink, swollen edges. When her wrists were untied she flung her arms outwards, tightening the chain between her shackles and pulling it fiercely against the front of her crack. She dragged the links sideways against it, opening it and exposing her clitoris then, in a frenzy, she rubbed the chain up and down and her clitoris throbbed and engorged under the pressure from the hard metal. She pulled against the rope that held her and dropped her weight against it until it tightened completely. She felt her chest tightening, and she bit onto the gag in her mouth, as a wave of scorching heat spread across her heaving, breathless

107

body.

Suddenly, the rope came free and she dropped to the floor. She gasped for air through her flaring nostrils as she pulled herself up onto her knees and, as she stared out into the crowd of men, her eyes widened as she felt herself growling like a dog.

"Chienne! Chienne! Chienne!"

Their chanting mesmerized her and she crawled on all-fours towards the edge of the stage.

"Chienne! Chienne! Chienne!"

She licked her tongue against the soggy gag in her mouth and raised her buttocks as high as she could then she turned them towards the crowd of men and opened her legs wide. She wanted them to see her shaved cunt and she pushed it out towards them, her head spinning with their chanting and her body flushing with the humiliating exposure.

"Chienne! Chienne! Chienne!"

She felt their hands reaching out and pawing at her. She dropped onto her elbows, scraping her hard nipples against the rough wooden floor and splaying out her shackled wrists as wide as she could.

"Chienne! Chienne! Chienne!"

A hand squeezed the splayed-out edges of her cunt, then another grasped her buttocks. She stretched her arms out wider as she felt an arm wrapping itself under her hips and lifting her off the ground. She felt her body boiling with heat as she was carried into the crowd and, as she was tossed amongst them then lifted above their heads, her head spun giddily as shivers of uncontrollable excitement coursed through her.

The men clawed at her tattered stockings, ripping them from the clasps of her suspender belt and pulling them off. They yanked at the suspender belt, twisting her around as they tugged at it in a frenzy, until it came undone. She fell beneath their overpowering hands, naked and filled with fear. They wrapped one of her stockings tightly around her eyes

108

and the other they bound around her shackled wrists. She could not see anything and her mind filled with images of their hands and her terrible exposure and frailty. She stretched her fingers out, grabbing the men's clothes and tugging at them frantically as if imploring them to violate her and degrade her more.

Suddenly, the breath was knocked from her as she was thrown to the ground. She did not have time to recover before she felt a painful jerk at her wrists as the stocking tightened around them and she was pulled roughly across the sandy ground. Her arms and legs flailed hopelessly as they hauled her between them on her back. She banged against them and did not know which way up she was as they dragged her about like a captured animal. The tightness of the stocking around her wrists and the clawing hands around her body made her head beat with the throbbing of her veins, then she felt a surging excitement pulsating through her as her ankles were held and her legs were spread wide apart.

Deborah threw her head from side to side and thrust her hips up at the men. She felt the burning sensation of her oncoming orgasm spreading deep inside her exposed cunt and she wanted them to release it for her. She wanted them to turn her over and beat her. She wanted bending over and whipping until she could stand no more and only then would she be able to feel the flooding release of her climax. She wanted to cry out to them to hold her down while they caned her and smacked her and beat her and she wanted to beg on her knees for them to punish her and deliver her to pleasure from pain.

She bit onto the gag and flung her head back against the sandy ground but no cane fell on her, no whip beat across her breasts and no hand smacked viciously across her buttocks. She twisted and turned, bursting with desire as her pent up orgasm burnt in her veins. She heard them shouting and she felt them pulling her legs wider but it was not enough. She struggled against them, hoping to anger them with her resistance, or even break free so that they would have to chase

109

her and catch her and punish her for her disobedience. But they were only excited by her frantic struggling and she did not have the strength to escape their clutching hands.

Everything they did was not enough to satisfy her. She felt fingers around the edges of her cunt but she wanted them to squeeze her labia and pinch them and send penetrating shocks of pain through her body. She felt her nipples being pulled but she wanted them pinched hard and bitten and thrashed and she went into a frustrated panic as she felt the scorching heat inside her and no way of releasing it.

She felt the heat of a body between her legs and she offered up her cunt. She raised it high, hoping to feel the stinging pain of a beating hand or the lacerating cuts of a cane across her swollen labia, but instead she felt the hot splash of semen flooding across her shaved crack. It ran down the insides of her thighs and trickled against her anus. She squirmed against it as more spurted onto her, spreading stickily across her engorged clitoris and running into the slit of her dilated cunt. She felt another gush of wet heat as more spunk flowed over her breasts, running down the sides of her chest and under her outstretched arms. She felt another splash of hotness against the side of her face and she smelled the salty tang of semen as it ran down the side of her neck and dribbled into her ear.

More spunk slashed onto her as they wanked over her one after another. Some finished in her tangled hair, some in her flaring nostrils, or under her arms. She felt some splashing into her ears and she tasted some as it ran across the tight-stretched gag in her mouth but still it was not what she needed to finish. She wanted to plead with them to beat her and thrash her but, as they dropped her to the ground, soaked and dripping with sticky spunk, she was still gasping desperately and writhing in the grip of her frustration.

Suddenly, the white stocking was pulled from her eyes and she was rolled over onto her front. Dust stuck to her face as she raised her buttocks, hoping at last to feel the pain

110

of a beating but still more spunk dripped down on her, falling onto her back and oozing between her raised buttocks. She wanted to cry out and beg to be thrashed but all she felt was more spunk splashing on her shoulders and underneath her arms.

She kept lifting her bottom and displaying her cunt but it was hopeless. She bit onto the gag and gurgled spit across it, letting it run into the sand then rubbing her face in it and burying her nose in it until her nostrils were plugged and she choked for breath.

They rolled her over onto her back again and, through her bleary, dazzled eyes, she saw the fat Arab standing above her. He turned to the crowd and, when he saw the cloaked man's arm held high, he smacked his hands together and rubbed them vigorously.

"Sold! All my bitches sold to the same buyer!"

The crowd of men drew back and stood in a circle around Deborah. She lay on the dusty ground, her head crooked to one side and her legs spread wide apart. She was drenched with sticky semen and it mixed with the mud that stuck to her reddened skin.

She rubbed her mud-caked eyes and saw the shiny toe-cap of a red, high-heeled shoe tapping impatiently in front of her face. She looked up along the slender leg and saw the sharp slit of a red dress falling each side of a pale knee. Her heart started pounding, but this time with fear, as she rubbed the spit and sand from her nose with the back of her hand.

"Ah, little bitch, and we thought you were lost," said Saab dropping her sunglasses down her nose. She turned to the man in the black cloak who stood beside her. Only his tightly squinting eyes were visible from a narrow slit in his heavy, black robe.

"Meet your new master bitch," said Saab, licking her glossy, red lips with her wet tongue. "Meet Theron."

The cloaked man stepped forward and pulled the heavy material away from his face. He was dark and swarthy and his white teeth shone in the sunlight as he opened his mouth to speak.

"So, I have bought back what was already mine!" He turned to Saab. "My dear Saab, Gross must be made to pay for this. He was in charge of her and because of his idiocy he lost her. Lost her because he was too frightened to do his duty and now I have had to buy her back. This little bitch has cost me too much and it's all his fault. Be sure you make his punishment entertaining though." He laughed then bent down and placed the palm of his hand against Deborah's wet and distended cunt. "And it looks as though she's too used to getting what she wants! I think we can put a stop to that though." He wiped his hand on a handkerchief then threw it down onto the ground as he turned back to the fat Arab. "Who did you buy her from?"

The fat Arab wrung his hands together and looked flustered.

"A man lord Theron. Just a man. He came last night and he left this morning. I did not know him. I have never seen him before. A man. Just a man ... "

The fat Arab bowed his head, desperately hoping that Theron would not question him further and find out that he was working for Jabari.

Theron pushed past him angrily and spoke to Saab.

"Put her with the others and have them all sent on. And please, my dear Saab, no mistakes this time!"

Saab smiled, pushed her sunglasses back onto the bridge of her nose then bent forward and smacked Deborah angrily across the face. Deborah reeled sideways, her spunk-smeared cheeks stinging from the sudden blow.

"That's the last time you'll cause me trouble bitch. Yes, I'll make that fool Gross pay but I'll make sure you pay more!" Saab turned to the fat Arab. "Send them on. And this time, send them with someone we can trust."

The fat Arab nodded obediently and ordered the boy to lead them away.

112

Deborah was still shaking all over and, as the boy dropped a rope around her neck and pulled her forward, she could not stop herself delving her semen-covered hands down between her squirming thighs in a desperate bid to relieve her burning frustration.

CHAPTER 8

Deborah had been thrown into the tent with Asia and Chrissie and lashed to the post for the night. She had struggled to undo her bonds in the hope that she could get free, release Chrissie and Asia and that together they could escape. But the leather straps around her wrists were too tight and, in the end, she fell into an uncomfortable and troubled sleep.

She dreamed of being back in the office and going out to lunch with Chrissie. They felt such good friends, almost like sisters. She saw them getting dressed up for the evening and riding in the back of a black limousine. She pictured them squeezed up together in the deep, leather seat, laughing and giggling and touching up their lipstick as they gossiped about what they would be doing. She smelled Chrissie's perfume and felt the thrill of her touch when she reached forward and wiped a mark from Deborah's cheek. Suddenly, the dream turned into a nightmare as she saw Saab pushing her way into the back of the car. Chrissie greeted her and they kissed each other passionately then both of them pointed at Deborah and laughed at her mockingly. Deborah reeled back confused as they pushed her out of the car and drove away laughing leaving her lying in the litter-strewn gutter shivering from fear. She woke with her heart thumping and sweat running down her neck. She could not get to sleep for ages and when she did she dreamed the same dream again.

Deborah was woken by the young boy walking over the top of them. His bare feet dug into her side as he bent down and clipped a heavy, iron yoke around each of their necks.

When he untied their wrists from the post in the centre of the tent he ordered them to stand. They struggled to their feet but Chrissie fell sideways under the weight of the heavy halter. Deborah wrapped her arm around her waist and held her up as she moaned pitifully.

"I can't stand any more. I just can't ... "

For a moment, Deborah thought of telling her about the bracelet. She wanted to share her disappointment with her only friend but, as she looked into Chrissie's sad, exhausted face, she realised that it would be too much for her.

The boy smacked Chrissie's buttocks with a short cane. She screamed out and arched backwards as he started punching her and he did not stop until she stood up to his satisfaction.

The boy laced a chain between rings in their iron yokes then yanked on it gleefully and pulled them outside the tent. He hooked the end of the chain into a ring on a horse's saddle then looked up at the rider obediently.

"Are these all lord Theron's purchases?"

"Oui. C'est tout."

The rider nodded to him then shook the reins of his horse and set off with the three chained women trailing behind.

The sun got higher as they plodded through the soft, hot sand. Deborah's lips were parched and her tongue was dry and, as it got hotter, she started feeling dizzy and kept stumbling. They trudged on and the iron yoke around her neck got so hot it burned against her throat and shoulders.

Deborah watched Asia and Chrissie struggling to keep going and when Chrissie fell to the ground the rider did not stop and she was dragged across the hot sand until Deborah managed to help her back to her feet. A little later, she fell again and this time Deborah had not got the strength to help and it was only when the sand mounded up around Chrissie

114

and the rider felt the resistance on the chain, that he stopped.

He jumped down from his horse and kicked at Chrissie but she was half covered in sand, completely exhausted and could not move. Asia and Deborah fell to their knees as he stood over her and held up his riding crop.

"Up bitch! Up!"

Chrissie's head was half-buried in the sand and she choked as she tried to breathe.

"Get up bitch!"

Thwack!

He brought the thin riding crop down across her buttocks and she flinched and choked. Deborah fell forward onto her hands as he brought the crop down again.

Thwack!

Deborah watched the hard, leather crop biting across Chrissie's taut skin and she gasped when she saw the thin, red stripe it left when he pulled it back.

"Get up bitch!"

Thwack!

The crop fell again, crossing the other red stripes and leaving another angry mark, but still Chrissie did not move. Deborah crawled forward slowly.

Thwack!

This time the crop cut across Chrissie's back and she turned slightly but still she did not have the strength to get up.

Thwack! Thwack! Thwack!

He laced her back with fierce blows and, as she rolled slowly onto her back, moaning and dribbling from her parched lips, he brought it down across her breasts.

Thwack! Thwack! thwack!

Spit bubbled from her mouth and she tried to cover herself with her hands but he kicked them aside and kept whipping her relentlessly.

Thwack! Thwack! Thwack!

Deborah clawed her way across the soft sand and reached out towards his feet. She grabbed his ankle and pulled at it as hard as she could. He looked down at her and kicked her away. She fell sideways and the yoke yanked against the chain and made her cry out.

Thwack! Thwack! Thwack!

The crop lashed Chrissie mercilessly and she rolled from side to side in hopeless agony. Sand stuck to her sweating body and was scored away in lines as the thrashing blows of the crop rained down.

Thwack! Thwack! Thwack!

Deborah grabbed his ankle again and this time, as he tried to shake her away, she clung on.

"Get away bitch!"

"Please, please stop. She's exhausted. Please stop beating her - "

"Get off bitch or you will get the same."

Deborah flinched as he threatened her with the crop but she did not let go.

"Please stop, she can't stand it any more - "

"You heard what I said bitch. Let go or you will take her place."

Deborah saw the anger on his face then looked across to Chrissie's limp body. She could not bear to see her suffering like this.

"I will take her place," she said faintly.

"What did you say bitch?"

She clung tightly to his ankle and looked up at him.

"Punish me instead. Beat me, but leave her alone."

He dropped the crop to his side and smirked. Chrissie rolled onto her back and groaned in pain. She stared at Deborah and smiled weakly.

"Boy! We will camp here. Unshackle them then bring this one to me."

Deborah stretched her arms as the heavy yoke was lifted from her shoulders. The boy released Chrissie and Asia and left both of them lying on the sand then grabbed hold of Deborah's hair and dragged her across to the rider who was

116

giving his horse a drink from a leather bucket. He turned around and grinned.

"So, you want punishing do you?" Deborah dropped her head. "Did you hear me bitch?" She looked up slightly and nodded. "I did not hear you. Do you want punishing or should I continue with the other little bitch?"

"Yes," she said quietly. "Yes."

"You do not sound very sure bitch. Louder!"

Deborah took a deep breath.

"Yes, yes, I want punishing."

He threw down the leather bucket and the horse reared back and whinnied. Deborah looked down at the water as it seeped into the sand.

"Thirsty eh bitch?"

She nodded and stared as the sand turned dark and the water disappeared. He bent down and scooped some of the moist sand into his hand and offered it to her.

"Here, eat this."

She parted her lips and he thrust the wet sand into her mouth, making her cough and choke before she spat it out.

He laughed loudly, opening his broad mouth wide and exposing a single gold tooth at the centre of his gleaming, white teeth. He pushed his cloak back onto his broad shoulders and threw his long, black hair back from his dark forehead.

"Come here bitch." He pointed to the side of the horse and she walked over slowly. "Stand against my horse."

She leaned back against the horse's side and felt the wide, leather stirrup strap between her shoulder blades. The horse shied back and she stumbled.

"Stand against it I said!"

He reached a leather lanyard from the pommel and tied it to a ring at the back of the saddle. He pulled it across her mouth, forcing her to open it and take the strap between her teeth. He bent his face to hers and looked into her frightened eyes as he yanked it tighter. She choked and felt veins in her neck throbbing and her face reddening as he increased the tension. She did not dare resist him for the sake of Chrissie and she stood still as he stretched the leather strap forward and secured it to the heavily tooled, leather pommel.

Deborah gasped as she fought for breath. The strap dug into the sides of her mouth and she gulped deeply, unable to ease the tension. She widened her eyes and pressed her head back against the saddle just enough to get a breath. The horse stamped its hooves and moved again and, as she stumbled backwards, all her weight dropped onto the strap and she bit into it and she started gulping again.

"Hold this bitch!"

He yanked the metal stirrup up between her legs, pulling the wide stirrup strap tightly between her buttocks and drawing the metal stirrup against the soft flesh of her cunt.

"Hold it bitch, if you do not want to fall."

Deborah bit into the strap in an effort to hold herself up and reached down and grabbed the metal stirrup.

"Pull it bitch! Pull it up!"

She grabbed it tightly and, in desperation, heaved it upwards. The wide strap cut between her buttocks but, as she pulled the metal stirrup up against her cunt, she was lifted onto her toes and some of her weight was taken off the strap across her mouth and she gasped in relief.

She clawed at the stirrup, struggling to hold herself up on the strap so that she could gulp in air. The horse moved again and, as she fell, she clung desperately to the stirrup, dragging the strap between her buttocks and holding herself off the tension of the strap between her teeth.

The man stood in front of her and grinned. He lifted his long robe and took his cock into his hand. It was hard and throbbing and, as he squeezed the shaft, she could see the heavy, pulsating glans swelling and beating. The veins stood out along its length and when he thrust his hand to its base it lengthened and throbbed and the pulsating glans enlarged even more. She felt the heat from it as he pressed it towards her and she struggled to keep a grip on the metal stirrup as he rubbed it against the back of her straining hand.

She heaved on the stirrup, lifting herself enough to relieve the tension. As she held it up tightly against her cunt, he pressed the tip of his massive cock through it and it was encircled by the tight-pulled metal stirrup. She gasped for air as she felt the intense heat of the throbbing tip against her squashed outer labia.

He pressed it further and she felt the engorged tip prising her fleshy edges apart then he thrust it in and she felt herself opening to take it as it drove in deeply. Her vagina tightened around it and she felt the pounding veins along its length as he tensed his buttocks and forced the swollen tip further.

She pulled on the stirrup to try and ease her weight from the strap in her mouth. He thrust his cock deeply, squeezing it through the metal stirrup. When he thrust it as far as he could its base filled the circle of metal and pressed onto her fingers so that she could barely hold onto it. The edges of the metal stirrup grabbed at her swollen labia and, as he thrust at her again and squashed her fingers against the metal ring, she felt herself losing her grip and she flushed with the heat of panic as she dug her teeth into the tight strap across her mouth.

She tightened her fingers and pulled on the stirrup. She managed to get a breath as he drove his cock in again and again she struggled to hold the stirrup as the thick shaft tightened inside the circle of metal. The horse whinnied and stamped its hooves and she pulled harder, desperate to keep her weight off the strap then suddenly she felt him grab her calves and yank her legs up high. She fell back onto the strap in her mouth and felt the tension in her chest as she heaved to get a breath. Her stomach filled with terror and she struggled to hold onto the metal stirrup but, as he drove his throbbing cock in deeper and heaved her legs onto his shoulders, she lost her grip completely and fell fully onto the leather strap, biting into it desperately as she felt herself slipping backwards against the sweating horse.

Panic-stricken, she heaved and gulped and smacked at him with her hands, clawing at his cloak and pulling at his wrist but he would not stop. He pushed his cock in again and she felt its tip swelling even more and when he drew it back the wide flanged edges of the throbbing glans pulled against her already stretched vagina. He forced it in again and she felt her arms going weaker as she stretched her hands down desperately towards the stirrup. He lifted her legs higher, holding her ankles above his head, then drove his cock in for a last time. She felt it swell and tighten against her vagina then she felt massive pulses of spunk spurting as far into her as he could drive them. He held his pulsating cock there until there was no more to come and, when he pulled it out and she felt the bubbling semen running down the insides of her thighs, she grabbed the stirrup again and with all her strength managed to pull it up enough to ease the tension of the strap.

She shivered and jerked as she hung there, gripping onto the stirrup and pulling it against her dilated, spunk-smeared cunt. The metal edges bit into her soft, wet flesh and she gasped for air whenever she could summon the strength to yank herself up enough on the strap to relieve the tension across her spit-smeared mouth.

"Boy! Let her down."

She fell to the floor as the horse stamped its hooves around her and she gulped for breath, drawing it in frantically as it seared her burning throat.

The boy stood over her, staring between her wide-spread legs. The man bent down on one knee and she shrank back from him fearfully.

"But you have had your pleasure before your punishment. Boy! Set some stakes in the ground! The bitch said she wanted punishing and we must not disappoint her."

The young boy ran off and pulled some long wooden

stakes and a heavy mallet from the pannier bags of his mule.

"Drive them in here!"

The man pointed to the ground with his foot and the boy wielded the heavy mallet and drove the stake deep into the sand. The man showed him where to put the others and soon he had them all in the ground in a square.

"Now bitch, you can have what you wanted. Crawl over here."

Deborah felt a wave of anxiety spread through her as she struggled up onto all-fours.

"Crawl bitch and come for your punishment."

Slowly, she crawled towards him, straining to move her aching legs as semen dribbled between her labia. She stopped at his feet and hung her head.

"On your back bitch! There!"

He pointed to the centre of the square of pegs. She crawled over obediently and stopped.

"On your back!"

She lay down and rolled over onto her back.

"Now, stretch out wide!"

She stretched her shackled arms out as far as the chain would allow then opened her legs until her ankles nearly touched the stakes near her feet.

The boy took some leather thongs and tied her ankles tightly to the stakes. He pulled her wrists out until the chain was taut across her breasts then he wound some thongs around them and secured them to the other two stakes. She pulled at her wrists and ankles but it was impossible to move them and, as she squirmed her buttocks against the sand, she felt it sticking to the spunk that still dribbled from her splayed-wide cunt.

The man ordered the boy to fetch a bucket of water and when it came he dipped a coiled-up leather strap into it. He pulled it out and let it uncoil, holding it above Deborah as water dripped from it onto her breasts. He flicked it behind his shoulder and water splashed from its edges, throwing tiny droplets out in a spray.

Deborah tensed herself waiting for the blow. She tightened her thighs and, as she squeezed her buttocks together, she felt the warm dribble of spunk that bubbled from her cunt.

He flicked the wet strap again and, as it cracked in the sunlight, she saw a fine mist of rainbow colours in the harsh light of the sun.

Swish-smack!

He brought the wet strap down across the front of her hips. It lashed across her skin and a mist of water sprayed up from its cracking end.

Swish-smack!

Another heavy blow across her hips and this time the edges of the coiling strap cut across the front of her exposed crack. She winced as the pain dug into her and she tightened her legs and buttocks even more.

Swish-smack!

The strap fell across her breasts and she screamed in shock and pain.

Swish-smack!

Another shocking blow across her breasts as the edge of the strap caught her hard nipples and bit into them agonizingly.

Swish-smack!

She screamed and tugged against the unforgiving thongs around her wrists and ankles as the strap laced across her breasts again.

He dipped the strap into the bucket of water then flailed her with it mercilessly, beating her across the breasts then working it down to her hips.

Swish-smack! Swish-smack! Swish-smack!

He dipped it in the water again then levelled it at her exposed cunt. She saw it coming down and tensed herself but, when it hit, she was not prepared for the sudden, shocking pain. It cut across her swollen, wet labia penetrating her with a deep and startling pain. She screeched and pulled her wrists and ankles wildly against their bonds but the strap kept smack-

122

ing down, each time harder and each time more painful.

Swish-smack! Swish-smack! Swish-smack!

She did not stop screaming in between the blows. She just kept howling and pleading and shouting frantically. She could not stand the pain, it was too much for her, and she felt herself becoming dizzy as the bright sunlight darkened before her misty eyes.

Swish-smack! Swish-smack! Swish-smack!

Now, she wanted it to stop while he fucked her again, then when his cock was deeply inside her cunt, and she was writhing on its swollen tip, he could start whipping her again and she would be able to finish. But the blows kept falling and the pain got worse and gradually she felt her muscles relaxing as she succumbed to the relentless punishment and the distress it brought.

After he had dipped the strap in the water several times and beaten her until she was silent, he threw the strap down and left her. She gasped noisily through her parched lips and lay, dazed and giddy and spread-eagled in the sand. She squirmed her buttocks together and squeezed at her swollen labia then she felt a hand caressing the inside of her leg.

She tensed as fingers ran along the inside of her knee and moved up slowly towards the splayed-out edges of her crack. She raised her neck slightly, expecting to see the man but instead she saw Chrissie's tangled hair and her naked, bruised shoulders.

Deborah tried to speak but her voice was hoarse with screaming and her throat too dry.

"Don't speak," said Chrissie softly. "Here, try and drink this."

She held out a large, skin water bottle with a broad, embossed silver spout. Deborah raised her head some more and opened her dry lips. Chrissie tipped the large water bottle and let some water dribble down into Deborah's mouth. It ran down the back of her throat and made her choke then, still with it spilling from her lips, she took some more and man-

123

aged to swallow it.

"You did this for me. Are you alright?"

Deborah nodded her head slowly as she took another sip from the dribbling water bottle.

Chrissie pulled herself up between Deborah's out-stretched legs. She smiled then dropped her face towards Deborah's red-striped breasts. She licked her tongue out and ran its wet end around one of Deborah's hard nipples. Deborah flinched as the warm tongue touched her but, as Chrissie lapped around the erect nipple, Deborah felt it soothing the soreness. Chrissie leant across to the other and licked that one as well.

"Is that better?"

Deborah nodded slowly as she licked water from her lips.

"Yes, please don't stop."

Chrissie licked both her nipples then took each one in turn into her mouth and sucked them. She pulled on them hard and, when she took one between her teeth and bit down onto it, Deborah felt a rush of heat flushing across her breasts.

"Please, please don't stop."

Chrissie moved her face down, keeping her tongue outstretched and letting its wet tip draw a moist line across Deborah's navel and down to the front of her shaved crack. She lapped around its edges, probing her tongue around Deborah's clitoris and making it throb and swell. She bit it gently then ran her tongue around the soft edges of her outer labia, lapping up the man's spunk and leaving her spit in its place.

"More, please, more."

Chrissie delved her tongue into Deborah's open cunt, slipping the tip around its inside edges then probing it at the entrance to her vagina. Deborah lifted her hips and widened herself as much as she could and Chrissie pressed her face hard against the moist, semen-covered flesh. She licked at it and probed it and pushed the tip of her tongue deeply inside

124

then ran it down and lapped around the tight muscle of Deborah's anus.

"Don't stop, push it in."

Chrissie pressed her tongue out as far as she could and Deborah relaxed her buttocks to let it in. She felt a wave of heat in her hips as Chrissie's tongue pushed through the muscular ring and she raised her hips higher as she penetrated her deeply.

"I need more, more."

Chrissie drew the skin water bottle away from Deborah's face and pulled it down the front of her stomach. It left a trail of water as it spilled out from the spout and Deborah felt it running into her open crack and down around her anus.

"Yes, more, more."

Chrissie held the skin bottle between Deborah's legs and pressed the embossed, silver spout around the edges of her cunt. Deborah felt the hardness of the spout and lifted herself towards it. Chrissie worked it around the soft edges, splaying them apart and watching them swell then she pressed the end of the spout against the pink centre and pushed it in.

Deborah gasped as the spout entered her. She felt it running in on the semen and spit that covered her flesh and, as it went in further, she felt the water dribbling from its tip and dousing her.

"More, more."

Chrissie pushed it deeply, squashing the skin bag with her hands and forcing a spurt of water into Deborah's cunt. Deborah's eyes widened as the flood of water squirted up inside her. It was warm and the flow was so great, it was like a massive surge of semen.

"More, more, give me more."

Chrissie squeezed the bag again and another flush of water spurted inside Deborah's vagina. Deborah felt her limbs filling with heat. She wanted the water to flow inside her so much. She wanted Chrissie to squeeze the skin bag and flush her completely with its contents. She wanted to imagine she was being fucked by a cock with an unlimited supply of spunk. She could see it in her mind, flowing from its tip, surging inside her and impossible to stop.

"More, give me more."

Chrissie squeezed the bag harder and forced the silver spout deeper and Deborah began tensing as her welling orgasm began rushing through her veins. She wanted to reach her arms around Chrissie and hold her by the throat and force her to empty the skin bag into her. She wanted to reach up and bite her neck as she splashed the water into her cunt, squeezing it out and spurting it into her without stopping. She opened her mouth to plead for more but, just as she tried to speak, she heard the sound of the cracking strap and Chrissie fell forward onto her with all her weight.

Swish-smack!

"Get off her bitch! I have not finished with her yet!"

Swish-smack!

The strap came down again across Chrissie's back and she fell forward heavily, banging her head against Deborah's and knocking the breath from her.

The man shouted angrily as he brought down the strap again.

"Leave her you bitch!"

Swish-smack!

Deborah felt the pressure of the blow through Chrissie's body and she opened her thighs as much as she could so that the spout of the water bottle was forced even deeper.

Swish-smack!

Chrissie fell forward again, unable to release the water bag and unable to roll away. Deborah felt Chrissie's ear by her lips and she grabbed it in her teeth and moaned into it.

"More. More. Don't stop. Keep it in. Please, please ..."

Swish-smack!

Chrissie fell forward again and the spout of the water sack spurted water deeply into Deborah's cunt. Deborah gasped as the breath was knocked from her again and she pulled herself around the deeply penetrating spout.

Swish-smack!

Chrissie screamed out loudly and, as she tensed her body against Deborah, Deborah felt the pain of the strap passing through her. As she heard the smack of the wet strap on Chrissie's back and felt Chrissie's tightening body against hers, she drew in the pain and it loosened the failing grip she held on her growing orgasm. At last, it was as though Deborah was taking the beating while she was being fucked and she screamed for more.

"More! More!"

Swish-smack! Swish-smack! Swish-smack!

The blows of the strap rained down and Chrissie screamed as every one landed on her back but she could not free her hands and the water bottle kept spurting into Deborah. Each burst felt like another surge of semen and each flushing wave brought Deborah's orgasm nearer to the surface.

"More! More! Beat her! Beat her!"

Deborah twisted and turned against her restraints and forced herself down on the bottle as the strap flailed Chrissie mercilessly.

Swish-smack! Swish-smack! Swish-smack!

Deborah felt the surging heat of her orgasm driving through her hips. She raised them as high as she could and, as more blows fell on Chrissie's back, she reared up and felt it explode.

Her head spun as it surged through her. Her veins pulsated with each blow of the strap and she jerked and shuddered with spasm after spasm as she felt the water bursting inside her. She drew in a massive breath of air, tightened her chest then, stretching out her fingers as wide as she could, she thrust her throbbing nipples against Chrissie's screaming mouth and was overtaken by a massive, convulsive paroxysm.

Deborah lay stretched out in the sand and, as the cold night air crept across her body and stars filled the sky, she began to shiver uncontrollably. She felt frightened of her exposure and she stretched her fingers out and clutched them repeatedly in loose fists. She tried to imagine that she was clinging to the bars of the cage and that it would not be long before her master came and taunted her with a stick and forced her to do his bidding.

She strained her bound ankles against the stakes that held them and felt the water dribbling from her splayed-out cunt. She felt so thirsty and so desperate and she tugged against the thongs at her wrists, hopelessly imagining that she could release herself and bend down and slurp at the water that ran down her thighs. She imagined herself lapping at it and quenching her thirst then running her tongue closer to her swollen outer labia and licking at them, poking the tip of her tongue inside, seeking out the inner petals and encouraging them to engorge and open. She pictured herself licking her clitoris as if she were a dog. She saw herself sucking at it and biting it and pulling at it as she held it tightly between her clenched teeth, then she dropped back in frustrated despair and fell into a fitful, dreamless sleep.

CHAPTER 9

It was dark as the three women trudged through the heavy wooden gates of a walled, desert town. A crowd of men circled around them, unyoked them from the chain that bound them to the rider's horse and dragged them down into a dark cell.

The next day they were brought food and later they were made to wash in bowls of water that some young women carried in on their heads. A small slit in the rock walls of their dungeon allowed in some light during the day and, when

Deborah climbed up to it, she saw crowds of people milling around the stalls of a market place. The place was ablaze with colour and packed with the goods of tradesmen hung up on wooden racks or strewn in piles on the ground. Men shouted and bargained over rolls of cloth or baskets of fruit and they huddled together in groups and passed notes and coins between their dark, grasping hands. The whole area was encircled by a high wall and at the one end an entrance arch spanned across thick, sandstone pillars. The ground was all red sand and, as the men walked about in their sandalled feet, it was thrown up in clouds which hung in the hot air and covered the whole market with a haze of ochre dust.

During the night they huddled together to try and keep warm. As they slept, wrapped in each others' arms, the heavy door crashed open and three robed men came in and dragged Chrissie away. Deborah pleaded with them to leave her, she could not bear the idea of being parted from her friend again, but one of the men kicked her in the side and she could only cry out hopelessly as Chrissie was pushed screaming through the door. The next morning, the same men returned, threw some bowls of water over Asia, tied a long leather leash around her neck and hauled her out on her knees.

Deborah was left alone until some veiled women brought some food. She asked them where she was and what was going to happen to her but they did not understand her or were too fearful to reply. They left without saying anything and Deborah picked at the food disconsolately, unable to eat properly because her stomach was so cramped with fear. When she slept she dreamed of the safety of the cage and when she woke up she felt exposed and frightened without the security of its surrounding bars.

The next morning she rolled over and saw the figure of a woman standing against the light from the small window. It was Saab. A long red dress with a slit up each side hung loosely from her square shoulders. Her hand was clutched in a fist around the thick end of a short cane the other end of which she flexed under her armpit. Two young boys stood at her side.

"Come on bitch. It's time to be presented formally to your master."

"Where am I? What's going to happen to me? What have they done with Chrissie? Why am I being - "

"Silence bitch, or you will feel this across your buttocks."

Saab twisted her wrist and bent the cane beneath her arm threateningly as Deborah struggled to her feet.

"Keep your head bowed bitch and follow me."

Deborah hung her head and, when Saab spun around on her black, high-heeled shoes and marched towards the door, Deborah followed obediently with the two boys behind.

They walked through several dark courtyards until they arrived at two huge polished, wooden doors. The young boys scuttled forward and strained to push them apart. Slowly, they swung back and revealed a long, marble floored room with massive polished pillars ranged along its sides. Between the pillars were heavy doors, some embossed with gold or silver and some covered in bright paintings or glittering gems. In the centre, suspended from a heavy iron chain, hung the cage. At the far end was an enormous, ornate chair with colourful drapes of cloth hanging above it. A figure in a blue and silver robe lounged back with his hands on the silver gilded arms of the chair. Half naked women sat at his feet and several young boys, holding silver serving plates on their laps, knelt on a step below the chair.

Saab pulled the tip of her cane from underneath her arm and prodded Deborah in the side.

"Crawl bitch! Crawl and be presented to your master."

Deborah dropped down onto all-fours but, as she began to move forward, Saab brought the short cane down viciously across her upturned buttocks.

Thwack!

130

Deborah shrieked in pain as the cane cut a thin red stripe across her taut skin.

"I said crawl bitch! On your belly!"

Saab slashed the cane down again

Thwack!

The piercing swipe sent a burning pain deep into her body and she fell forward onto the shiny, marble floor.

"I said on your belly bitch!"

Thwack!

The cane cut across her buttocks again and she tensed and pressed the front of her hips against the floor, gasping for breath as she waited for the throbbing burn on her skin to subside.

"Now crawl bitch!"

Deborah kept her body flat against the shiny floor and started pulling herself forward. The coolness of the marble tiles spread across her squashed breasts and her hard nipples tingled as she squirmed forward. Saab walked slowly beside her, her high heels clicking on the floor as her thighs stretched out from the slits in her red dress.

Deborah tried to look up as she crawled beneath the shadow of the hanging cage but Saab noticed her and whacked her again with the cane.

Thwack!

Her buttocks stung as the sharp edge bit into her and she felt the front of her shaved slit pulling against the smooth floor as she struggled to follow Saab's orders.

Saab drove her forward, slashing at her with the cane if she slowed too much or tried to look up until finally, she lay with her stretched-out fingertips touching the edge of the step below the massive chair.

Theron stood up and the women at his side shrank back as if afraid.

"So, finally, the last of our latest purchase is here."

"Lord Theron, this is the bitch called Deborah."

Deborah tried to look up but Saab pressed the heel

131

of her shoe against the back of her head and all she could see was the edge of the shiny, marble step.

"Well Deborah, you have been very expensive for me." He came closer to her until she saw his bare feet in front of her face. "And you have caused such trouble for poor Gross. He is to be punished of course, and you must watch, after all it is because of you that he is to suffer."

He prodded his toes beneath her chin and lifted it slightly. Spit was smeared across her mouth and cheeks and she felt filthy and ashamed.

"Hello little slave," he said mockingly. "You do look miserable. I hope you are not sad to be with us. Of course not, how could you be!"

She looked up through bleary eyes and saw his white teeth flashing as he grinned. His full lips were pink against his dark, swarthy face and his long black hair fell loosely onto his muscular shoulders. He brushed his hair back with his large hands and turned sideways, staring upwards and showing her his sharp profile. His chin was square and his nose narrow and pointed and his features blended together into a strikingly handsome face. He was tall and slim and black hairs covered the upper part of his chest where it was exposed by the open neck of his robe. When he turned back and stared at her closely with his dark eyes she felt his menacing power and had to turn away.

He laughed and went back to the huge chair, standing in front of it and arranging his robe before sitting slowly and resting his hands on the silver embossed arms. The women on each side pulled up close to him and one draped her head onto his lap. He stroked her hair unthinkingly and poked his finger into her mouth. She sucked at it eagerly, pulling her mouth down onto it and drawing it in to the knuckle as she stared up at him hoping for his approval.

Suddenly, he jumped up and pushed her aside.

"Oh, I quite forgot. Gross is waiting for us. Boys! Boys!" Several of the young boys leapt up and clamoured

132

around him. "Bring poor Deborah. I think we can let her stand, but lead her properly, we don't want her getting away again do we? No, that would never do."

Saab eased her heel from the back of Deborah's head and kicked her in the side of the chest.

"Get up bitch, but keep looking at the floor."

Deborah struggled to her feet as the boys surrounded her. They poked their fingers at her, prodding her legs and buttocks and feeling her breasts. One of them pulled on the chain between the shackles on her wrists and another prised her knees apart and looked up at her cunt.

Theron pointed at them all one by one, as if counting them, then placed his hands on two of the boys' heads.

"You two, Kahlil and Ahmad, you may bring her, fetch your leads."

They rushed behind a curtain and when they came back each was clutching a coiled cord with something shiny and metal fixed to the end.

Theron brushed the other boys aside and they scuttled away and sat on the step beneath the chair.

"Now, let my little servants clip our new slave into her traces."

Kahlil and Ahmad reached up towards Deborah and held out shiny, metal clasps attached to the cords. They pressed the backs of the clasps and they opened, revealing sharply serrated edges, like small metal teeth. Kahlil thrust the clasp at Deborah's nipple and she drew back in fear.

Theron put his hand on her shoulder.

"Now, little slave, that's not very good behaviour is it? I told you to stand up but, as far as I remember, I did not tell you to do anything else. Did I tell her to do anything else Saab?" Saab shook her head. "Oh dear, this is so annoying. Saab, show her that I mean what I say."

Saab nodded and brought her cane down across Deborah's buttocks.

Thwack!

Deborah twisted sideways but, before she could catch her breath, another swipe of the cane came down.

Thwack!

She thrust her hips forward to try and ease the burning pain but, as she moved, Saab wound her elbow around Deborah's neck and bent her forward, leaning her across her outstretched knee and flailing her repeatedly.

Thwack! Thwack! Thwack!

Theron bent his head and looked up into Deborah's pain-racked face.

"Perhaps that is enough. Yes, I think she will do as she is told now."

Saab released her and she stood as still as she could as the throbbing pain from the cane continued to penetrate her and course through her burning flesh.

"Now, little slave, stand still and the boys can fit your traces."

Kahlil reached forward again, holding the clasp open and placing the serrated teeth around her hard, extended nipple. She looked down in fear as he released it and it clamped tightly around her.

The sharp teeth sank into her flesh and she shrieked in pain. Her eyes widened as the metal clamp kept tightening under the pressure of its spring and she folded forward to try and ease the piercing pain.

"Please, please let me go, please - "

"Did I say speak? I don't think so. Oh dear, Saab, I think our little slave needs some more help to make her obedient."

"No, please, no - "

Thwack!

Again the cane lashed down across her buttocks and the stinging pain surged through her body and mingled with the searing burn that penetrated her breasts and surged through her throbbing veins.

Thwack!

She gulped breathlessly as her whole body filled with an agonizing fire and she tensed herself, trying to stand upright and show that she was obedient in the hope that Theron would order Saab to stop.

He bent his face to hers and smiled.

"Fix her other trace, I am getting impatient."

Ahmad offered the open clamp to her other nipple and let it go. It snapped shut around her dark flesh and she shrieked again but this time she did not move. The veins in her neck throbbed and her head spun dizzily as she held her body taut, absorbing the pain from the serrated clasps and letting it run through her as it set her nerves on fire and overwhelmed her with anguish.

The boys took up the other ends of the uncoiled cords and stretched them tight. The clamps pulled against her nipples and stretched them out, lifting her firm breasts and sending shock waves of pain deep into her chest. The boys flicked the cords and pulled her forward. Her eyes widened with fear but she moved at their command, allowing them to lead her forward like a captured, suffering animal.

The other boys ran to one of the doors that were between the tall pillars and pushed at it with all their strength until slowly it opened. They dashed through it, laughing and poking each other as they disappeared into the darkness that lay behind it. Deborah was led through the entrance and told to stop once they were inside.

In the middle of the room was a deep pool with a pillar at its centre. Gross was bound to it by heavy chains. His clothes had been stripped from him and, as Deborah was led further in, she saw how his naked, muscular body strained in panic against his unforgiving bonds. Chrissie knelt in front of him, his huge, flaccid cock lying limply against her open mouth. Water splashed in over the sides of the pool, washing around Chrissie's thighs and pulling heavily at the flimsy dress that hung in tatters from her shoulders. Her blackened eyes stared emptily ahead and she did not seem to notice Deborah.

Theron jumped into the pool and water splashed around the bottom of his blue and silver robe.

"Well, here is Gross, and still looking very sad I must say. Poor Gross. Perhaps this will cheer you up. Look, it's your little charge. Yes, here's the reason for your punishment. Oh, poor, poor Gross, you were so bad for letting her go. It has cost me a lot to get her back you know, and I don't even know yet whether she's worth it."

He reached down and held Gross's heavy, black cock in his hand.

"Oh my dear little Chrissie, you've not been very successful with poor Gross. But look, your little friend Deborah has come to watch, perhaps that will encourage you. I do hope so. This is your last chance to show if you can be like a man. And if you can't, well, I think I will have to get rid of you, permanently."

He prised Chrissie's lips open with his fingers and placed Gross's weighty glans into her mouth, then he climbed out of the pool, folded his hand into the crook of Saab's arm, and sauntered over to Deborah.

Spit dribbled from the corners of her mouth as she stood, afraid to move, with the painful clamps biting into her stretched-out nipples.

"Kahlil! Ahmad! Take our little slave nearer so that she can get a good view!"

The boys ran each side of the pool, tugging at the cords that led to the clamps on Deborah's nipples. She staggered forward, crying out with the pain as they drew her forward into the pool. She stumbled down the side and stood with the water lapping around her calves then they pulled her forward again, stretching the cords each side of the pillar in the centre of the pool, until she was in front of Gross.

He looked at her and struggled against the chains that bound him to the pillar.

"Gross must not touch. Saab is very angry if Gross touches."

136

He pulled at his chains frantically but they held him fast. Chrissie reached up and took his huge cock in her hands and massaged her fingers along its length. She sucked at it and pulled its flaccid shaft deeply into her mouth as the rising water splashed around her hips.

Theron laughed loudly.

"Poor Gross. How sad." He shouted down to Deborah. "Oh I do hope your little friend can get him excited. You see I will not let him go until his cock is hard and spurts with spunk. Poor, poor Gross."

Chrissie sucked Gross's cock hard and pulled her fingers along it desperately. She held his balls in the cups of her hands and lifted them and squeezed them and pulled the flesh that enclosed them but he struggled against her and threw his head from side to side in panic.

"Gross must not touch the girls. Saab would be very angry with Gross."

Theron held onto Saab's arm and walked around the pool.

"My dear Saab you have been too severe with poor Gross. He cannot think of anything but you. Oh dear, it looks as though he will be going for a long swim soon."

Deborah dropped her shoulders to try and ease the pain in her nipples as the water lapped above her knees. She looked at Chrissie's anguished face and saw her hopeless desperation. She stepped forward and the boys took up the slack of the cords but Theron shouted angrily.

"I did not tell you to move bitch! Stay where you are!" He pressed his fingers to his lips in thought. "Ah, I see, perhaps you want to take your little friend's place. Of course, how silly of me. How inconsiderate I am. Boys! Drag the bitch out! She has failed and will have to be punished."

Several of the boys jumped down into the pool and dragged Chrissie away from Gross. She struggled against them, reaching out for Gross's cock and splashing frantically in the rising water. Finally, they got her to the side and Saab started caning her. She managed to crawl away and cowered against a wall with her arms folded across her breasts but Saab did not stop the thrashing until Chrissie went quiet and stayed still.

Kahlil and Ahmad pulled on the cords and drew Deborah forward until she was almost touching Gross.

He was seized with panic.

"Gross must not touch! Must not touch! Saab will be angry! Saab will be angry with Gross!"

He screamed frantically as Deborah reached down and took hold of his cock. It was hot and, as she lifted it, she felt its full weight. She took hold of the loose skin that folded closely around the heavy glans and pulled at it. It came forward and she squeezed it tightly between her fingers.

Without letting go of his cock, she edged closer to him and pressed her hips against his heavy chains. As she squirmed the front of her slit against the iron links of the chain, she bent forward and placed her face against his ear.

"Gross, you must let me, you must ... "

She remembered how kind he had been to her, feeding her in the boat and trying to save her from the men who took her from the lorry, and now she knew she had to save him from the Theron's threatened punishment. She pressed her mouth against the side of his neck and felt his blood pounding in his veins as he tried to squirm away in fear.

She shrieked as the cords were pulled hard and she was drawn up tightly against him. As he struggled to keep himself away, his chains dug into her hips and pressed her slit open at the front.

"Gross, let me, you must ... "

Another yank on the cords and this time, because she was already tightly against Gross and she could not move any further forward, the serrated clips pulled tightly on her already stretched-out flesh. The pain in her nipples was too much to bear and she shrieked wildly and let go of his cock as she tried to reach up to her agonized nipples. She grabbed hold of one of them and tried to force the biting clasp apart but it was impossible. The spring that held it was too strong for her and even though she pressed as hard as she could it would not release.

A sudden wave of panic flooded through her. She could not get free and now the water was splashing at the tops of her thighs and lapping against the soft flesh of her shaven crack. Desperately, she squeezed his cock and ran her hands down to his balls. They hung heavily and she cupped their weight and squeezed them as she looked into his face. His eyes were wide with terror and spit ran freely from the sides of his full-lipped mouth.

"Gross, let me suck your cock, let me lick it and make it hard so that I can wank it and finish it."

He tossed his head wildly from side to side.

"Gross must not touch! Gross must not touch!"

She pressed herself harder against his chains and felt the sweating heat of his body.

"Gross, you must let me, it's your only chance."

She bent down and held his cock to her mouth. The clasps pulled at her nipples, and she winced as she bent further, but she managed to get her lips against it. Water splashed around his balls as she took the soft tip into her mouth. She licked at the skin of his foreskin. It was fleshy and full and she closed her teeth around it and bit into it.

She felt his balls tighten in his scrotum as she bit him harder. She sucked the flesh of his foreskin then probed the tip of her tongue inside it and touched the open end of his broad glans. She pressed her tongue against it and pushed the pointed end into the tight hole. Again she felt his balls pull back into their fleshy sack so she probed further. She pulled her hand along his soft shaft and squeezed her fingers around the base of his wide-flanged glans. She opened her mouth to move it further down and water splashed in and she started choking.

She pulled herself up and breathed deeply then

plunged her face back down and again wrapped her mouth tightly around his cock. She sucked as hard as she could and she squeezed his balls and ran her hand along the soft flesh but she could not make his cock hard. She pulled away and clasped herself to him.

"Gross, you must let me. Tell me what you would like to do. Tell me what you would like to do to me."

She reached down and, when she held his cock, she felt it hardening. She squeezed it hard and felt the veins filling and throbbing along its surface.

"Tell me Gross. What would you like to do to me? Would you like to fuck me?"

His cock hardened even more and she felt the glans swelling inside her hand.

"Would you like to put this inside me and fuck me?"

She held onto it as it swelled and lengthened. She bent down to suck it but the water was now at her waist. She hesitated for a moment then, as she felt the pressure of the metal clasps on her nipples and the pulsating throb of his cock in her hand, she took a deep breath and drove her head beneath the surface.

She closed her mouth around his cock and sucked it hard. She felt it swelling and, as it lengthened, its broad tip forced against the back of her throat. She held her breath as long as she could but, in the end, she could hang on no longer and her ears started drumming and her head was spinning as she burst to the surface gasping and choking.

Still she held onto his cock. It was huge and throbbed massively in her hand. She clasped her fingers around it as hard as she could but she could not encircle it. She pulled along its length, feeling the throbbing veins against the palm of her hand then squeezing the engorged tip as it heated and swelled beneath her grasp.

She pressed her wet face against his ear again.

"Gross, would you like to stick this in me? Would you like me to open my legs so that you can get it in? I can if you want, I can spread my legs as wide as you want. My cunt is shaved. It's shaved especially for you. It's all smooth around the edges. My labia, they're so soft and smooth. They're wet as well, not just with the water but with my juices. Yes, they're wet with my juices, wet and slippery and ready for you to ride me. Gross, if you want, I'll open my legs now and you can plunge it in."

She squeezed his cock hard and climbed up onto him. The heavy links of his chains bulged out around his muscles and she wrapped her legs high on his hips.

"Stick it in Gross. I want your cock inside me. Right in. It's so huge but I can take it. Yes, I can take it all. I want it deep. I want to feel it at the top of my cunt, as far as it will go. I want to drive myself onto it and I want to feel it exploding with spunk. Stick it in. Gross, stick it in."

She drew herself up higher and opened her legs as much as she could. She felt the smooth flesh of her shaved cunt opening and she felt the throbbing heat of his massive cock as it pressed against her distended labia.

"Stick it in! Stick it in! I want you to ride me and fuck me until you come. I want you to plunge it deep into me and fuck me until I scream that I cannot take any more. Your cock is so huge, so massive, and I want to feel it all. I want to feel every throbbing vein against the wet flesh of my open cunt."

She dropped herself against the throbbing tip and its broad-flanged end spread her fleshy edges wide. It sank in and she raised herself slightly against its pressure then, as her vagina tightened around it, she dropped down and took it in.

The water flooded around her breasts and she clawed against his chains to try and thrust herself down on his cock even more but she kept slipping and falling away.

"Fuck me Gross. Fuck me with that huge cock. Fuck me like I was an animal. I want your spunk inside me and I want to feel the veins on your cock expanding and throbbing inside me as you spurt it out."

She tried to drive herself down again but she lost her grip and fell backwards, smacking her hands out in the foaming water as it splashed over her face and into the her mouth.

"Fuck me Gross! Fuck me!"

Still with his cock inside her, and with her legs wrapped tightly against the chains that bound him, she thrashed about frantically. She shrieked in agony as the cords pulled tight, yanking at the clasps on her nipples and sending shooting pains through her outstretched body. Water splashed into her mouth and, unable to keep up the strain on her neck, her head went back and ducked beneath the water. The clasps bit into her nipples and she flailed her arms wildly to try and get upright but every time she came to the surface she gasped for breath only so that she could keep yelling to Gross.

"Get it in me Gross. Stick it as far as you want. I want it all. Fuck me! Fuck me!"

The boys holding the cords pulled at them and yanked her up out of the water. The tension on her nipples was unbearable but, as the pain burned deeply into her breasts, she felt herself screaming louder and wanting more.

"Get your cock into me Gross. Get it deep and ram it home. Ram it right in so that the end swells and sticks tight. Fuck me! Jam it in as hard as you can and fuck me! Stuff it up into me and fuck me for the bitch I am!"

Some of the other boys dived into the water and grabbed her by the arms. They pulled her upright and held her against Gross. Water splashed around her neck and she watched it foaming around Gross's mouth as the boys forced her up and down his hard, throbbing cock.

"Get it deep Gross! Get it deep!"

She kept shouting to him as the cords pulled on her nipples and the pain in her breasts drove her into an uncontrollable frenzy.

"Pull the cords! Pull the cords! I want more! More! More!"

The boys pulled on the cords and her body burned in

142

agony as she was lifted then thrust down onto the still swelling cock. It was so tight inside her that they could hardly force her up and down its length and, as it expanded even more and forced against her tightly-stretched cunt and she felt the pressure of the water around her neck, she shouted in a wild frenzy.

"Fuck me down onto it! Stretch my cunt around it! Pull my nipples! Stretch them out! Drive my cunt down and ..."

The rising water splashed around her face and she started choking as it flooded over her head. She ground her teeth together and held her breath as repeatedly she was plunged down by the boys onto Gross's pulsating cock.

Her ears drummed as the bubbling water foamed around her but she held her breath until she felt the cock inside her swelling and filling her completely. She tightened her hips and squeezed herself around the throbbing veins of his huge shaft as it bulged and pulsated against her flesh. She raised herself enough to grab a breath as she felt a fiery heat running up the length of his cock then she screamed like an animal as a tremendous burst of spunk shot against the top of her tightly filled vagina.

It flooded her and she felt drowned by its huge, soaking bursts. She bit her lips and dropped herself back against the strain of the cords that held her nipples and she felt herself spinning dizzily as her body tensed in a muscle-seizing spasm. For a moment, she felt consumed by pain but, as the seizure gripped her fully, it also released her into a delirium of ecstasy. Everything went dark as she reared up for a last time against the biting clasps at her nipples and fell backwards into the gurgling water as she was consumed by a massive, heaving orgasm.

Deborah did not remember being dragged from the pool and only slowly came around as she was hauled along the marble floor. The boys pulled her by the hair into the pillared hall, dragging her beneath the steadily swinging cage before throwing her against the step below Theron's massive chair.

She lay before him with her shackled arms outstretched, still gasping for breath and still twitching with the remnants of her orgasm. She pulled her legs up and felt Gross's spunk running from her cunt and, as she reached her arms down to clasp her knees, she glanced them against her nipples and recoiled in pain as their ends ignited deep and fiery pains inside her.

Theron bent forward with his elbows on his knees. He smiled as one of the half-naked women at his side ran her hand inside his robe and started fondling him.

"Well, you're beginning to earn some of your high price already little slave. Take her and lock her in the cage!"

CHAPTER 10

Deborah had not realised how welcome the enclosing bars of the cage would feel. She shivered with remorse as she remembered how she had acted with Gross and she felt degraded by the way she had screamed at him to fill her cunt with his cock. But, when she thought of his chained body, his fear and her desperation to have his throbbing shaft inside her, she felt the edges of her cunt swelling and running wet. She pushed her shackled hands down to the base of her stomach and probed her fingers into the front of her shaven slit then, as if realising what she was doing and feeling an overwhelming wave of shame, she yanked her fingers away and flung herself down onto the hard, iron bars. She crouched down like an animal and cowered in the corner of the cage feeling as though she had been captured and shut up to prevent her from any more wrongdoing.

Some veiled women entered the hall and, as the cage swung lazily on the heavy chain, Deborah squatted on the open floor and watched them. They carried wound-up rolls of cloth which they laid on the floor in a large square then they brought in plates and dishes and set them around the edges. Young boys carried in huge silver plates laden with food and set them down on heavy, wooden trestles that they dragged from behind the pillars.

After a while, Theron and Saab entered with a group of women surrounding them. Saab was wearing a tight, red dress that clung to her breasts and hips then parted in a wide slit at the front. When she sat on a large cushion and folded her legs the dress opened to the tops of her thighs and Deborah could just make out the dark shape of her neatly trimmed, black pubic hair.

Theron looked up at Deborah and ordered the cage to be lowered. It swung from side to side then crashed to the smooth, marble floor with a jolt.

"Take her out. She can work with her little friends keeping our important guests happy. Nothing must go wrong with the entertainment. My clients and my wealth are all that matter. A good feast and my guests will only be too pleased to buy the products of my mines and, of course, the drugs that are routed from the south."

The young boys reached in and tried to drag her out of the cage but she clung to the bars and would not let go. She bared her teeth at them but they pulled at her arms and legs and poked at her with canes until, finally, they prised her hands away. She clawed her fingers out emptily as they held her shackled wrists to the floor, tied a tight collar around her neck and clipped a leather leash to it. They pulled her up onto her hands and knees and dragged her out.

She dribbled from her mouth and pulled against her collar as they led her to one of the huge pillars. When she tried to look up they kicked her then they pulled the leash up tight and kept her on all-fours as Chrissie and Asia were led in by more boys. Chrissie looked exhausted and kept dropping onto her elbows but, every time she fell forward, the boy leading her lashed her with a short cane and made her get up.

145

Asia hung her head and struggled to move. Her black eyes were wet and smudged with dirt and her buttocks were laced with angry red stripes. A boy ran across and started whacking her upturned bottom with a cane and, as the blows fell onto the criss-crossed weals on her skin, she scuttled forward in blind panic until he stopped.

The three of them were made to wait on their hands and knees as guests arrived then, when everyone was seated around the feast, the boys drove Deborah, Chrissie and Asia forward on their leashes. They paraded them amongst the guests, yanking on their leads and making them crawl wherever they were commanded. As they were led around, men in flowing robes pawed at them, feeling their breasts, rubbing their hands up between their legs and poking their fingers into their mouths. Some men made them sit up and beg for tit bits of food and, if they were not pleased with them, they kicked them or smacked them across their buttocks.

A tall man in a long, black robe grabbed hold of Deborah's hair and pulled her face between his outstretched legs. She fell onto her elbows and the collar at her neck tightened as the boy tried to haul her back up so that she could serve the man properly. The man pulled her hair tight and pressed her face against his hard cock and, as the boy still pulled back on the leash, it forced her mouth to gape wide. Her tongue poked forward between her wide-stretched lips, forcing bubbling dribbles of spit to run across her chin and down the front of her throat.

"The bitch is hungry for it. Look how she salivates like a dog. Here bitch, feed on this."

He grabbed more of her hair in a bunch and forced her head down until the end of his hard cock was against her gaping mouth.

"Go on, eat it up bitch."

Deborah's mouth dripped spit and her eyes widened as she tried to pull against his grip on her hair. The more she pulled the more the leash dragged her back and she froze with terror as she realised she was hopelessly trapped. The boy started lashing her buttocks with the free end of the leash but the blows were too weak to overcome the dizziness and confusion which was engulfing her. Her face and neck reddened then, as the lashing seemed to fade away completely, she felt her hair falling loosely around her face as the man released her and she was snatched backwards under the unremitting pressure of the leash.

The boy kept lashing her and slowly, as she gulped for air, the pain returned and she started flinching under the frenzied blows.

Lash! Lash! Lash!

She began to roll from side to side as the stabbing pains cut into her and, as the boy yanked insistently on the leash, she felt her body throbbing back to consciousness.

Lash! Lash! Lash!

He dragged her around the floor until she struggled back onto her knees and only then did he hold back the stinging lashes from the flailing, leather leash.

Deborah hung her head and felt humiliated and degraded as the boy continued to lead her around. When the men shouted for more food she was made to pick it up in her mouth and carry it over to them. Asia was too weak to carry a large basket of fruit that one of the boys pushed into her mouth and she collapsed. The boy leading her thrashed her with the other end of the leash and then took a cane to her but she could not get up. Theron ordered her to be tied upside down against one of the pillars and, when they had finished securing her, she hung by her ankles on tightly pulled ropes with her head cocked to one side and her face pressed against the shiny, marble floor.

As the feast progressed, the guests became more demanding and Deborah and Chrissie were made to work harder. They were made to carry plates in their mouths and, after the men had used them, they were forced to lick them clean. The boys forced them down onto their elbows and the men laughed at them as they lapped the plates. Bits of food stuck around their mouths and on their chins but the boys would not let them stop and thrashed them whenever they slacked or did not clean a plate well enough. When Theron thought the guests might be unhappy with their performance he told Saab to make sure they worked harder and she went to each one of them and kicked them until she was satisfied.

Deborah was knocked sideways as a man lunged at Chrissie.

"Clean it properly bitch!"

He held his plate out in front of her and she licked out her tongue and started again.

"More bitch! Lick it more! I am not satisfied!"

Chrissie licked more but her tongue was dry and sore and her jaw ached and she could not get the plate clean enough.

"Hold her boy! She needs a lesson!"

The boy snatched the leash and pulled the collar up tight. Chrissie gasped and threw her head back as the man picked up the plate and smacked it across her upturned buttocks.

Smack!

Chrissie howled as the flat, silver plate smacked against her taut skin.

Smack!

He brought it down again and she tightened her muscles as it smacked loudly and knocked her forward.

Smack!

She cried out again.

Smack! Smack! Smack!

Deborah kept her head low but looked up under her eyes as the silver plate struck Chrissie repeatedly.

Smack! Smack! Smack!

Every time it came down against her skin the loud smack made Deborah wince. She watched Chrissie's face screwing up in pain as she gasped for breath and she watched her buttocks becoming redder each time the plate came down across them.

Smack! Smack! Smack!

Deborah pulled forward against her leash. She wanted to get closer. She wanted the smacking sound of the plate to fill her ears and she wanted to hear Chrissie's gasps as the pain surged threw her. Deborah felt the tension on her throat urging her forward and she pulled more against it, opening her legs slightly and pushing her knees hard against the shiny floor. She wanted to drag the boy forward, straining on her lead like a dog, and she wanted to snarl at Chrissie and drive her aside and stand in her place.

Smack! Smack! Smack!

Chrissie screeched every time she managed to suck in air but her face became redder and her eyes bulged as her throbbing veins stood out against her straining throat. She threw her head back and yelled once more then fell sideways on the shiny, marble floor.

Deborah pulled harder against the leash, poking her tongue out from her open mouth and letting spit dribble from its tip. She opened her legs wider and felt her wet outer labia peeling apart. She felt the opening to her vagina exposed and she felt her wetness dripping from it and running along her swelling slit and around her engorged clitoris.

Chrissie started screaming as some men rolled her onto her back, held her by the arms and legs, lifted her off the ground and stretched her out. They poured a bowl of honey over her face and it ran down into her hair and dripped from the sticky, tangled ends. They fetched more and dripped it over her breasts then dribbled it over her stomach and into her splayed-out crack. It ran between her buttocks and fell in sticky drips down onto the floor. Several of them started to lick it off her breasts and stomach then one of them got between her legs and played the bulbous tip of his cock around the sticky edges of her honey-covered cunt.

Deborah strained forward against the leash as she watched Chrissie's hips rising and falling as the man plunged his cock in and pushed it in as deeply as he could. He thrust it hard inside her then, as the men holding her arms and legs pulled her wider still, he reared back and grabbed his cock by its base. Deborah felt wetness dribbling down the insides of her thighs as he pulled it out and shot his spunk across Chrissie's honey-smeared breasts and into her gaping mouth.

The boy yanked on Deborah's leash and pulled her harshly. She resisted for a moment, feeling the tension at her neck and feeling her breasts flushing with heat as she stared at Chrissie taking a cock into her mouth as another one sank deeply into her cunt. The boy yanked the leash viciously and Deborah turned to him and snarled then, as he pulled her forward against his knees, she submitted to his control and dropped her head obediently.

He led her to a tall jar of oil and ordered her to pick it up. The large, tapered stopper had been removed and the long neck ended in a wide, rounded flange. Deborah bent her head and closed her sore lips around the wide lip of the neck and pulled at it. It was heavy with oil and so slippery that she could not pick it up. The boy yanked her collar impatiently and the flanged end slipped from her mouth but, when he started thrashing the other end of the leash down on her buttocks, she bent and closed her lips around it again. She bit behind the flanged end and, as the boy snatched at her lead, she managed to lift it.

He pulled her forward with the jar hanging in her mouth and she saw the men holding Chrissie's legs high while one of them thrust his cock into her anus. Another one brought a belt down across her breasts as two more stuffed their hard cocks into her mouth. Chrissie tried to suck them but they were too big to keep in her mouth and they wanked over her instead and filled her gaping mouth with spunk.

The boy yanked at Deborah's collar but she resisted again. She felt the heat in her cunt as she watched the spunk dribbling down Chrissie's cheeks and she felt the jar of oil slipping from her mouth. She tightened her teeth around the wide flange but she could not hold it and it fell from her grasp. It landed on the floor and, spilling oil from its neck, rolled towards one of the men.

He jumped up as it splashed oil on his red robe and he grabbed it and glared at Deborah angrily.

"Bitch! Stupid bitch!"

It was Jabari! Jabari, the rider who had stolen her from the men in the alley and had then sold her to the fat Arab to be auctioned.

She shrank back, sensing that he recognised her. She opened her mouth to speak but, as he realised that she could expose him, his face coloured with anger and he lunged at her and grabbed her by the hair. He could not risk Theron finding out that not only had he stolen and sold Deborah but that now he had infiltrated Theron's feast in the hope of stealing some of Theron's clients for himself. He masked his fear with outrage and shouted at Deborah.

"You have tarnished the robe of Jabari! You'll pay for your clumsiness bitch!"

He tipped the jar and poured oil down over her head. It stuck to her hair and pulled it down heavily across her face. She crouched fearfully on all-fours until he emptied the jar.

He threw it down angrily on the floor.

"More oil! Bring more oil! I want to give the bitch a real drenching!"

Boys scuttled around picking up jars of oil and brought them to him.

"Hold the bitch down!"

Deborah was thrown down face-forward on the shiny marble floor and held by the arms and legs. A wave of desperation flooded through her. It was as though she had suddenly woken up and found herself living in a nightmare. She panicked, opened her eyes wide and started screaming.

"Let me go! Let me go! I can't stand any more! Let me go!"

The men took no notice of her cries and pinned her

151

down to the ground as Jabari took another jar of oil, pulled out the tapered end of the large stopper, and emptied the sticky contents over her shoulders. It ran underneath her outstretched arms and around her squashed-out breasts until it formed a shimmering pool on the shiny marble floor.

"More oil! More oil!"

He took another jar and poured it over her buttocks, opening the crack between them and letting it dribble down over her anus. She squirmed and tried to pull away but the men gripped her wrists and ankles tightly and held her fast. Jabari poured more oil between her buttocks and it ran around the edges of her cunt and down the insides of her thighs. As she twisted against the men's grasp, the oil moistened the soft edges of her labia and she felt them sliding against each other as she tightened her muscles. He took another jar and drenched her legs and feet then held it over her arms and hands until she was completely soaked.

"Turn the bitch over!"

They threw her on her back. The sticky oil ran into her mouth and nose and stung her eyes. Jabari emptied another jar over her breasts, trickling it onto each of her nipples and letting it spread over her breasts and run down the side of her chest and under her arms. He took the round headed stopper from another jar, slowly drawing out the long, tapered end, and held the flanged neck of the jar above her glistening cunt.

"Hold her legs wide!"

They pulled her ankles wide and exposed the pink flesh of her cunt. Its edges were covered in oil and the dark pink centre gleamed as she lifted her hips and fought against the tight grip of the men as they pulled at her ankles. Jabari sloshed the oil around her shaved crack then lowered the spout of the jar until it touched the front of her glistening flesh. Still with the oil running over the wide flange, he poked the neck of the jar against the front of her cunt, opening it and running the oil copiously over her hard clitoris and along the soft edges of her inner leaves.

She felt the saturating warmth of the oil flooding over her flesh. Its soft stickiness drenched her and ran inside her and her whole body felt heated by its sticky ooze.

Jabari pressed the wide flange of the jar harder and prised her oily outer labia apart. She tensed her legs as she felt her flesh being stretched then she cried out when it would go no further. He held her labia wide and ran more oil from the spout around them then he pressed in the neck of the jar again but still the wide flange was too much for her.

Jabari threw the jar down with a crash. He grabbed the leash from the boy and yanked at the tight collar around her neck. She gasped and tried to reach up to release the tension. Her oily, shackled wrists slipped from the men's grip but Jabari did not give her chance to get hold of the leash as he yanked it again viciously and started to drag her across the marble floor.

He pulled her the length of the hall, yanking on the leash as she twisted and turned uncontrollably. Her oil-covered body slid across the floor and she banged into men's legs and crashed into the pillars as he dragged her around in a frenzy. She kept trying to grab the leash but her shackles were so heavy, and her limbs so slippery, that it was impossible.

He pulled her amongst the remnants of the feast and she smashed into one of the trestles, knocking the heavy board from its low legs as she was flung sideways against Chrissie. The leash slackened then fell away loosely as Jabari tossed it down onto Deborah's shaking body. Deborah looked at Chrissie as she lay, dissipated, with her legs spread wide and spunk still running from her mouth. She reached across to pull the hair from Chrissie's face but was knocked aside as Jabari reached down, grabbed Chrissie and pulled her up onto her knees.

"Perhaps this one will do better!"

He took hold of a jar and held it over her head. She stared at Deborah, her dark eyes half closed and her mouth dripping with creamy spunk. She tried to speak but winced with pain and, as Jabari dribbled oil over her face, Deborah reached out her oil-smeared hands and took hold of the bottle.

"I can take it," she said quietly. "I can take it."

Jabari laughed and let go of Chrissie. She fell back to the floor and tried to smile to Deborah.

"Then you'll take a beating first. I want to make sure you're ready this time. Bend her over! And make sure she cannot slip away!"

Some of the men grabbed one of the heavy trestles and, holding it above the ground, threw her across it so that her arms and legs hung over each side. They wound the chain between her shackles at her wrists around her ankles and pulled them tight with leather thongs. They used more leather thongs and lashed them around her waist, taking them underneath the trestle, bringing them back between her legs then leading them up to her waist again. They pulled on the thongs until she was held fast then they lifted the board high and presented her to Jabari.

He ran a finger between her shoulder blades and down onto her glistening, taut buttocks.

"Hold her up! Present her for her punishment like a captured animal."

He grabbed a silver plate and rubbed it against her oil-covered buttocks. The shiny, metal surface ran smoothly across her skin and oil dripped from its edges as he rubbed it against the backs of her thighs.

"Hold her tight!"

He pulled back the still dripping plate and held it behind his head.

"Let us see how much you need before you are ready for a fucking bitch!"

Smack!

The metal plate smacked down across her upturned buttocks. Oil sprayed out from its sides as it struck her wet flesh and she was knocked heavily against the unforgiving trestle by the pressure.

Smack!

The plate hit her across both cheeks of her buttocks and, as he pulled it away, it stuck to her skin. She felt it pulling at the backs of her legs and she sensed the pressure tugging at the soft flesh of her cunt.

Smack! Smack! Smack!

He smacked her repeatedly and her buttocks reddened but the pain was diluted by the sticky oil and not enough to penetrate the glowing warmth she already felt across her tingling skin. A wave of anxiety coursed through her stomach. It was as though he was letting her down, as though he was not doing enough to punish her.

He bent forward to her face. Her mouth was wide open and her oil-drenched hair stuck in wet strands to her cheeks.

"Are you ready now bitch?"

She turned her head slowly, licking her hair from her lips and dribbling spit from the side of her mouth. She screwed up her eyes and stared at him.

"No."

The men shouted and jeered and Jabari smacked the plate down across her buttocks angrily.

Smack! Smack! Smack!

"Enough bitch?"

She paused and watched her spit falling in a sticky stream to the floor.

"No. Not enough."

"Indolent bitch!"

Jabari smacked her again but even though spit flew from her mouth and her bottom reddened even more, when he asked her the same question she gave him the same reply.

"Not enough."

She wanted more and she raised herself against the metal plate as he rubbed it against her flesh. When he pulled it away she raised herself more, hoping he would bring it down harder and beat her with it until she cried out in agony. But she knew it would not be enough and she twisted against her bonds in a growing frenzy of frustration.

As she squirmed her oily body against the hard trestle, she felt him parting her buttocks. They peeled away from each other and she felt her oil-covered labia exposed to his gaze. She raised herself more, trying to encourage him to smack her harder then she drew in breath sharply and gaped wide as he forced the tapered end of a hard rubber stopper against her oily anus.

It prised the muscular ring apart and a searing pain shot through her. He screwed the taper against the inside of her anus, covering it with oil that dripped down the crack of her reddened buttocks, then suddenly thrust it hard. She yelled loudly as it penetrated her but she did not dare move as he forced it deeply inside until the rounded end was squeezed firmly against her splayed-out anus.

She gasped for breath and opened her mouth wide to scream to him to stop. She wanted to tell him that now she was ready but, as soon as she summoned the strength to yell out, her mouth was filled by the rounded end of another stopper. It was thrust into her mouth and held there by the long tapered end and, when she tried to close her mouth, it was held so wide she could not move it at all. She felt a wave of nausea swelling up inside her and when she tried to breathe her throat tightened and gagged.

"Enough bitch? Is that enough?"

She threw her head from side to side in panic, fighting back the nausea that burned inside her gagging throat.

"No? I thought not."

She reared back, her lungs exploding, as she fought to breathe through her flaring nostrils but, as she tensed herself, the pain in her anus increased and she fell forward against the trestle, burning all over with the heat of terror.

She felt Jabari rubbing the plate against her buttocks and she felt the sticky surface smoothing her skin then he pulled it away and she heard him hold his breath as he brought it down again.

Thwack!

The metal plate smacked hard across her buttocks and struck the rounded end of the stopper that protruded from her distended anus. She bit onto the stopper in her mouth in agony and shock as the smacking plate drove the tapered neck of the stopper in her anus deeper inside.

Thwack!

He struck her again and the stopper went further as the metal plate smashed against its still protruding rounded end.

She could not move. Her body felt filled and she shuddered all over with the shock of the blow as he smacked the plate down again.

Thwack!

Her throat tightened completely and she flushed all over with a sickening heat as her head spun in giddy horror.

Thwack! Thwack! Thwack!

Every blow drove the neck of the stopper deeper and, each time the plate struck it, the rounded end pressed harder and more forcibly against her anal ring.

Thwack! Thwack! Thwack!

She felt the rounded end opening her up and she went rigid as the final blows came down.

Thwack! Thwack! Thwack!

Her head reeled and foaming spit burst from the sides of the stopper in her mouth as now she felt the hard neck of the jar pressing against the swollen edges of her exposed cunt.

"Ready now bitch?"

For a moment she felt it opening her up then her eyes widened as it drove in and her mind was filled with the screams that she could not make.

When Deborah slowly returned to consciousness, it was to feel her cunt and anus still burning from the penetrations, but at least her mouth was free. Theron and Jabari stood over her. Theron bent down to Deborah and flicked his fingers slowly up and down her swollen lips.

"Well little slave you are a sorry sight."

"Please master, Jabari - "

Jabari pushed forward not wanting Deborah to speak.

"Lord Theron. You have acquired a fine and entertaining bitch here. Perhaps you would like to sell her?"

Deborah sensed his nervousness and she reached out and grabbed Theron's ankle. Perhaps, she thought, Jabari could take her out of this hell.

"Please master, Jabari - "

"You see lord Theron. She is keen to be in my company."

Theron looked confused.

"Yes indeed. Strangely keen." Deborah gripped her fingers tightly around his ankle. "What is it my little slave. Do you like my friend Jabari?"

"Please, it was Jabari - "

"I will offer you the best price for her Theron. The very best."

"You are very keen. Perhaps you have seen her before?"

"No Theron. How could that be possible?"

Theron looked down at Deborah and smiled.

"Perhaps she has been riding with you? Yes, I think she knows you. Look how she grips my ankle and repeats your name. Oh dear Jabari. How could you deceive me like this?"

"Theron, I promise I have never - "

"And perhaps you have got an eye on some of my clients? Perhaps you are looking to take over some of my business?"

"Theron, I assure - "

"Jabari, you must think me a fool! You will not threaten my empire again. I know you have been plotting

158

against me but it is the end for you now. Take him! I do not want to see him again!" Several men grabbed him by the arms and pulled him away. "I do not want to see him again, ever! Finish him!"

They dragged Jabari away. He struggled and protested and looked fearfully around him but no one came to his assistance then, in desperation his fear turned to anger.

"You will not get rid of me that easily Theron. And you bitch, " he glared at Deborah, "just you wait. You will pay for this! You will pay for this!"

As they pulled him out of the hall his shouting faded.

Theron looked down at Deborah.

"Boy! Keep her on a tight leash. She may eat some of the scraps but do not let her fall to sleep."

He turned to Saab who was smoothing down the front of her tight, red dress.

"Accompany me Saab. I need a rest. I am so upset. Later, we shall return and see what other ways we can think of to entertain our little slave."

He slipped his hand into the crook of her arm and walked away, giggling to himself and squeezing himself tightly to Saab's side.

CHAPTER 11

The boy led Deborah around on the leash for hours. When he got tired, he allowed her to stop and pick at some of the food that had been thrown down by the men, but he did not relax the tension on the leash and he did not allow her to get off all-fours. Asia was still tied upside down to the huge pillar and Chrissie still lay spread-eagled amongst the remains of the feast.

Deborah felt dizzy and exhausted, her knees were sore and she felt filthy and degraded. Her hair was tangled in knots and oil still dripped from its ends. She tried to wipe her eyes with the back of her hand but the boy kicked her and dragged her forward so that she had to put her hand back down to the floor to keep her balance. She felt ridden with guilt about Jabari. She had hoped he would be able to get her away from this nightmare but, by showing she knew him, she had sealed his fate with Theron. If only she had kept quiet and let him buy her then she could have been free. It was as though everything she did went wrong. Tears welled up in her eyes and dripped down onto the floor.

Suddenly, the huge doors of the hall crashed open and Theron came in holding onto Saab's arm. The guests followed behind surrounded by the crowd of boys.

"Still here little slave? I'm so glad. Saab has thought of something for you to do. She is sure it will entertain you."

He strolled over to her and took the leash from the boy.

"I do hope you haven't been bored little slave. That would never do."

He pulled himself close to Saab then, with his hand draped loosely across her crooked arm, walked towards his huge chair leading Deborah alongside like a dog. She had not got the strength to resist and crawled on her hands and knees without tugging against her lead or holding back.

Theron stopped beneath the slowly swinging cage and some of the boys ran around and started pulling at Deborah's oily hair. He smiled down at them then handed the leash to Saab.

"Here my dear. Entertain us. I rely on you to provide me with the good things in life. Dear Saab, if it was not for you I would be very miserable. Very miserable indeed my dear, dear Saab."

Saab smiled with satisfaction then pulled the leash tightly against Deborah's neck as Theron flopped down heavily in his huge chair.

Deborah looked around nervously. She stared at

Chrissie as she lay on her back with the spunk, that had run so freely across her face, dried and caught in her tangled hair. Her eyes were barely open as one of the men bent down and sucked at her nipples and, when he reached down and played his fingers around the edges of her crack, she did not move. Deborah stared at Asia hanging upside down against the pillar, her head more crooked than before as the full weight of her bruised body pressed down on her neck. Her pitiful form filled Deborah with dread.

Saab snatched at the leash and Deborah turned away.

"Kneel up bitch!"

Deborah hesitated, petrified by her confusion and fear. Saab let the free end of the lead fall to the floor. She held out her hand and one of the boys dropped a short cane into it. She crooked her hand across the thickest end, tucked the thin end under her armpit and flexed it impatiently. She glanced across to Theron then strutted around Deborah and smiled.

"I said kneel up bitch!"

Deborah looked up at her beseechingly. She felt defeated and hopeless and could think of nothing except begging to be released.

"Please, no more, please - "

"And when I say kneel up that is what I mean!"

"Please let me go. I promise not to - "

"Silence bitch!"

Deborah knew she had no alternative but to obey and, as Saab lifted the cane threateningly, Deborah slowly raised herself up onto her knees.

The cage swung above her and she stared up at the enclosing bars. She imagined herself locked inside it, clinging to its iron rails and gripping them so tightly it was impossible to prise her away.

"Lift your arms up bitch!"

Deborah reached her hands up towards the cage and held them high until her fingers nearly touched the bars. She could hardly hold the heavy chain between her shackles as it looped down across her breasts. It glanced against her hard nipples and sent shivers through her taut breasts. Her arms felt so tired and weak but she tightened her chest and struggled to obey Saab's orders.

"Now, stay like that bitch, and do not move!"

Deborah struggled to keep her hands as high as she could but her shoulders ached and soon she felt her elbows bending. Saab glared at her and flexed the cane under her arm.

"Keep them high bitch!"

Saab lowered the cane from her armpit and pressed the end against one of Deborah's nipples. It dug into the hard flesh and Deborah felt a deep sting shooting through her breast. Saab pressed it harder then pulled it back and circled the tip around the base of the engorged nipple.

"High bitch."

Deborah clenched her teeth and started to force up her arms. Her breasts tightened under the strain and her nipple was forced out against the sharp end of the poking cane but she strained as hard as she could until her hands were stretched as high as she could get them.

Saab ran the cane around the nipple then pulled it back suddenly and lashed at one of the boys who reached out at Deborah's breasts. He fell back and, when she bent down to him and glared into his blinking eyes, he shrank back in fear. She pressed her face against his cheek and whispered something in his ear. He smirked and scuttled off.

Saab ordered Chrissie to be brought over. The boys dragged her by the hair and threw her down at Saab's feet. She was filthy and covered in dried semen. Her nipples were hard and red and her hair stuck to her cheeks and mouth. Saab ordered her dragged to her knees then instructed the boys to pinion her arms at her back. Saab hoisted her red dress slightly then drew her thigh up between the slit. She placed her foot on Chrissie's shoulder.

"Lick this bitch."

Saab dropped her knee sideways and revealed the dark triangle of black, pubic hair. She pushed her fingers down into it, pulled at it until it lifted her skin then she parted it by stretching her fingers and exposed the front of her pink crack. She thrust it down towards Chrissie's face as she peeled it wider and exposed the engorged folds.

"Lick it!"

Deborah looked at Chrissie as she eased herself up and lifted her full-lipped mouth towards Saab's exposed cunt. For a moment, Deborah thought she saw a knowing and confident smile on Chrissie's face as the two women exchanged glances. As Saab stood over her, it seemed as though, instead of Chrissie being Saab's submissive slave, she was her compliant equal, as though they were sharing some secret unknown to Deborah. She felt frightened and shivered and her stomach surged with nervousness as a strange wave of loneliness passed over her. She looked again at Chrissie's face but the expression had gone and Deborah jumped with shock as Saab screamed out angrily.

"Lick it bitch!"

Chrissie poked out her tongue and laid its tip against the fleshy opening. Deborah watched as Chrissie's tongue ran along the front of Saab's crack, pressing the flesh wider, licking spit onto it and making the swelling edges glisten. Deborah strained to keep her hands high as she watched Saab lifting her hips and opening herself more for Chrissie's probing tongue. She felt the edges of her own cunt swelling as the tip of Chrissie's tongue licked eagerly around the base of Saab's engorging clitoris.

"I said keep your hands high bitch!" yelled Saab as she brought the cane down sharply across Deborah's breasts.

Whack!

Deborah yelled and fell forward as the cutting pain bit into her taut breasts.

"High!"

Whack!

The cane came down again, slashing across Deborah's nipples and sending a deep, penetrating sting through her breasts and into her stomach. She fought against the pain and managed to pull herself upright and strained her arms as high as she could lift them against the weight of her heavy shackles. She stretched her fingers higher and just managed to touch the bars in the floor of the suspended cage. Their hardness sent a thrill through her arms and she reached up more and managed to bend her fingers over them.

Deborah hung on the bars as she watched Chrissie licking deeper into Saab's cunt. Chrissie's mouth was wide and her tongue probed around Saab's swollen outer labia, pressing them sideways and opening them to expose the soft inner flesh. Deborah watched the wetness from Saab's cunt dripping onto Chrissie's cheeks and mixing with the dried spunk that stuck to her pale skin. As she watched it dribbling down Chrissie's chin and across the front of her throat, Deborah felt the edges of her own cunt moistening and her clitoris hardening and pressing between the fleshy furrow of her distending slit. Again, she could hear the words of the men as they described the woman in the cage and how she had been made to lick Saab. She imagined that the woman was Chrissie and the thought of it made the swollen flesh of her cunt beat with a fresh and overpowering excitement.

Saab stood impassively as she was licked then smiled eagerly as the boy returned carrying something. He held it up in front of her and grinned and she snatched it from him and dangled it in front of Deborah.

"A little present bitch."

Deborah stared at the tangle of leather and cocked her head slightly as she strained to keep her fingers wrapped around the bars in the floor of the cage.

"Ah, I see you don't know what I have for you."

Saab started to pick at it, parting the leather straps and revealing three long, leather-covered shafts. She handled each one in turn then selected one and drew her hand along

164

its length.

"These are all for you bitch. Big aren't they?"

She laughed and pushed them into Deborah's face as Chrissie licked her tongue frantically up and down Saab's open slit, lapping at her flesh and smearing spit and wetness against the insides of her open thighs.

"Part your legs bitch!"

Deborah slid her knees wider and strained up even more to keep her fingers latched over the iron bars.

Saab called over two of the veiled women and handed the tangle of leather straps to one of them. Saab watched impassively as the woman untangled some of the straps. The woman tightened a strap around Deborah's neck and hung it down between her shoulder blades. She took another and wound it around Deborah's neck then pulled it down between Deborah's breasts and led it into a buckle on a flat leather panel to which was attached one of the huge leather shafts. The woman pulled the panel down across the base of Deborah's stomach and drew it between her legs so that the leather shaft stuck out like a massive, hard cock from her groin. The smooth leather pressed against Deborah's skin and clung to the soft flesh of the front of her crack and she opened her legs wider, and strained her hands higher, as the woman yanked it closer.

Deborah felt a circular clip on the inside of the panel clasping around her clitoris and, as the woman pulled the leather panel closer against her, the clip encircled her clitoris and held it fast. The woman let the panel dangle between Deborah's legs as she unwound something else from the tangle of leather straps.

Deborah felt a wave of pain as the metal clasp dug into the edges of her swollen clitoris but, as she bent forward to try and ease it, she felt her fingers slipping from the bars and, fearful of Saab's anger if she did not keep her arms at full stretch, reached up again to hold them. She panted as the pain surged through her and she felt sweat running underneath her armpits and dripping down the sides of her chest.

165

The woman took hold of another one of the huge, leather shafts and pressed its end against the centre of Deborah's wet cunt. Deborah lifted herself on the bars as she felt the rounded tip probing the edges of her swollen flesh then she gasped as the woman drove it in.

Deborah's labia were parted by its smooth girth as it entered and her vagina tightened around it as it penetrated her fully. She clutched the bars of the cage and clenched her teeth as the woman grabbed hold of the dangling leather panel between her legs. She drew it over the widened base of the shaft in her cunt and, as she pulled it up between Deborah's buttocks, she drove the shaft in fully.

Saab smirked as Deborah breathed heavily between her clenched teeth.

"Now bend over bitch!"

Deborah could not let go of the bars of the cage. It was as though her hands were frozen around it and would not open. Saab raised the short cane and brought it down across her erect nipples.

Whack!

Deborah yelled out but still could not let go.

Whack!

She tried to force her fingers apart but she could not release the bars and, as she tightened against the pain of the cane, her cunt closed around the penetrating shaft and drew it in further.

Whack!

Still she could not let go and, as she tightened her legs and pulled at the shaft in her cunt, she felt the clasp around her clitoris biting even deeper.

Whack!

She felt her fingers loosening and suddenly she dropped forward, reaching out to save herself and falling heavily onto her elbows. The stiff, leather cock hung down from her groin and she panted through her nostrils as the clasp around her hard clitoris sent waves of pain deeply into her hips.

Saab opened her legs wider as Chrissie probed her tongue against her anus, licking around the tight muscular ring then driving it into the centre and forcing it as deep as she could.

The veiled woman eased the leather strap between Deborah's buttocks, took the last stiff shaft and pressed it against Deborah's exposed anus. Deborah felt the pressure of its smooth, rounded end and she felt her anus dilating to encircle it. The woman drew the strap that hung down between Deborah's shoulder blades into a buckle on the strap between her buttocks and yanked it tight. Deborah gasped as she felt the shaft sinking into her anus. The woman kept yanking on the strap and pulling it tighter into the buckle, each time driving the shaft deeper until it was as deep as it would go.

Deborah knelt on all-fours, spit dripping from her mouth and sweat running down her arms. The two straps around her neck pulled tightly and dug into her skin as they pulled down between her breasts and shoulder blades to the panel between her legs. She did not dare move, she felt the penetrating pressure of the leather shafts tugging at the linings of her vagina and rectum and she felt the clasp around her clitoris driving a burning pain deeply into her hips. She dropped her head slightly and saw the huge leather cock hanging down from the panel strapped across the base of her stomach and she felt a flushing surge of heat as she felt its weight.

Saab prodded the end of her cane into Deborah's back.

"Show me how you wank it bitch!"

Deborah lifted one of her hands from the ground and, as she tipped sideways, her hips squirmed around the shafts. This time she tightened herself on them, squeezing her thighs together and gripping the panel between her legs so that she forced the shafts even deeper and the clasp around her lengthening clitoris to bite even more.

Deborah reached her hand down to the black, leather

167

cock and touched the end of it. It was bulbous and rounded and she took it between her thumb and finger. She lifted it and held its weight in her hand then ran her fingers along the underside and felt the heavy, sewn creases that lined it like veins. She reached down further and wrapped her fingers around its base, tipping it upwards and sensing its length and heaviness before she ran her fingers slowly back to its tip.

She tightened herself onto the shafts in her cunt and rectum as she encircled the leather cock with her hand and drew it back down along its full length. Her sweaty hand caressed the shiny, black leather and the raised creases pressed lightly against the palm of her hand. She held her hand at its base, watching the tip rising and falling as she twisted her wrist, and squeezed her fingers against its underside. She imagined it throbbing as she clutched her hand around it and lifted it up to feel its weight.

"Wank it bitch! I want to see how you make it finish!"

Deborah drew her hand up its length then pulled it down again and squeezed it at the base. She held it there for a moment then drew it up again, covering its tip and pressing her thumb against its end. She dropped her head and watched it as her hand ran along its length and she squeezed her hips tighter and opened herself against the probing shafts that were deeply inside her.

She listened to Chrissie's slurping tongue as she licked into Saab's anus and pressed her nose into the pink furrow of flesh of her cunt. Deborah imagined the cock in her hand thrusting into Chrissie's cunt and fucking her as deeply as she could get it. She pulled at it harder and squeezed it tighter and began panting and breathing with the rhythm of her wanking hand.

Saab grabbed the back of Chrissie's head and drew it in closer. Chrissie pulled against her restrained arms and buried her face deeply between Saab's open thighs as Saab turned and shouted.

"Who's first? Who wants to be fucked by the bitch?"

Several men crowded around Saab. She stared at them as she grabbed Chrissie's hair in a bunch and pulled her face fiercely against her cunt. Saab reached the short cane down Chrissie's back and smacked it between her shoulder blades and a slight flush spread across her pale cheeks as she nodded to one of the men.

"You! You can be first."

She smacked the cane across Chrissie's back again as the man knelt down on all-fours in front of Deborah.

"Fuck him bitch! Fuck his arse and fuck it hard!"

Deborah let go of the leather cock and felt its weight pulling heavily against the tight leather panel. She moved forward but, as she felt the shafts in her cunt and anus, she stopped and felt a burning heat swelling through her hips and flushing across her breasts. The clasp pulled around her clitoris and she felt it swelling under the painful tension then, as she grew accustomed to the still increasing heat, she moved forward again and lifted the man's robe and exposed his upturned buttocks.

His heavy balls hung down between the tops of his thighs and his hard cock raised and lowered in rhythmic, beating throbs as it pulsated and hardened. Deborah reached forward to his muscular buttocks and spread them with out-turned palms. She exposed his dark, anal muscle and pressed her fingers against it. It dilated and opened under her touch and she bent her head over it and dribbled spit down onto it. She rubbed her spit around it with her fingers then crawled further forward until the rounded end of the leather cock touched his buttocks and her breasts pressed down flat against his back.

She reached down and took the leather cock in her hands, squeezing it and pulling at it then placing its tip against his spit-smeared anus. She felt the pressure at the base of her stomach as she pushed it hard and she squeezed her buttocks together and drove it forward until she felt his anus open and let it in.

As he tightened his buttocks and pulled the shaft in, she rode in behind it, wrapping her arms around his chest and letting him draw it in as far as he could. The shaft went deeper and she pressed it in hard until she felt his anus against the flat leather panel and she knew it would go no more. She gripped her arms around him and began to pull it back, tensing her own buttocks and squeezing down around the shafts inside her as she slowly drew it out. She gasped for breath but, as she felt his buttocks rising underneath her, she clenched her teeth and drove it in again. This time she pushed it in faster and she felt him tense beneath her grasp. She drew it back and reached down the front of his stomach and grabbed his hard cock in her hands. It was heavy and massive and she could hardly encircle it with her sweating fingers. It throbbed and pulsated as she squeezed it and she could feel the raised veins along its length beating against her hands as again she drove the leather cock back in and pushed it even deeper.

She held onto the base of his throbbing cock and fucked him hard, pulling the leather cock out until its tip allowed his anus to tighten around it them thrusting it in again, forcing his muscular ring to widen and take her again. All the time the shafts in her cunt and anus drove against her flesh and, as she squeezed the tops of her thighs against the tight, leather panel, the clasp around her clitoris bit deeper and sent shocks of pain coursing through her sweating body.

She gripped his cock as hard as she could then felt the surging rush of spunk as it expanded and swelled beneath her grasp. She squeezed it as tightly as she could and thrust her leather cock as deep as it would go and, when she felt the spunk splashing from his cock, she reared up and drove her own cock in to the hilt and thrust him in time with his heavy, pulsating orgasm.

She rubbed her hands around his swollen glans, spreading his spunk between her fingers. When there was no more to come, she pulled the leather cock out of his tightening anus and dropped forward onto his back, panting and gasping for breath. He threw her off and she fell onto her elbows.

Another man lay down on his back and she crawled forward, wrapping her arms beneath his knees and lifting his legs as she went between them. She pressed the tip of the leather cock against his exposed anus and drove it in. He tightened his legs as she pushed it deeper and she reached her arms around them and grasped his hard cock in her hands.

She thrust him wildly, pulling his cock in her hands and squeezing the throbbing shaft until she felt it filling with spunk. She drove her leather shaft in as deeply as she could, arching her back and reaching her head down to the swollen end of his cock. She wrapped her mouth around it and sucked frantically as spunk surged up and sprayed in massive pulses onto her tongue and down her throat. She swallowed it all until there was no more left.

Deborah pulled herself away and took another, wanking his cock so hard he cried out in pain before finishing into her hands. Another one lay down in front of her and she was given two more to suck while she fucked him until he finished. As she reared back against the tension of his swelling cock, the other two flooded her mouth with spunk. She sucked them both frantically but there was so much that, even though she swallowed it in hungry gulps, some spilled from her mouth.

Spunk dribbled down her chin and her body ached with the strain but when she rolled on her side, gasping for breath and unable to carry on, Saab thrashed her with the cane and drove her back to fuck another. She gasped for breath as he finished in her hands and his spunk bubbled from her overflowing mouth as she bent forward and struggled to suck it up.

Sweating all over, she crawled to Saab's feet and clutched onto the hem of her red dress. She wanted to beg and plead with her to let her stop but she did not have enough breath to speak.

Chrissie hung between Saab's legs, her face covered

in Saab's juices and her lips swollen and reddened. Deborah felt the heat from Chrissie's body and smelled the sweet musky odour of Saab's cunt on her lips. Deborah dropped against Chrissie and her skin tingled as she touched her shaking body.

Deborah turned to Chrissie and looked into her wet, exhausted face. Again, she saw the strange, knowing smile on Chrissie's face as she stared up at Saab and a shiver of apprehension ran through Deborah's stomach. Deborah opened her mouth and moved her face closer to Chrissie's, hoping that she would turn to her and smile, but still she gazed up at Saab with a confident and satisfied stare. Deborah felt confused and tried to speak but, suddenly, Saab grabbed Deborah by the shoulders, pushed her backwards onto the floor and started kicking her angrily.

"Get off her bitch! Leave her alone!"

Deborah shrank away from the blows and crawled closer to Chrissie. She needed to be close to her, she needed to know that her friend had not abandoned her. She felt Chrissie's legs part and she felt the leather shaft pressing between Chrissie's outstretched thighs. She lifted her hips and pressed the tip of the shaft against Chrissie's distended cunt and, as she touched it, Chrissie's soft flesh opened more and the leather shaft sank in.

"Get off her bitch!"

Whack!

Saab brought the cane down across Deborah's buttocks but the shock and pain made her tighten her muscles and thrust her hips forward. The leather shaft went further into Chrissie's cunt and her gasping cry sent thrills of excitement through Deborah's body.

Whack!

Another stinging blow and Deborah thrust deeper.

Whack!

The burning pain cut her deeply but it only caused her to drive the leather shaft into Chrissie's cunt until it would go no further.

Whack!

Deborah tightened her buttocks and squeezed onto the shafts in her cunt and anus and, as she drew the leather cock back and felt it running against the silky smoothness of Chrissie's vagina, the surging heat of her orgasm began to flow at last.

Whack! Whack! Whack!

Each cutting lash of the cane made the flood of her orgasm grow. All she wanted was to thrust her cock into Chrissie's cunt and finish as the cane thrashed down on her squirming, stinging buttocks.

Whack! Whack! Whack!

Deborah could not keep it back and her body filled with overwhelming heat as her orgasm ran through her in huge, convulsive waves. She cried out in pain and delight as she pushed Chrissie's arms high above her head and tightened the chain between her shackled wrists across Chrissie's screaming mouth. She held it there, tensed herself then dropped down against Chrissie's breasts, jerking fitfully in a massive seizure of agony, suffering and ecstasy.

Her head pounded as she fell sideways and rolled onto the shiny, marble floor. The cane kept thrashing her but each blow only caused another flush of heat and another jerking orgasm. She crawled away, unable to stand the fits of pleasure and the searing, unforgiving pain until finally, her head spinning giddily, she collapsed in front of Theron's throne.

He looked down at her shaking body.

"Oh my dear little slave, don't you want to play any more? Are you getting bored? Perhaps we are not entertaining you enough. And I thought Saab tried so hard to give you some pleasure." He reached down and lifted her spunk-smeared chin. "Oh, and what a messy little slave you look and your little friend as well. You must think me a terrible host." He turned to the veiled woman. "Have the bitches washed. I do not want to see them again until they are clean."

Deborah looked up at him and stretched out her hands

in breathless desperation.

"Please, please - "

Her head was ringing and she was gasping desperately for breath and her body kept jerking with involuntary spasms as though she was in a fit.

"Of course, little slave, there is no need to beg, of course you can play again later."

He stood up in front of her and she reached her shaking fingers around his ankles.

"Please, please let me - "

"Oh, how sweet. You are so keen to please. How very, very sweet. But you are very naughty not to obey me. However, I will be kind. Very well, just a little more before you have to go. You see I have to entertain my guests. My guests come from all around the world and they all have different tastes. I am always looking for women who they can degrade. Yes, and you are so good to them. How wonderful! They are happy and I am rich. I re-direct the grain we are sent as aid and, after feeding my workers, I sell it on for drugs which my clients purchase and then, the most wonderful saving, I export it to them with the phosphates from my mines in the same ships that they sent the grain to me in the first place. Oh I do love economics. Marvellous! Everyone is happy! Everyone is pleased and everyone is satisfied. Are you satisfied little bitch?"

Theron grabbed the chain between the shackles at Deborah's wrists and dragged her across the hall. Guests shrieked and laughed as he pulled her along on her knees like a frightened dog. Some of them wanked over her as he hauled her, twisting and turning in panic and desperation, across the shiny marble floor. Finally, he dropped the chain to the floor and Deborah collapsed against Chrissie. Some of the men were holding her legs wide apart and licking her cunt.

Theron stared at them both and started shouting.

"What filthy little bitches. On your knees bitches!"

Deborah got up onto all-fours, still with the leather

cock hanging from her groin. The men released Chrissie and she crawled away from them but the boys grabbed her leash and drove her back to Theron's feet. She struggled to stay on her knees and swayed from side to side as he patted each one of them on the back of the head.

"There my little slaves. I will see you again when you are more respectable. Saab!"

He laughed as he took Saab's arm and strutted out of the hall.

A veiled woman undid the straps that held the panel between Deborah's legs. She felt it peel away from the wetness that was spread across her naked flesh then gasped as the shafts were removed from her cunt and anus. The women argued about who would hold the leashes but in the end Deborah and Chrissie were led away.

CHAPTER 12

They were led into a small dark room. The veiled women tied their wrists with ropes then pulled them up to hooks in the ceiling. Water was brought in large bowls and emptied over them then young girls came and combed their hair and rubbed oil into it.

A woman stood guarding the door while two of them lifted their veils and sucked Deborah's nipples. Deborah felt them hardening under the pressure from their full lips and, when she felt the women's teeth biting into them, she felt a deep tingling running inside her breasts. The woman at the door shouted something and they all left with the young girls running behind giggling.

Deborah and Chrissie hung on the ropes all night and, just as it started to get light, the door burst open and Theron strode in with Saab and the young boys.

"Ah, my beautiful, sweet-smelling slaves. You have

made such an effort to please me. Saab, don't you think they are beautiful?"

Saab scowled at them dismissively as Theron ran his fingers around Deborah's mouth.

"Come," he said turning away abruptly, "I want to take my beautiful slaves out. Bring them!"

They were released from the hooks in the ceiling then their hands were bound behind their backs and the leashes clipped back into the collars at their necks. The chain between the shackles around Deborah's wrists pulled heavily across the front of her thighs. Theron walked ahead with Saab as the boys pulled on the leashes and dragged Deborah and Chrissie out of the small, dark room.

They were led out into an enclosed courtyard filled with market stalls. Saab picked up a wide-brimmed hat and adjusted it carefully to protest her pale skin from the hot sun. The stall holder wrung his hands together and ran around her shouting the price but when she scowled at him he shrank back unpaid. Crowds of men milled around Theron and Saab, some holding their hands out for gifts and others pointing and poking at Deborah and Chrissie.

Deborah tried to twist herself away from the pawing hands but when she did the boys yanked on her lead and pulled her forward roughly. She felt ashamed and humiliated as the leering men ran their hands across her body and she looked down to the ground. As they came close to a stall covered with cakes and bread, Deborah saw Chrissie twist her back towards the trestle and snatch a small cake from a wooden bowl.

Suddenly there was shouting as a large hand smashed down on the heavy trestle and a bearded man pushed his way forward.

"Chiennes! Chiennes!"

His eyes blazed with anger as he shouted and charged towards them. He knocked the stall aside and grabbed at them but a crowd quickly surged around and he could not reach them. He pointed at Chrissie as she clutched the cake behind her back and pressed herself against a wall. Deborah squeezed against her side as the furious man lunged forward, grabbed Chrissie by the hair and started to shake her. She squirmed against his grip and he got angrier when she slipped from his hands and crouched down behind the collapsed trestle.

Theron turned back and strode over. The bearded man shouted and ranted but, when Theron fixed him with a stare, he calmed down. Theron bent down to Deborah and Chrissie who still huddled together behind the broken stall.

"Ah, there you are. I thought I had lost you again. What are you doing skulking about like that? I hope you haven't done anything naughty?"

Deborah felt Chrissie's arm at her back then she felt the cake being pressed against her hands. For a moment, Deborah hesitated but, as she looked into Chrissie's heavy-lidded eyes and saw the fear on her face, she took the cake and closed her fist around it.

Again the bearded man struggled to get at them but Theron held him back with an outstretched arm.

"Come along my little slaves. Come out and show yourselves."

Chrissie went first and Deborah followed. Chrissie clung to Deborah's side as they emerged and stood naked in front of Theron.

"Well, my little slaves, are you thieves?"

They both stood frozen with fear as the crowd of men pawed at them and the bearded man shouted angrily.

"Speak up!"

"Please, we didn't mean to cause any trouble, please - "

"I said are you thieves?"

"No, honestly, we just want to - "

"Then let me see what you have in your hands! Un-tie them!"

Deborah dropped her head and looked at the floor as

177

she was untied. Her shaking hands fell free but she kept them behind her as the chain between her wrists looped down below her naked crack.

"Your hands!"

Chrissie reached forward and held out her hands. Theron smiled at the bearded man then turned to Deborah.

"And you? What about you?"

Deborah pulled her shackled hands from behind her back and held them out.

"Oh dear, oh dear. So, you are a thief."

She looked across to Chrissie but Chrissie was staring down at the ground.

"Yes, yes, but - "

"Oh dear little slave, oh dear."

"Please, I'm sorry, I did not mean - "

"Quiet bitch! Your first lesson will be obedience!"

She opened her mouth to speak but saw the angry look on his face and hung her head.

"And your second lesson will be how to tell the truth! Now, crawl to my feet. Crawl to the feet of your master my little, thieving slave."

Deborah knew she must obey. She dropped to her knees and crawled forward on the dusty ground.

"Lick my feet until I tell you to stop."

She poked out her tongue and started licking his bare feet. She ran its tip between his toes and tasted the dust-encrusted sweat that lay between them, then she lapped across the top of his foot and around his ankle. The crowd gathered around and laughed at her.

"Stop! Now tell me what that feels like."

She looked up at him unsure what to say.

"I did not say look up bitch! I said tell me what licking my feet feels like."

She hung her head again.

"Good, it feels good."

"It feels good master!"

178

"Yes, it feels good master."

"And why does it feel good? Does it feel good because you are humiliated and degraded?"

"Yes, yes master."

"Do it again then."

She bent her face to his foot and began licking it again. This time she licked along its side, picking up dust from the ground around her lips and mixing it with her spit before running it over her tongue. She raised her buttocks higher and reached her hands forward and held onto his ankles as she took his toes into her mouth one by one and sucked them.

"Stop! Now tell me again."

"Good master, it feels good."

"What else?"

She raised her buttocks higher and felt them parting and exposing her flesh to the gaze of the staring men.

"I enjoyed my ... "

"Yes, my little slave? What else?"

"I enjoyed my bottom being looked at!"

"Oh, what a slut you are."

"Yes, yes I am master."

"And sluts do what they're told don't they?"

"Yes master."

"And sluts always tell the truth don't they?"

"Yes master."

"Open your legs wider. Stay on your knees but open your legs."

Deborah widened her knees and felt her moist outer labia peeling apart. She felt the men staring at her and she dropped her back lower, raising her hips and opening the crack of her buttocks even more.

"Tell me what you feel now little slut."

She felt a dribble of spit running from the corner of her mouth as she opened it to speak. She knew she must tell him the truth and the thought of speaking out so publicly embarrassed her but, at the same time, it also sent a shiver of excitement through her stomach.

"I want them to see my cunt. Please master, I want them to see my exposed cunt and I want them to see my anus." With each word a fresh and even more intense thrill ran through her stomach and she wanted to say more. "I want to lift my cunt up to them so that they can see my flesh and I want them to watch how it dribbles with wetness because I am so excited."

"Ah! So you want to exhibit yourself do you?"

"Yes master. I want them to look closer. I want to lift my bottom and show them every part of my cunt. I want them to get close to it and breathe on it and then, and then I want them to lick it and bite its edges and pull the flesh out between their teeth."

Theron smiled at Saab then turned sharply back to Deborah.

"Yes, and then bitch? What do you want then? Tell me the truth now!"

"Master, please I want them to lick my anus. I want to feel their tongues going in one after another and I want to feel the wet, probing tips pushing deeply inside me."

"Yes, and?"

"And I want them to lift me up and parade me to the crowd, holding my bottom up and showing it to everyone. I want to feel their hands all over me and I want to feel humiliated and ashamed as they display me like a prize."

"Yes, yes and what else?"

"Oh master, I want to be dragged around in the dirt and I want my legs held open and my arms stretched wide. I want every one of them to stick his cock inside me and fuck me hard. I want them all to finish inside my cunt and I want to feel their spunk running down my legs. Then I want to be made to bend my head between my thighs and lick it up."

"How? How would you want them to do that?"

"I want them to hold my head forward and make me

180

lick every drop and then I want them to hold my mouth closed and pinch my nose tightly while I swallow it all down. I want to feel it running down my throat and I want to gulp and gag as it runs down me."

"What would you want them to do then?"

"They would roll me in the dirt until I was covered in dust and mud then they would bend me over and tie me to a timber beam by the wrists. They would tell me I had not sucked enough and that I must be thrashed until I pleaded for more."

"Would you want them to thrash you?"

"Yes, I want them to thrash me. I will suck them all they want and I would beg them to fuck me as long as they thrash me enough."

"How much thrashing would you need?"

"A lot. They would take a whip to me first and lash me across the bottom and it would sting so much that I would shriek in pain but that would not be enough."

"Why not?"

"Because I want to finish and I can't until I feel more pain."

"Go on, go on."

"Then they would flay me with a rope, then a cane, but every time they asked me if I was ready I would shake my head. I would hardly be able to bear it but still I would keep begging them for more."

"What would you want them to do?"

"I would want them to turn me over on my back and hold my legs wide while they caned me across the flesh of my cunt. I would want to feel the slashing cane cutting into my flesh and I would want to feel ny body stretched out tight so that I could not move. But they could thrash my breasts and beat me all they wanted and still it would not be enough."

"What would you need?"

"I would need more than a beating, I would need more than their cocks in my cunt and I would need more than their spunk running down my throat."

"What then? What would you need?"

"Oh master, please master, I need so much, I'm so ashamed, but I can't help it, please master, please - "

"What would you need? You must tell me."

"Oh master ... "

She could not carry on. Her heart was pounding wildly in her chest and a burning flush of shame was running up her neck and across her face. She could hear what she had been saying, her words were ringing in her head, and she could not bear to think about it. She did not know what had happened to her. She felt so dirty and degraded and she wanted to run away and hide her face. She fell onto her elbows and pushed her face into the dusty ground, wishing she was locked in the cage and clinging to the safety of its iron bars.

Saab bent down and grabbed her by the hair.

"Tell your master what you would need bitch!"

Deborah looked up at Saab's face, her pale skin cool and shaded by the wide brim of her hat. She looked so confident and assured, she looked so in control and Deborah felt like a confused and shamed child in her hands. She could not hold back.

"I would need to be gagged and blindfolded. I would want my clitoris pinched in a metal clasp, my nipples tied with thin wire and pulled out on heavy weights and my cunt filled with anything. Yes, anything, I want them to fuck me with their cocks but I want them to bring anything they want and stuff it into me. I want to be blindfolded so tight and held down so fast that I do not know what they are doing, so that I cannot tell what I am being fucked with and how deeply they are driving it. I want to hear them shouting and pushing and arguing about who should go next and I want to hear their shouts and the noises of my cunt being filled. I want to hear their roars and snarls and I want to feel their coarse hair against my flesh and I want to be lifted onto them and ravaged and driven into ecstasy like an uncontrollable animal."

"Would you finish then?"

"No, oh no, I could not finish yet. I could not finish unless I was beaten as I was fucked. I would need so much thrashing and so much fucking and only when I could tell there was no more to come would I let it go. Yes, only when I had taken everything from all of them and have been beaten until they are exhausted would I let it go."

She dropped back against Saab's grip and started yelling and screaming. Saab shook her viciously but she did not stop.

"Bitch! Bitch!!"

Saab kicked out at her and knocked her sprawling amongst the crowd. Dust flew up into her face, choking her and stopping her ranting screeches.

Hands reached down and grabbed her and she struggled against them in sudden panic. She felt so confused by what she had said and she fought against the men hysterically. She wanted to plead to Theron for forgiveness. She wanted to tell him she had lost control and had not meant what she had said. She wanted to beg him to let her go. She wanted to throw herself at his feet and plead with him to lock her in the cage.

For a moment, she saw him standing in front of her and she reached out to him but he turned away and she lost sight of him as the hem of his robe was engulfed in dust. She realised he had deceived her. He had made her ready for men who would pay him handsomely for their fun.

Saab laughed as the men dragged Deborah around the dusty courtyard. Some of them wrapped their arms around her waist and held her up as others pinched her nipples. Sharp pains stabbed through her breasts and she threw her head from side to side as the men pushed their faces at her and tried to kiss her. They bent her over and held her buttocks high and paraded her around the courtyard, holding her up so that everyone could paw around her exposed cunt and smack her buttocks.

They hoisted her upside down onto one of the men's backs. He grabbed the backs of her knees and pulled them down to his chest, pinning her open legs against the sides of his head and squashing her cunt against the back of his neck. He strutted around with her and she screamed as pinching fingers pulled at her nipples.

They fought over who should carry her next until, finally, she was dropped on the ground and they flicked at her with swatches of cloth. She curled up and cowered as the whipping ends of the cloth burned her skin and she felt a draining swell of hopelessness running through her. Shame overwhelmed her and she covered her face with her hands.

"The bitch is too ashamed to look at us!" shouted Saab. "Put a bag over her head and cover up her embarrassment!"

They yanked her hands away from her face and hauled her to her feet.

"Yes, cover the bitch's head, and make sure it's tight!"

A black, velvet bag with a drawstring was held in front of her. She struggled and tried to break free but the men held her tightly and pulled it down over her head. She could not see anything as it pulled close to her face and, when she breathed, the thin material drew in against her mouth and was sucked inside. She choked and poked her tongue out to make a space to breathe and, when she sucked it in, it was hot and sweaty.

They pulled the drawstring tightly and she flared her nostrils, breathing noisily through the soft material as it clung against her face. She tossed her head from side to side to try and break free but the men held it tightly and she could not escape. She widened her eyes, hoping to see something, but no light came through the material and she threw her head about in panic as she felt herself first being dragged around and then held up off the ground.

She felt dizzy and disorientated, as though she was being thrown through the air or turned upside down and she thought she was going to be sick. Suddenly, the movement stopped and it went quiet. She felt the pressure of hands on her back and an arm across the front of her hips. The pressure on her back increased and she was bent forward roughly. She opened her eyes wider, flashing them from side to side, and tried to listen to what was happening, then she felt her arms being stretched out wide and the chain between the shackles at her wrists tightening across her breasts. Her arms were pulled wider, tensioning the chain until its hard links dug into her breasts and trapped her nipples.

She felt hands on her shoulders as she was pressed forward until her outstretched arms and her neck were pressed against a hard surface. It felt like a wooden bar of some sort but she did not know what it was. She felt tight bonds being wound around her elbows, pinning her to whatever it was she was bent against, then more were bound around her wrists. She extended her fingers to see it she could touch anything and straight away she felt something thin being wound around each one and pulled tight so that her fingers were stretched out and she was unable to move them.

Seized with a fresh wave of fear, she turned her covered head but it was grabbed and held fast as something hard was pulled down across the back of her neck. The sound of a heavy bolt sent a tremor of fear through her and, when she tried to move her head again, it was impossible, she was held fast, bent over and bound with her neck and arms trapped between two hard and unforgiving surfaces.

She felt her ankles being held and pulled outwards, stretching her legs wide until they were lifted off the ground and she was suspended by the fastening at her neck. Something was lashed around her ankles and tied tightly then her knees were pulled wide and bound to something as well. She twisted her body but another binding was wound around her waist and pulled out at each side, pinioning her and making it impossible for her to move.

Her face was hot and soaked with sweat and, when

185

she licked out her tongue, she tasted the salty moisture as it ran down her nose and into her gaping mouth. She did not know where she was or exactly how she was pinioned but she felt the horror of exposure and the desperation of being completely captive and utterly helpless.

She poked her tongue out to push the material away from her mouth but, as she pressed it against the wet material, she felt something pushing against it from the other side. It bulged against the material, forcing it against her lips and driving her tongue back into her gaping mouth until it was filled. She felt a throbbing heat on her tongue as the bulging material forced deeper into her mouth then she tasted the saltiness of spunk as the sweat-covered material was soaked with a pulsating spurt of semen. It frothed and bubbled through the material, dribbling across her tongue and running to the back of her throat.

The pressure of the material was released as the cock pulled back but, as she swallowed, another forced its way in, this time pushing even deeper and filling her mouth even more. She felt the pressure of a hand against her nose then her jaw was forced wider by the throbbing heat in her mouth and she felt another surge of spunk oozing through the tightly pressed fabric. It dribbled through and dropped on her tongue and she licked it up and swallowed it just as her mouth was filled again.

She sucked at more spunk as it spurted against the material across her mouth and, when there was no cock filling it, she chewed at the material and sucked it wildly to get all she could from the semen-drenched velvet. She breathed heavily through her nostrils, thinking only of the surges of spunk and her desperation to suck it all in and swallow it as fast as she could.

She sensed warmth around her buttocks and felt liquid dribbling down them but she could not move to expose herself more. She felt her buttocks being forced wide and she felt wetness against her cunt and around her dilating anus but she was bound so tightly she could not move as it ran across her flesh.

She sucked in a frenzy and, when there was nothing filling her mouth, she squeezed her buttocks together and felt the hot, dribbling spunk that ran between them and covered the swollen flesh of her distended cunt.

Her head spun in the darkness of the velvet bag. The tension in her arms and legs and the pulling on her fingers sent deep shivers through her. She felt so exposed and captive. She did not know whether her cunt was being filled with a cock and although she felt pressure deep inside her rectum she could not tell if she was being fucked in her anus. Everything was confused, all she could see were the images in front of her straining eyes and all she could feel were the surges of heat boiling up inside her and sending shivering waves of delight across her tautly outstretched limbs.

She sucked as much as she could but now she did not even know she was sucking. Everything in her mind was muddled as her body throbbed and burned. She did not know if she was being thrashed and beaten. She did not know if the lashing blows she imagined were really falling across her burning buttocks. She could not tell whether spunk was being splashed down her back and along her arms and she was not sure if it ran down her calves and over her feet.

She heaved and gasped and imagined herself tied out across a wooden bar with another clamped across her neck. She pictured the crowd of men wanking against the bag that covered her head and was pushed so deeply into her mouth by their throbbing cocks. She saw them clamouring to wank over her and she saw them fighting each other for possession of a cane and a whip so that they could beat her across the buttocks and the backs of her legs. She saw Saab standing behind the men, barking instructions at them and telling them to thrash her hard and she saw Chrissie, sprawled against a trestle in the market, held by the arms and legs and taking all of the men in turn inside her widespread cunt. She saw images of Theron as he bent over her and traced his fingers between her

187

shoulder blades and down her back until he pressed them against her spunk-covered anus then forced them deeply inside. She pictured him bending down and licking up the spunk that oozed from her stretched-out anus as he drove in his fingers as deeply as he could.

She saw it all in the blackness and she felt herself tightening against her bonds as the images flashed in front of her wide, staring eyes and condensed into one huge picture of suffering and delight. Everything she saw she imagined was happening to her. She tensed her buttocks and strained her bound and extended fingers, sucking like an animal and swallowing in huge, satisfying gulps.

Her orgasm started running within her, tugging at her nerves as it surged through her veins and into her tightened muscles. She took one last swallow then opened her mouth and went rigid as she submitted to the irresistible pressure that overwhelmed her. Her ears drummed and multi-coloured lights flashed in the darkness of the velvet bag. She thought she was screaming but if she was her cries were lost in the thunder that exploded in her pounding head as she gave way to her climax and let it consume her. Her body filled with it, every nerve burned as though she was on fire and she was devoured by it: ignited by its flames and consumed by its penetrating heat.

When, finally, it released her, she fell forward against her bonds and heard nothing except the throbbing of her drumming ears then even that faded as she drifted into a deeper, more profound blackness.

"Deborah, poor Deborah, let me try and release you."

Chrissie worked quietly to undo the bolt that held the heavy bar of the stocks across Deborah's neck until finally she got it loose. Looking behind her, and being as quiet as she could, she drew it back then lifted the bar and held it up as Deborah pulled herself free. Chrissie untied Deborah's outstretched fingers and released the ropes which bound her legs and waist. Deborah clawed at the bag over her head but her fingers felt so strained and weak she could not get it off so Chrissie undid it and pulled it away.

Deborah's face was red and covered in sweat and spunk and her wet hair stuck to her cheeks and into her mouth. She tipped forward dizzily but Chrissie grabbed her shoulders and stopped her falling. Deborah nestled in Chrissie's arms, blinking her bleary eyes in the purple, dusky light as she slowly came to her senses. Suddenly, she jumped up and started pulling at Chrissie.

"Quickly, we must get away from here. Quickly, before anyone comes. Before they capture us again and take us back."

"No, it's too risky. They're bound to catch us and that will mean more punishment."

"No, this is our chance to escape. No one can help us. We must try and escape by ourselves. Quickly, we must get away!"

Deborah pulled at Chrissie and dragged her reluctantly across the square and down a narrow, dark alley.

CHAPTER 13

"Quickly, as fast as you can before they find we've gone."

Chrissie stumbled and struggled to keep up and, when they emerged into the light, she slumped against a wall exhausted.

"Please, I must rest, please - "

"No time. We must keep going. Come on!"

Deborah grabbed Chrissie's hand and pulled her along the alley.

Chrissie kept stopping and gasping for breath but Deborah urged her on, pulling at her when she slowed and holding her up when she stumbled. Deborah's mind was racing. At last they were free. At last they could escape from the clutches of their tormentors. At last they could return home and put all the terrible things that had happened behind them. Her heart pounded with excitement and fear as they dodged into an entrance and threw themselves against a heavy, wooden door.

"Quick! In here before anyone sees us!"

Deborah pushed at the door and it flew open. She dragged Chrissie inside and they stood together in the darkness, panting and bending with their hands on their knees to try and get their breath back.

Deborah spoke in gasps.

"We can hide in here, until it gets dark. Chrissie, oh Chrissie, we're free!"

Chrissie looked up at Deborah. Her eyes were filled with tears and she was shivering all over.

"Deborah, we must go back. They'll catch us and then things will be worse. Please, let's go back. I'm afraid."

"No, we'll be alright. Anything's better than going back there. This is what we've been waiting for. Don't be afraid. We'll be alright. We're free!"

Chrissie slumped down on the floor.

"Please, let's go back."

Deborah could not understand her reluctance, it was as though she did not want to escape. She bent down and ran her hands into Chrissie's tangled, black hair.

"Chrissie, it will be alright. I know it will."

Chrissie looked up into Deborah's face and more tears welled up in her eyes and began to trickle down her flushed and dirty cheeks. Deborah wrapped her arms around Chrissie and held her tightly until she went to sleep.

Deborah sat by the half-open door as it went dark. She thought of the long journey on the ship, then the terrible trudge across the desert and wondered how they could possibly find their way back. It seemed hopeless but she knew they had to try. Anything was better then the ordeals they were

190

being subjected to, anything.

She dozed and dreamed and occasionally woke up with a start. Again, she had the dream of going out in the car with Chrissie and again she was tormented by the appearance of Saab and the terrible feeling of treachery as Saab and Chrissie laughed at her and mocked her.

She was woken by the sounds of people in the alley and when she peered around the door she saw it was getting light. An old woman wearing a heavy robe walked past with some children running behind her. Deborah looked over to Chrissie. She seemed fast asleep and Deborah decided not to wake her. Another noise outside startled her and she jumped back in surprise as she saw Gross ambling down the alley. He looked miserable and lost and his arms hung heavily at his sides. For a moment, she thought of hiding from him then she realised that this was their chance. Gross would surely help them. She pushed the door open and rushed out into the alley.

"Gross! Gross! I need help. I've got away. I need help to escape." He looked confused and backed away as she ran towards him. "Gross, please, I need your help."

He looked around, his eyes darting fearfully about him.

"Gross must not touch. No, Gross must not touch little slave."

"Gross, don't be frightened. You must help me. I need to get back to the harbour. You're the only one that can help me. You're the only one who knows how to get back. Please, oh please, Gross, please."

He cocked his head from side to side and reached his hand forward slowly.

"Gross must not touch. Saab will be angry. Gross has been punished."

Deborah took his hand and, even though he resisted, drew it towards her. He looked around in fear then smiled anxiously and let her place the palm of his hand on her firm breast.

"Gross, you may touch. It's alright. There's no need to be frightened any more. We can escape. Yes, we can escape. We can be free and you need not be frightened of anyone again."

His smile softened and he relaxed his arm. He let her rub his hand around her breast until her nipple hardened under the pressure. She parted his fingers and drew them across her smooth skin until her nipple poked out between them.

"Gross like little slave."

"Yes, I like you as well Gross. But I need your help. I need your help to escape. Will you do it?"

He stood, looking quizzically at her, then he looked down at his hand as she rubbed it around her breast and he squeezed his fingers together until they trapped her nipple tightly between them.

"Yes, squeeze it hard Gross. Squeeze it as hard as you want." He squeezed his fingers and pinched her hard nipple tightly. "Yes, as hard as you want. I don't mind how hard you do it."

He squeezed his fingers together and she gasped in pain as her hard nipple was squashed between his thick, black fingers. She took his other hand and drew it down between the tops of her thighs. She held it against her shaved crack and squirmed around it so that he could feel the soft, wetness of her swollen labia.

"Gross like little slave."

"Yes, you can squeeze that as well Gross. Pinch it as hard as you are pinching my nipple. Pinch it and make me cry out and I will not stop you. I will only ask you for more. Go on, pinch my cunt. Pinch it! Pinch it!"

He pinched her fleshy labia between his fingers and she rose up on his hand as the pain sent hot, penetrating shocks deeply inside her cunt.

Suddenly, he pulled back.

"No, Gross is afraid."

"Don't be afraid Gross. Please don't be afraid. You will help me won't you? Please Gross. Please."

He stood back and looked at her.

"Gross will be back. Tonight. Gross will come back to little slave tonight."

He turned and ran off down the alley. Deborah looked around to see if they had been seen then rushed back behind the door.

Chrissie was waking and rubbing her eyes.

"Chrissie! Chrissie! Gross is going to help us. He's coming back tonight. He's going to help us escape!" Chrissie looked anxious and worried. "What's the matter Chrissie? Don't you hear me. We're going to get free! Please don't be worried. It'll be alright. I promise you. It'll be alright."

Chrissie turned her head and looked down at the floor. Deborah snuggled up beside her and tried to comfort her but every time she mentioned the plan to get away Chrissie looked down at the ground and would not say anything.

After it went dark Deborah heard a scratching at the door and rushed outside. Gross was holding out a bowl of food. Deborah snatched it from him, spilling some of its contents onto the floor.

Gross reached forward to touch her but pulled back in fear.

"Tomorrow. Gross will come when it gets light. Take little slave back to big ship and home."

"Oh Gross! You're so good!"

Deborah grabbed him around the neck and kissed him but he pulled away embarrassed and ran off down the alley into the darkness.

Deborah shared the food with Chrissie then tried to sleep but she was too excited and only dozed. Finally, the sunlight started to cast a weak shadow through the half-open door and Deborah jumped up when she heard a soft knocking on the door.

"It's Gross! He's come for us. Chrissie, wake up!

Wake up! At last, we're going to get away!"

"What, what's happening?"

"Come on! Gross has come for us. We're going to get away!"

Deborah grabbed Chrissie's arm and yanked her to the door. They both shielded their eyes from the glare as they emerged into the alley. Gross was holding some clothing and pushed it forward towards Deborah then suddenly shrunk back as he saw Chrissie. He dropped the clothing to the ground and started mumbling and shaking his head.

"No, no mistress. Gross did not touch. Gross did not touch." Deborah stepped forward and grabbed his arm but he yanked it away in fear. "No, no mistress. Gross has not been bad."

"What's the matter Gross?" Deborah laughed. "Don't be silly. It's alright. It's only Chrissie. She's my friend. Please Gross don't be afraid."

"No, Gross must not touch. Gross would not disobey ... "

Chrissie moved towards him and he dropped to his knees in front of her. Deborah tried to pull him up but he pushed her back fearfully.

"Please mistress, please ... "

Deborah turned to Chrissie and saw a strange look on her face. It was a confident smirk, as though she knew why Gross was so afraid and she was enjoying his fear and subservience. Deborah could not understand what was going on.

"Chrissie, what's the matter with him? Why is he so afraid? Chrissie what's happening?"

She felt panicky as her body flushed with a confused mixture of anxiety and foreboding. She had felt in control and now things were happening that she could not understand and it made her feel isolated and threatened. She looked at Chrissie again and, as she threw back her long, black hair haughtily and wiped her forehead with the back of her hand,

194

Deborah saw someone that frightened her and she shivered all over and felt a wave of nausea flooding into her stomach.

Chrissie turned to Deborah and, still with the strange look on her face, wrapped her arm around Deborah's waist.

"I think we should go back now."

Gross lurched forward, grabbed Deborah's wrist and tried to pull her away from Chrissie.

"Gross take little slave. Quick! Escape! Chrissie not friend!"

He pulled at Deborah frantically but she fought against him. She could not understand what was happening.

"Gross what are you doing? Chrissie is my friend. You must help us both. You said you would."

"No, just little slave. Get away! Get away!"

He yanked at her wildly but she kicked out at him and held onto Chrissie. He went to push Chrissie away but shied back when she turned to him and scowled. Deborah kicked him again and he fell to the floor shouting and blubbering.

"Gross help little slave. Gross help ... "

He made another grab for Chrissie and held onto her ankle. He pulled her onto the ground and she fell on her side. He rolled across her and shouted to Deborah.

"Run! Run!"

Deborah tried to push him away and reached down and grabbed Chrissie's outstretched hand. Chrissie took hold of it but Gross threw himself across her, breaking her grip and pinning her down.

Suddenly, a crowd of men and boys came chasing noisily down the alley. Deborah turned towards them fearfully and again tried to pull Chrissie up but, as Gross rolled in front of her, Deborah was knocked off balance and pulled onto the ground, panting and gasping for breath.

She struggled to her feet and tried frantically to pull Chrissie free but, as she strained to drag Chrissie away from Gross, some of the men pulled her away and flung her to the ground again.

Chrissie broke free and started to run away but some boys surrounded her and started baiting her like a captured animal. They pawed at her and pinched her and slowly closed in around her. She fought against them as they pulled her onto the floor but, when she started to scream, they stuffed a large, leather ball into her mouth then bound it in tightly with a leather strap. She threw her head from side to side and her eyes widened in terror as they dragged her down by the hair and held her on the ground. She kicked her feet out at them but they sat on her legs and pinned her down.

Deborah summoned up all her strength and scrambled to her feet. Gross stood by her side and made another attempt to pull her away but all she could think of was saving Chrissie. She rushed at the boys but they dodged aside and she fell to the ground in a cloud of dust. She choked and coughed and wiped her eyes as the boys taunted her and jabbed their fingers in her sides. Some of them bent down and pinched her nipples and others pulled at the naked edges of her shaved cunt. She screamed as they pulled at her swollen labia but her cries only made them laugh louder and pinch her flesh harder.

She strained her eyes to see through the billowing dust and, for a moment, she glimpsed Gross standing dazed and looking from side to side anxiously. He took a step towards Deborah then froze, turned and ran away.

Some of the men pushed the boys aside. They held Chrissie's legs wide apart then one of them knelt between them and pressed the engorged tip of his hard cock against the outspread flesh of her cunt. She bit hard onto the leather ball as he pushed the throbbing glans inside and spit dribbled from the edges of her mouth as he drove it deeply inside her. He thrust his cock up and down her and her face reddened with the strain of every lunge. The other men gripped her ankles tightly as the man fucked her wildly and they stretched her out as the man reared back with the onset of his orgasm.

Deborah watched his body tense as he strained back,

pulling his cock out and spraying his spunk from its throbbing end across Chrissie's stomach. He held the pulsating shaft in his hand and, still with spunk splashing from its end, he was pushed aside and another man took his place between Chrissie's widespread knees. The men raised Chrissie's legs high, exposing the dark ring of her anus, covered with the wetness that dribbled down from her sopping cunt. The man pressed his engorged glans against it and, as it opened, he drove his cock straight in.

Deborah pulled against her captors but she could not get free and she watched helplessly as Chrissie was fucked repeatedly. Suddenly, they stopped and Deborah felt the tight grip around her arms slacken. She rolled over on the ground and wiped her dust-encrusted eyes. Theron stood above her with Saab by his side.

"Oh my little slaves, you do cause me so much trouble. I hope you weren't thinking of leaving me. No, of course you weren't. How could you think of leaving me when we were having so much fun."

He bent down to Deborah and ran his fingers around her swollen lips.

"What a pretty little slave, but so ungrateful. Saab! Have these two put back on their leashes and brought to me. Their trip out has lasted too long."

Saab shouted to the boys and they pulled Deborah and Chrissie to their feet. The leads were clipped to their collars and they were both dragged along the alley and through a heavy, wooden door. Deborah had not got the strength to resist and her feet trailed behind her as they were dragged back into the large hall and held on their leashes in front of Theron. She felt defeated and hopeless.

Theron sat on his huge chair with Saab standing by his side. Several women crouched at his feet and one them was licking Saab's shiny, leather shoes.

"Really my little slaves, you are starting to prove rather troublesome. In fact I'm fed up with both of you. Saab

197

you told me they would please me but I find them very disappointing. Troublesome and disappointing! I don't want to see them again until you can promise me they will please me."

He got up and strode down the long marble floored hall with the young boys following him.

Saab stared angrily at them both and Deborah dropped her head, afraid to meet her gaze as she walked over menacingly.

"Bitches!" Saab walked behind Chrissie and draped her hands across the tops of her shoulders. "Sweet little bitches." She kissed Chrissie's forehead. "What shall I do with you? Let me see." She ran her hands down across Chrissie's breasts and pinched her hard nipples between her fingers. Chrissie tightened herself and tried to pull back but Saab squeezed her nipples tighter. "Now, I promised Theron that he would enjoy you and now he says he is displeased. If he is displeased with you then he is displeased with me and I do not like that."

Deborah looked up slightly and watched as Saab squeezed Chrissie's nipples as hard as she could and Deborah felt the edges of her cunt swelling as she watched Chrissie tensing herself against the pain. She looked into Chrissie's eyes and again saw the fear on her face. Her dark eyes were wide and the leather strap pulled deeply into her tightly stretched cheeks. Spit dribbled from the edges of her mouth as it was forced wide by the leather ball and, when Deborah looked down across Chrissie's stomach, she could see spunk still running from her cunt and flowing down the insides of her trembling thighs.

Deborah felt a wave of guilt flooding through her. She felt responsible for what had happened and could not bear to see Chrissie suffer any more. She pulled against the hands at her arms and stepped forward.

"Punish me mistress. Punish me and I promise to do anything you wish of me."

Her own words shocked her and she felt a nervous

shiver run through her body.

Saab looked up and spoke mockingly.

"How would you like to be punished bitch? Would you like to be beaten?"

"Anything mistress, anything."

"Perhaps you would like something stuffed in your mouth like your little friend?"

"Yes, mistress, yes, I would, but please let her go."

"And perhaps you would like me to ride you while I whipped you until you could stand no more."

"Yes, yes I would."

Saab pinched Chrissie's nipples viciously and pulled them forward.

"Would you like this bitch?"

Deborah stared at Chrissie's outstretched nipples.

"Yes, mistress, yes. Please do it to me instead."

Saab let Chrissie's nipples go and ran her hands down Chrissie's spunk-smeared stomach. She stretched her fingers into the top of Chrissie's crack and opened the soft, fleshy leaves.

"And would you like me to do this bitch?"

Deborah felt a surge of heat in her stomach as Saab exposed Chrissie's hard clitoris. It shone, glistening and proud between the swollen folds of Chrissie's cunt.

"Yes, as wide as you wanted mistress. Yes."

Saab ran her fingers into Chrissie's crack and delved them deeply into her vagina.

"And this?"

"Yes, as deeply as you could."

"Now bitch. Tell me what else you would want me to do with you. Tell me!"

Deborah strained against the hands that gripped her arms and felt the edges of her cunt swelling as she pulled against their restraining tension. She wanted them to hold her tighter. She wanted to feel their fingers digging into her skin. She wanted to feel them controlling her, pulling her back and holding her away from what she wanted. She wanted to be punished and frustrated and she wanted to feel hopeless and driven to more desire by pain.

"I want to be gagged."

Saab pushed Chrissie's thighs wide and pulled her wet fingers out of her vagina.

"Yes, bitch, then what?"

"I want to be gagged so that I cannot scream and I want my hands to be tied to my sides. Then I want to be tied by the ankles and pulled up high on a rope."

Saab pressed her wet fingers towards Chrissie's anus and ran their tips around its hard edge.

"Go on bitch. What else?"

"I want to be suspended on the rope and spun around until I am dizzy and sick."

Saab pushed the tips of her fingers into the centre of Chrissie's anus and Deborah felt a surge of heat in her hips as she watched them go in to the knuckles. She saw Chrissie's eyes widen as the fingers penetrated her and Deborah felt another wave of heat across her still swelling cunt as she watched Chrissie dropping down for more.

"Tell me bitch!"

"I want to be held by my ankles over a bucket of water. I want to be held above it and I want to see spit dribbling from my mouth and falling on the surface. Then I want men to wank into the water and I want to see my spit mixing with their spunk then I want to be dipped into it and I want to lick up the spunk with my tongue."

"Go on. Go on bitch."

"I want to be lifted away from it and see it dribble from the end of my tongue. But I need the taste of their spunk and I want to plead to be lowered into it again."

"Yes, yes, what next bitch?"

"I want to see more men wanking into the water and I want to beg and beg to be lowered down. I want to lick my tongue out as far as it will go until I can just touch the surface

200

and taste the spunk then, as I begin to lap it up, I want to be snatched back again. I want to feel frustrated and tormented and I want to feel hopeless and desperate and ashamed."

"What else bitch?"

"Then I want to be thrashed."

"What with?"

"First with a cane. I want to feel its hard, cutting lashes across my bottom. I want to feel it flailing me across the back and I want to be spun around and caned across my breasts. I want to feel the cane coming down across my hard nipples and I want to feel the pain as it penetrates my breasts and makes me scream like an animal. Then I want to be ducked in the water again so the spunk covers my face."

"That's not enough bitch. What else?"

"I want to be lashed with a whip. I want to feel the hard leather smacking across my flesh. I want to feel its burning cuts and I want to feel the raised, red stripes it leaves across my skin."

Saab pushed her hand between Chrissie's shoulder blades and pressed her forward. She forced her to bend down onto her knees then she grabbed her hair and yanked her head back. Chrissie's nostrils flared wide as she gasped for breath.

"Go on bitch. Then what?"

"I want to be beaten with a split rope. I want its ends to tangle around my hips and cut into me and make me spin when it is pulled back and then I want to be ducked back down into the water and drink up the spunk as men keep wanking around me."

Saab straddled Chrissie like a horse and wedged her knees tightly into Chrissie's waist. She wound Chrissie's hair around her hand in a bunch and pulled it back viciously.

"Go on bitch. What else?"

"I want to be left hanging with my face on the surface of the water and I want to keep drinking the flows of spunk as the men drench me with semen. I want to be thrashed again, as hard as possible. I want to feel the tangled rope cutting into me and throwing me into gulping spasms of pain. I want to be overcome by it and I want to pass out with my mouth full of spunk. Then I want to be cut down and dragged around by the rope at my ankles while I am still unconscious and, as I come around, I want to be humiliated and degraded and flailed and spat upon."

Saab reached her one hand behind her and pushed her fingers between Chrissie's buttocks. She pressed their tips against Chrissie's anus and drove them in. As Chrissie gasped, Saab pulled her hair back even harder and began thrusting her fingers in deeply and riding her like an animal. Chrissie's nostrils flared wider as spit bubbled from the sides of her mouth and ran down over her chin.

"Would you like me to ride you like this bitch?"

Deborah stared at Chrissie's sweating face and pulled frantically against the restraining hands at her arms.

"Yes, I want to be ridden and I want your fingers in my anus. I want them in as deep as you can get them. I want to feel them pressing out my flesh and probing right inside. Yes, I want you to ride me and thrust me with your fingers and I want you to thrash me with a whip and beat me and flail me until you are satisfied."

Deborah pulled hard against the men who held her and managed to get an arm free. She reached it out towards Saab, pulling at the other in frenzied desperation.

"Please, please, take me like that. Ride me and thrash me, fuck me in the arse, fuck me and whip me, ride me and punish me, thrash me and ... "

"Let the bitch go! Set her free!"

The men released Deborah and she fell forward onto her knees. She held her buttocks up high and, with her eyes fixed on Chrissie as she bucked beneath Saab, she clawed her hands on the ground and pulled herself forward.

She hung her tongue out over her bottom lip and spit dripped from it and fell in a sticky strand onto the floor. It dribbled onto the backs of her hands and she lapped at it and sucked it back in before spitting it out again. Saab shouted as Deborah got closer.

"Hold the bitch by the ankles!"

Some of the men grabbed Deborah's ankles and held her back. She strained forward and tensed her body against their grip but they held her fast.

"Please mistress, please let me take her place."

"Beg more bitch."

"Please, oh please mistress, I want to serve you, I want you to ride me. Please take me between your legs - "

"Keep begging bitch! I may let you if you beg enough."

"Please, please, let me feel your knees digging into my sides. Let me feel your fingers inside me, probing me, poking into me. Please, please ... "

Saab pulled back Chrissie's hair even harder, straining her neck and making her choke as the spit ran down the back of the gag and gathered in her throat. Saab reared back, throwing her head back and thrusting her fingers even deeper into Chrissie's anus. She shouted out to the men.

"Strip me, strip me and thrash me, I'm starting to come!"

Several men ran to her and began undoing the front of her long red dress.

"Strip me I said! Strip me!"

One of them grabbed the front of the dress and tore it down exposing her breasts and her smooth stomach.

"Strip me! Strip me bare! Make me naked!"

They pulled at her dress and tore it from her back as she reared frantically on Chrissie's back.

"Now whip me! Whip my naked flesh! Whip me until I finish!"

One of them brought a short leather whip down across her back.

Whack!

"Harder!"

He lashed the whip down as hard as she could and, when he pulled it back, it left raised, red stripes across her straining back.

Whack!

"Harder! Harder! Whip me harder!"

Whack! Whack! Whack!

He brought the whip down viciously and she rode Chrissie in a frenzy, plunging her fingers deeper and squeezing her knees hard into Chrissie's waist.

"I'm coming! Beat me! Beat me!"

Anther man lashed a cane across her buttocks, thrashing it as hard as he could, while the other continued to beat her across the back with the whip.

Whip! Thrash! Whip! Thrash! Whip! Thrash!

Deborah pulled as hard as she could against the hands around her ankles but she could not get near enough. She watched Saab's frenzied face and the lashing of the whip and cane and, as she strained her legs against the hands at her ankles, she felt her own orgasm building up inside her. She began screaming, begging, pleading to be ridden but Saab's cries and the thrashing of the whip and cane drowned the sound of her voice as she fell forward, jerking and squirming as her orgasm gripped her and threw her into a convulsive fit.

The men kept beating Saab until finally she slackened her grip on Chrissie's waist and fell sideways to the ground. Some of the men rushed to her and covered her with a large sheet that she wrapped slowly around her still pulsating body. She leant back on the floor and wiped away the spit that dribbled from her lips. Deborah looked up at her and held out her hand, still hoping that she would mount her and ride her and punish her as she wanted, but Saab ignored her and motioned to the men.

"Take me and bathe me." She pointed at Deborah. "And use her how you want."

They tied leather straps to Deborah's ankles then lifted her up and, keeping her legs as wide as they could, laced

204

the free ends of the straps around the bars in the floor of the suspended cage. They held her up by the shoulders as they worked and she strained to see what they were doing as the veins in her neck started pounding and her head buzzed. She twisted against their grasp and, as she pulled against them, her oily skin slipped from their hands and she dropped backwards.

She shouted out as she plummeted towards the floor then had the breath knocked out of her as her full weight fell jarringly onto the straps. As the straps caught her weight, they tightened against her ankles and cut into her skin. She threw herself about on the straps at her ankles and the cage swung wildly and spun on the chain that hung from the high ceiling of the hall. The boys reached up and bound her shackled wrists tightly to her sides. She struggled against them but they pulled her arms so tightly to her sides that when they had finished she could not move them at all.

Hands reached up and set her spinning on the straps. She felt giddy and sick as they spun her faster then, when they stopped her suddenly, she was left gasping and terror-stricken. Her head hung backwards and, as everything continued to spin and spit dribbled from her mouth she saw a bucket of water being placed below her.

They lowered her down and she felt the water bubbling around her face and, when they lifted her out, it ran back down her nose and made her choke. The men stood around her and some of them wanked across her breasts and their spunk ran across her throat and over her face. It dripped into the bucket and when they lowered her again she lapped at it hungrily and swallowed it down. When they hauled her up again she held her tongue out longingly and, when she felt her skin burn as the cutting edge of a leather whip came down harshly across her buttocks, she strained to reach it like a starved, ravenous animal.

Deborah hardly felt the tension released as the straps were

untied from her ankles and she could not open her eyes. She only vaguely felt herself being lifted up into the cage and, as it was hoisted back up on the chain, she could only just hear the shouting voices of the men below.

She lay on the hard bars of the swinging cage, sleeping fitfully, dreaming of being free, of returning home and being warm. She imagined selecting clean clothes and smoothing them down across her skin but, as she drew her arms up and they pressed against the unforgiving bars of the cage, she knew she was still a hopeless captive. Her only chance of escape had faded away and disappeared. She rolled onto her side and pushed her hands down between her legs. She shivered with cold as her fingers peeled apart the swollen flesh of her cunt and she felt the dribble of wetness running into the palms of her eager hands.

She felt the inner edges of her labia and poked the tips of her fingers against the warm entrance to her vagina. She pressed her nails against the soft lining and a deep thrill sent shocks of excitement up into her chest. She dug her nails in again and threw her head back as the surge of excitement ran into her throat and onto her tongue. She felt the cage spinning and it seemed to fall as she dug her nails deeper then, as he felt the jarring jolt of the cage hitting the floor, she also felt aware of a large, black face pressed against the outside of the bars.

Gross peered in at her, tilting his head from side to side. He reached forward and pawed at her with his hands, rubbing them against her wet cheeks and pulling gently at her tangled hair. He smiled at her uncertainly and she grabbed his fingers and pulled his hands down against her breasts.

"Gross, we were so close to getting away, so close."

"Gross will care for Deborah. Gross will look after little slave."

She felt her heart beating against the palms of his large, black hands as she splayed his fingers apart and pushed them around her aching nipples.

206

"Here Gross, squeeze them. Squeeze them like you did before. Feel how they get hard under your touch. Squeeze your fingers as around them as hard as you can. Do not be afraid to hurt me. You know I do not want you to hold back. The more pain you give me the more I will want and if you give me enough pain I will want you to fuck me like you did before."

He squeezed her nipples and they hardened under the pressure. She cried out as pains shot from them and penetrated her breasts but she held his hands there so that he knew she was not yet satisfied and that he must not take them away.

"Gross will look after Deborah."

"Yes, look after me by giving me what I want. Squeeze hard. Hurt me."

She lifted her knees and dropped them wide.

"Look at that Gross. Look at my cunt, my naked cunt. Take hold of the sides, the shaved sides of my cunt, and pinch the edges. Pinch them as hard as you can. Don't hold back. The more you pinch them the more I will want you to do it."

He moved his hands down and slowly took hold of her swollen outer labia between his thumbs and forefingers. He started to squeeze them and, as the pain bit, she opened her legs and lifted her hips higher, exposing her glistening cunt fully to his pinching fingers.

"More Gross. Harder. Harder. Pinch me harder. Pinch me until I scream and cry out in agony but when I do you must not stop, you must not let me go. Hold the edges of my cunt until I demand your cock inside me then open me wide and thrust it in. Push it in as deep as you can and keep pushing it as I scream for more. Yes, yes, more! More!"

He squeezed the stretched-out flesh as hard as he could and she threw her head back in a fresh ecstasy of pain and suffering.

"Gross. You must not leave me. I need you always. I can stand it all as long as you are there."

He pinched her labia until she howled.

207

"Gross will always be there for Deborah," he said as she screamed for him to open her cunt and fill it to the hilt.

CHAPTER 14

The cage was lowered and Deborah was pulled out by some men. Saab stood against the wall, smoking a cigarette and petting one of the boys who clung to her thin, black dress. She lifted one of her feet and casually rubbed the high heel of her black shoe against the back of her calf.

"Put the bitches on their leads and bring them. I will make sure that when Theron sees them next that they are ready to please."

The men dragged Chrissie from behind one of the huge pillars and clipped the lead to her collar. Deborah looked into her dark eyes and saw the hopelessness in her face.

The boys made them get down on all-fours then led them out of the huge hall and into a covered entrance to the market square. Men gathered around and stared at them as they were held tightly with their collars pulling at their necks.

Saab grabbed hold of Chrissie's hair and pulled her head back. Chrissie gasped and spit dribbled from her mouth.

"String the bitch up! And make it tight!"

Some of the men grabbed Chrissie and turned her back to face the square. They pulled her arms high and tied them tightly to ropes that hung from the covered entrance. They wound some leather straps around her ankles and pulled her legs wide then tied them off to iron rings that hung from the walls on either side.

"Tight I said!"

They pulled harder on the ropes and straps until she was strung out tautly. Saab tugged at the ropes to check their tightness then held out her open hand.

"My cane."

One of the boys dropped a long cane into her up-turned palm and the crowd of men gathered around excitedly. Saab pointed the tip of the cane between Chrissie's shoulder blades and pressed it against her skin.

"This bitch has failed to please her master. How shall I punish her?"

The men surged forward, shouting and pointing, holding up their fists and spitting at Chrissie's outstretched body. Deborah shrunk back as they pushed around her and she winced as some of their spit splattered on her back and in her hair.

Saab pulled the point of the cane down into the small of Chrissie's back.

"Shall I beat her until she begs to serve her master properly?"

The men cheered and waved their arms in agreement. Deborah tried to lift her hands from the ground as the men's feet stamped around them and she coughed and choked as dust was kicked up into her face.

Saab flexed the cane as she pressed it against Chrissie's back.

"Very well." Saab bent her face to Chrissie's ear, kissing it as she whispered quietly. "I want to hear you beg."

Saab stood back and laid the cane against Chrissie's taut buttocks. She smoothed its thin edge across Chrissie's skin, leaving a white mark where it was pressed. She ran it back up across the small of Chrissie's back then onto her shoulders, touching each one in turn before resting it against the side of her neck. She lifted Chrissie's tousled hair with the tip and twirled it in a knot then suddenly snatched it away and drew it back behind her head.

Chrissie turned her head slightly and looked back and Deborah saw the fear in the eyes as the cane came down.

Whack!

Chrissie's body tightened against its bonds as the cutting cane fell across her buttocks. She cried out and Deborah

209

saw spit spraying from her mouth.

Saab drew the cane back leaving a thin red stripe across Chrissie's pale skin. Deborah saw Chrissie's buttocks relax then tense again and she watched her closing her hands into fists as the cane came down again.

Whack!

Chrissie screamed loudly as the cane cut another bright red stripe across her buttocks. Deborah's stomach filled with fear as she heard Chrissie's high-pitched scream and she pulled against the collar at her neck and dug her hands into the dusty ground to try and pull herself forward.

Whack!

The cane came down again and Chrissie let out another piercing screech. The crowd of men shouted loudly and Deborah pulled harder on her leash, pushing her knees into the ground and digging her toes into the dusty soil.

Whack!

The cane cut another line across Chrissie's buttocks and Deborah watched her fingers stretching out in agony as she twisted against the ropes at her wrists and the straps around her ankles.

Saab ran the tip of the cane up between Chrissie's shoulder blades and Deborah listened to Chrissie's desperate gasping as she fought to tense herself for another blow.

Whack!

The cane cut across Chrissie's back and, when Saab pulled it back, it left a harsh red line that ran from shoulder to shoulder. Deborah pulled harder, and dribbled from her open mouth as she strained to move forward.

Whack! Whack! Whack!

Chrissie screamed with every blow until Deborah saw her outstretched fingers slowly curling up and her hands dropping loosely against the tight-pulled ropes at her wrists.

Saab screeched at Chrissie.

"Are you ready bitch? Are you ready to please your master?"

210

Chrissie's head fell forward. She tried to speak but could not make a sound.

"I did not hear you bitch!"

Deborah pulled frantically against her lead and, as the crowd jostled around her, the boy holding her let go. She crawled forward, dodging the men's stamping feet until finally she emerged from amongst them.

Chrissie blubbered a few words, but they were weak and pathetic.

"I can't stand any more. Please ... "

Deborah crawled towards her and looked up at Saab.

"She can't take any more. Please, please stop ... "

Saab's face reddened with anger and she held the cane above Deborah threateningly. Deborah shrank back on her hands and knees and waited for the cane to fall but Saab held back.

"You want to save your little friend do you bitch?" Saab pulled the cane back and Deborah flinched. "Well, perhaps you can. Yes, perhaps if you are a good little bitch, perhaps you can." Saab parted her legs, pulling her long, black dress tightly against the outsides of her thighs. "Crawl between my legs bitch. Perhaps if you can distract me I will not want to flog your little friend so hard."

Deborah glanced at Chrissie as she hung on her bonds with her head held forward and spit running in a stream down onto the ground. She crawled forward between Saab's legs.

"That's right bitch. Now take my mind off your little friend."

Deborah craned her neck back and looked up the insides of Saab's thighs. A tight, black thong was pulled between her legs and Deborah could see the mound of flesh that was drawn within the thin, narrow gusset. She reached her head up and felt the heat from Saab's thighs as they pressed against the sides of her cheeks then she stretched up further until her lips touched the tight, filmy material that covered the flesh of Saab's cunt.

Deborah licked across the material and, as she tasted the salty moisture from Saab's cunt, she felt a thrill of nervous excitement running into her own hips. She licked her tongue out and laid it flatly across the material then dragged it forward until she felt the hard bulge of Saab's clitoris pulsating between the covered flesh at the front of her crack.

Suddenly she heard Chrissie cry out as Saab brought the cane down hard across her red-striped back.

Whack!

"I want it licked bitch! I want to feel your tongue against my flesh! Pull my panties away!"

Deborah reached her hands up the insides of Saab's thighs and took hold of the edges of the thin material, already soaked by the spit from her lapping tongue.

"Not like that bitch! With your teeth!"

Deborah dropped her hands obediently and took the material between her teeth. She bit into it and, as she pulled it away, she felt the hot flesh of Saab's cunt exposed against her lips. She bit harder and pulled more and, as the material peeled away from Saab's wet flesh, Deborah bit into it harder and ripped at it until it tore. The torn material hung on the thin edges of the thong and Deborah reached her tongue up and laid it flatly across the swollen flesh of Saab's wet, outer labia. She tasted the salty moisture on her tongue and let it drain to the back of her throat.

"Lick it deeply bitch! Lick it deeply or your little friend will get some more!"

Deborah plunged her tongue between the wet flesh and licked along the inside edges, prising the inner folds back and exposing the entrance to Saab's dripping vagina.

"Stick it in bitch!"

Deborah sank her tongue in deeply, tasting the sweet flow of moisture that ran from it as she sucked it over her tongue and swallowed it eagerly. She pressed her nose against the front of Saab's crack and felt the pulsating clitoris beating and throbbing against her flaring nostrils. Deborah reached down and stretched her hands between her own legs, pressing the tips of her fingers against the swelling edges of her cunt, opening them and probing inside.

She opened her mouth wide and sucked at Saab's flesh. She moved her head sideways across Saab's swollen labia, rubbing the wetness that ran from them across her cheeks until it dribbled down and stuck to her tangled hair. She buried her face as deeply as she could into the warm, wet flesh and ran her fingers deeply into her own cunt as she squeezed the throbbing tip of her engorged clitoris, pinching it hard and pulling at it to make it grow harder.

She felt Saab dropping her hips lower and she sucked harder, licking her tongue in as deeply as she could and straining to lap up all the moisture that ran so freely from the fleshy folds. She felt Saab tensing herself and she sucked harder, licking her wildly and probing her deeply, with a building desperation to draw Saab's orgasm onto her aching tongue.

Suddenly, Saab pulled away and left Deborah on her knees, her hands between her own writhing legs and her still lapping tongue hanging out of her wet mouth.

"Bitch! Bitch!"

Saab pulled the cane back and brought it down onto Chrissie's back.

Whack!

Chrissie moaned and Deborah fell back startled and afraid.

"You want to feel yourself do you bitch?" She turned to the crowd of men. "Look, the bitch wants to feel herself! Look at her feeling her cunt. Bitch!" The men crowded around. "Show them bitch. Show them your cunt. Show them how you are feeling it. Give them some pleasure. Make them come. Yes, make them all come or it will be the worse for your little friend."

Deborah felt the heat of the men's bodies as they gathered around her. Her fingers were still inside the wet folds of her cunt and, as she felt the glare of their staring eyes, she lay back on the dusty ground and opened her legs for them to see.

"Yes, show them your lovely little cunt bitch. Make them come and listen for the sound of my cane across your little friend's back if you fail to please any of them."

Deborah lay in the dusty ground and prised wide the outer leaves of her cunt. The men jostled to get closer and pushed at each other and she felt suffocated by them as they leant over her and pawed her. But her exposure and humiliation caused a thrill to shoot through her stomach and, as she pinched her engorged clitoris tightly between her grasping fingers, she felt the wave of excitement running down into her hips and across the fleshy edges of her splayed open cunt.

One of the men pulled up his robe and knelt across her chest.

Saab drew the cane back threateningly behind Chrissie. "Here's your first bitch. And make it good or your little friend gets more."

The man took his hard cock in his hand and held it above Deborah's breasts. He pulled the skin up and down the veiny shaft and the engorged glans swelled and throbbed. Deborah stared up at it and, as she watched his balls hanging down loosely in their fleshy sack and the veins pulsating on the heavy shaft, she drove her fingers deeper into her throbbing cunt.

She raised her chest, lifting her hard nipples towards his cock as she squeezed her breasts together with her arms. The man pulled his hand up and down his cock and Deborah watched his hard, engorged glans swelling more each time he brought his encircling fingers up to behind its wide-flanged edge. She delved her fingers deeply into her cunt and squeezed her upper arms tightly against the sides of her breasts, lifting them and offering them to be covered in his spunk.

Whack!

Deborah's ears filled with the slashing sound of the cane as it came down across Chrissie's buttocks.

"I said make him come bitch! Make him come!"

Whack!

The cane came down again and Deborah flinched with the noise it made and the picture she had in her mind of the cutting stripes it laid across Chrissie's taut buttocks.

She opened her mouth and lifted it towards the end of the man's cock.

"In here! In here!" she shouted frantically. "Stick it in here!"

He moved higher across her chest, dropping the full weight of his heavy balls across her breasts and offered the tip of his cock to her open mouth.

"Yes, stick it in. Stick it in my mouth. Let me suck it! Let me suck it!"

Deborah licked her tongue out at it, poking the tip into the dilating hole at its end and lapping at it hungrily.

"Stick your cock in my mouth. Wank it over my tongue and let me suck your spunk down my throat."

The man pulled his hand along the length of his cock and she felt a dribble of spunk then he held the throbbing shaft tightly and his spunk shot from the end of his cock and splashed stickily across her stretched-out tongue.

She wrapped her mouth around the end and sucked frantically, drawing the creamy liquid out and swallowing it as fast as she could get it. Then she heard another lacerating blow from the cane.

Whack!

She raised herself higher as she heard Chrissie screeching and she pulled the end of the still pulsating cock as far back into her throat as she could. She blubbered and choked as the spunk filled her mouth and she delved her fingers deeply into her cunt as she felt the heat inside increasing and the wetness from it flowing across her hands.

Whack!

She heard another blow and reared up until the end of the throbbing cock closed her gulping throat. Her head was spinning and her ears were drumming but she could hear Saab screaming at her.

"More bitch! More!"

Deborah pulled her head away from the man's cock and pushed him off. He fell to one side and she sat up on her elbows and opened her legs as wide as she could.

"Another! Give me another!"

Another man straddled her and, as he held out his cock above her face, for a moment, she saw the flash of a red robe and thought it was Jabari. Perhaps he had escaped from Theron's clutches and had come to save her? She looked up at him, thinking that he would smile down at her and whisper that she was safe but she saw it was not him and, without a second thought, lurched forward and took the cock into her spunk-smeared mouth. She sucked frantically, running her lips along its throbbing shaft and licking at the pulsating veins that beat along its length. She felt it filling and swelling and drove herself onto it and gulped at it as it finished.

Her mouth filled with spunk and she dribbled it down her chin as she fought to swallow. Then she heard the cane again and, as its noise filled her with desperation, she pulled back and shouted for more.

Another cock was driven into her mouth, then another as each man took his turn and filled her mouth with hot spunk. She kept screaming for more and each time she heard Saab bring down the whip on Chrissie's buttocks she was filled with a frantic anxiety for more. Her cunt ached and she held her legs wide and shouted for them to fill it.

"Stick your cocks in here. I want fucking as well!"

She heard the cane again as she took two massive cocks into her mouth and one inside her burning cunt. She raised herself up against them, tightening herself around them and squeezing them tight until they swamped her with gushes of creamy spunk but still she was not satisfied.

The sound of the whacking cane and the scent of the spunk in her mouth was driving her into a frenzy. She wanted the cane as well. She wanted to be fucked and wanked over but she wanted to be beaten and thrashed. Her cunt was hot and overflowing with spunk and she could feel the pressure of her orgasm building up in her veins, but she knew she could not finish until she felt the cuts of the cane across her body.

A huge spurt of spunk was emptied across her neck and breasts as she turned on her side and clawed her way across the dusty ground towards the sound of the whacking cane.

Whack!

She could hardly see through her bleary eyes but she kept moving forward, drawn to the cracking sound of the cane as it cut into Chrissie's flesh.

Whack!

Deborah pulled herself across the ground as two men chased her. They grabbed her ankles and started wanking over her back but still she clawed her way forward in the dirt.

Whack!

She reached out and clutched hold of Saab's ankle as Saab brought the cane down across Chrissie's buttocks with another sickening blow.

Whack!

Deborah reached up Saab's calf and hung onto her leg desperately as Saab wielded the cane again.

"Please, I need it. Please beat me. Please, I need beating ... "

Whack!

The cane fell across Chrissie's back but this time she did not yell out. Deborah sensed Chrissie's hopelessness and clung to Saab's leg as she begged to take her place.

"Please, give it to me, please ... "

Saab looked down at her and sneered.

"Bend over bitch!"

Deborah got onto her knees and knelt before Saab. Her heart raced and the veins in her neck pounded as she heard the cane swishing back behind Saab's shoulder. She tensed herself and felt the heat of her orgasm streaming through her hips as she squeezed her thighs together and tensed herself.

Whack!

The cane came down across her buttocks and her orgasm was released. It flooded through her, drowning her in pleasure as she dropped forward in a sudden, convulsive spasm of ecstasy.

Whack!

The cane came down again and her orgasm ran like a massive tide. Her head spun and she reared back like a whipped horse then fell forward again, shuddering and shaking as the fit set her body jerking and shaking in a delirium of joy.

Even though Saab kept bringing the cane down across her buttocks and back, Deborah did not feel the blows. She felt herself pulled around the dirty ground and she felt cocks pushing themselves into her cunt and anus and she sucked the ones that were forced into her mouth.

Clouds of dust billowed around her as they dragged her from one side of the square to the other and she felt the heat of the men's bodies as they caned her and drove her on her hands and knees from one to the next. and when she was lashed with a rope she lay on her back and opened her legs so that she could take it fully across her swollen cunt.

She did not see Chrissie cut down from her bonds and she did not hear Saab's last orders as she instructed the men to stretch out Deborah's arms and tie her up under an archway so that anyone that chose to could fuck her or wank over her.

Deborah hung hopelessly on the tight ropes with spunk dribbling from her mouth and cunt. It ran over her chin, trickled across her breasts and dripped down the insides of her thighs. A man came to her in the darkness and licked her cunt then, later, another stood behind her and fucked her in the anus, filling it with his spunk as his cock swelled and throbbed

218

against her dilated anal ring.

As it got darker, she felt cold and began to shiver but as her limbs trembled she realised that she was also shivering with fear. It was as though she had suddenly realised how degraded she had become, how eager for humiliation and how desperate to be made to feel so dirty and shamed. She felt like a used slut. She could hear herself begging for more punishment, pleading for cocks to fill her mouth and cunt and she shook all over in disbelief at what she had come to. Yet, as she shivered and felt the spunk dribbling from her anus, she also felt the thrilling heat of excitement burning into her hips and again swelling the sore edges of her distended, dripping cunt.

Suddenly, she felt hands on her shoulders and opened her eyes wide. It was Gross! He cocked his head from side to side and pawed at her arms and breasts then he jumped back and pushed his hands under his armpits.

"No, Gross must not touch again."

Deborah's closed her gaping mouth and tasted spunk on her tongue.

"Please, Gross, please take me back to the cage."

He reached forward nervously and undid the ropes at her wrists. She fell forward and he caught her in his arms. She felt his heart pounding and clutched onto him tightly. He pushed her back and untied her ankles then lifted her up in his arms and carried her back through the dark passageway and into the huge hall. He let the cage down on its heavy chain, opened the door and laid her on the floor.

Her head spun as she lay against the hard bars then she thought of being beaten and straight away felt her heart quicken. She thought of Saab's cane lashing across her buttocks and she felt the heat building in her cunt. She imagined again the flailing ends of the rope tangling around her hips and burning her skin and she felt the pressure of her engorging labia as they swelled around the entrance to her vagina. She pictured her back covered in red stripes from the sharp whip and her stomach surged with a wave of excitement and she knew she could not hold it back. Her need for pain had taken her over. She did not want anything unless it was accompanied by the delights of pain and humiliation. She wanted beating, she wanted fucking and she wanted humiliating and she also wanted the unfathomable pleasure of knowing that her suffering would never stop.

Gross reached into the cage and laid his hand across her breast. He took her nipple between his splayed-out fingers and tightened then around it.

"Little slave want Gross to squeeze?"

"Yes, as hard as you can. And please don't stop. Don't ever stop."

CHAPTER 15

For the next few days Deborah was left locked in the cage. Once she was brought food and once the veiled women came and took her away for washing. She woke up one night and thought she heard Gross creeping through the hall towards her but when she peered into the darkness she could only see a young boy carrying a silver tray.

She slept fitfully, sometimes dreaming of being free, sometimes of being in the limousine with Chrissie and sometimes of being punished as she begged for more. Once she woke up covered in sweat and shivering with fear but she plunged her hands between her legs and thought of ways that Theron could order her to be punished and she fell back to sleep.

The idea of escape now seemed impossible and she felt resigned to her captivity. The idea filled her with fear, yet, at the same time, when she thought about it, her heart quickened and images of the suffering she might be subjected to caused her labia to moisten and swell. One night she thought of Gross pinching her nipples and squeezing her labia between his fingers and she wrapped her legs around one of the iron bars and pulled herself up and down it until she finished. Later that night she dreamed of Theron escorting her through the market and selecting silver trinkets for her to try on and when she opened her eyes she saw him standing below the cage as it swung slowly on its heavy chain.

"Hello, little slave. I have missed you. What have you been doing? Nothing bad I hope?" He walked over to the ornate chair and slumped down with his hands on the carved arms. "Let the cage down! Let me see my little slave."

The cage dropped to the floor and some of the men opened the heavy door. Deborah clung to the bars too frightened to move. She did not want to leave the safety of the cage and, when they reached in and tried to pull her out, she curled up to stop them grabbing hold of her. The men prodded her with canes and the tips dug into her skin but still she clung on, locking her fists around the hard bars and tightening her elbows against her chest. One of them grabbed her and pulled at her and when another brought his cane down across the side of her legs, she lost her grip and they dragged her out.

Theron got up from the huge chair.

"Come, my little slave, don't be frightened," he said as he patted her head. "Now, on your hands and knees and follow me. Here, let me clip your collar around your neck so that I can lead you."

She felt tired and confused but his orders excited her and she raised her head and extended her neck for the collar. He pulled it softly around her throat then yanked it tightly against the buckle. She could think about nothing else but serving him. It was as if that was her only purpose in life and she welcomed the secure feel of the collar around her neck and the protection that her controlling master afforded her. As he turned and walked before her, the hem of his blue and silver robe skimmed across the marble tiled floor and she was mesmerized by the colourful swirling of the fine cloth. She crawled behind him as the leather leash dangled loosely from his hand and hung in a loop beneath her neck. There was no need to pull her, her only desire was to follow.

He led her into the market place and walked slowly from stall to stall looking absently at pieces of jewellery and small, decorated pots. Deborah crawled at his heels, following him when he moved on and waiting obediently when he stopped. She watched for him to start walking and moved straight away so that he did not have to pull on her lead. She measured her pace to fit his and hoped he was pleased with her obedience.

As she crawled, naked and exposed between the crowds of people, she felt ripples of excitement running through her. She lifted her bottom high so that any men who wanted to could stare between her buttocks and see her anus and cunt. She knew that, in the end, she would want Theron to punish her, but the thrill of being led about so publicly was enough to satisfy her for the moment. Even if her master decided not to punish her for a long time she knew that Gross would come and service her with the pain she needed to stem her frustration at not being with her master.

Theron talked to a man at one of the stalls and the man pointed at Deborah and laughed. Deborah felt another thrill of excitement at being humiliated by their mocking and lifted her bottom higher. The man laughed again and when he asked Theron something Theron nodded.

"Suck him little slave. Suck him because I tell you."

Deborah did not hesitate. She reached up her still shackled wrists and ran her hands up the inside of the man's robe. She held his heavy balls in her hands and squeezed them lightly then reached up to the base of his thick, flaccid cock. She lifted it and felt it weight before encircling it with her fingers and drawing the loose skin forward along its length. She held it against her lips then placed her mouth around its end and sucked at the folded skin of his foreskin. She felt his cock thickening and lengthening and, as she ran her tongue around the soft folds of skin at its end, she felt his swelling glans emerging from its fleshy cover. She pressed her fingers down to the base of his shaft and, as it grew harder, she licked the throbbing glans as it engorged and filled her mouth.

Suddenly she felt a snatch on her leash and her mouth was pulled away. She held onto the cock in her hands but Theron snatched the leash again and dragged her back to his side. She felt guilty for making him pull her lead a second time and she pressed herself against the side of his leg to show him that she was sorry for resisting him. The man nodded to Theron and they both laughed then Theron flicked lightly at Deborah's lead and led her to another stall.

She could still taste the musky scent of the man's cock in her mouth as she crawled forward obediently with the leash hanging loosely from her neck. A sudden wave of excitement passed through her stomach as she realised that she was not being dragged or forced to crawl but that she was crawling because the only thing she could think of was pleasing her master. She hoped he would ask her to suck another cock or get someone to wank into her mouth and splash spunk across her tongue. She raised her head and dropped her jaw, showing him her tongue and how she wanted it washed down with spunk but he took no notice of her. She looked up at him appealingly, poking her tongue out as far as she could and his ignnoring her filled her with more excitement as she felt completely humiliated and worthless.

He walked over to some heavy doors in a large wall, motioned for someone to open them and, as they swung open, he walked inside. She crouched on all-fours and watched him disappear into the darkness of the building. She sensed her nipples hardening as she realised that even though he was not there to hold her lead she was still obeying him. She would wait there as long as he wanted or, even if he had forgotten about her, she would wait for as long as it took for him to think of her again. Even if he forgot about her and never returned she would still wait and still be thrilled by being his slave.

He re-appeared and beckoned her with his finger. She crawled forward, her knees covered in dust and her hair hanging down over her face as men gathered around her and taunted her.

"Come little slave. I would like you to see my other little friends."

It was dark inside and, to start with, Deborah could hardly see anything. As her eyes slowly became used to the light, she saw that they were in a huge, low roofed and heavy-beamed building. She looked around anxiously. Dozens of women were chained and tied or hung up around its edges. She drew back in fear but he pulled her forward as he walked down the middle of the rows of women.

"Ah, my little friends. My dear little friends."

He stopped and Deborah stopped as well when she felt the leash go slack and hang in a long curl down to the floor. A woman was bent face-forward over a trestle, her arms and legs pulled down tightly at its sides and her wrists and ankles secured by leather thongs to iron rings fixed to the floor. A naked man behind her was fucking her. He turned to Theron and drew his cock from the woman's cunt. It stood out, thick and glistening with her moisture. He looked down at Deborah.

"When will this beauty be available Theron?"

Theron laughed and tugged on her lead.

"A little while yet."

He bent down to Deborah and ran his fingers across her open lips. She knew he sensed her thoughts and parted her lips so that his fingers ran inside them.

"Very well," he said, "you may suck him."

She crawled to the man and took his weighty cock between her lips. She tasted the woman's juices on his throbbing glans and ran her tongue along its underside as she pulled it in further. She felt the veins throbbing as she took it to the back of her throat and when she gulped onto it she felt it thickening and pulsating with the surge of his spunk.

Theron grabbed her hair and pulled her away. Spit dribbled from her mouth as she licked her tongue out towards the throbbing cock but when her master snatched her lead and walked on she followed him obediently.

She crawled past the ranks of women. One was pulled against the wall on chains and was being thrashed by a huge black man, another was hanging upside down by her ankles as a man licked her splayed-out cunt. Two women had their heads in barrels and were being fucked from behind. Theron stopped occasionally and looked at the women. If they saw him they dropped their heads as though they were too ashamed or too frightened to meet his gaze. A young woman was being driven forward on her knees by a man with a whip. She fell on the floor at Theron's feet but he ignored her, dropped Deborah's leash and walked to the other side of the huge room.

The woman turned her head to the side. It was Asia! She looked pale and drawn and spit ran amongst the caked mud that stuck to her anxious face. She gasped for breath as she stared into Deborah's eyes.

Deborah glanced around quickly, worried in case Theron saw her, but he was too far away.

"Asia, are you alright?" Asia looked frightened and lifted her head slightly but did not speak. "Asia, have you seen Chrissie? Is she here?"

Asia's eyes widened as slowly she opened her spit-smeared mouth.

"Don't talk to me. Please don't."

"Chrissie, have you seen her? I need to know she is safe."

"Don't trust the bitch. Don't trust the bitch. You must not - "

Suddenly, the man who had been driving Asia whacked her across the buttocks with his whip and she screamed out in pain. He whacked her again, then pulled her up onto her knees and drove her away from Deborah.

Theron came back and Deborah hung her head, Asia's

words still ringing in her ears and sending waves of confusion and anxiety through her stomach. He lifted the lead, led her to the far end of the room and stopped.

"Look up my little slave."

She raised her head and saw the cage hanging from a heavy chain. It was empty and swung slowly in the dim light.

Theron laughed then led her back outside, handed her lead to one of the boys and strode back under the archway.

The boy yanked on her lead and pulled her back to the cage. She crawled inside and crouched against the bars as it was hauled back up on its heavy chain.

The next day she was pulled out again and taken away by the women to be washed. When they led her back into the long, marble pillared hall she was made to stand in front of Theron's ornate chair.

Two figures stood in the shadows behind him. One stepped forward, it was Saab. The other hung behind a pillar but, when she stepped forward and brushed back her long, black hair, Deborah shrank back shocked.

Chrissie looked radiant. A long, black dress hung from her shoulders and her hair fell loosely in soft curls about her face. Her skin was smooth and her nails were painted with a shiny, red varnish. She smiled broadly at Deborah and her white teeth flashed between her full, sensual lips. She took Saab's hand and walked lazily down the smooth, sparkling steps.

Chrissie had that same haughty look of confidence that Deborah had seen when they had met Gross in the alley. Deborah realised now why he had been so frightened of her. He had known that Chrissie was not Deborah's friend. That was why he had tried to get Deborah away from her. She thought he had been frightened and confused but all the time he had been trying to save her. Her heart sank as she realised how she had not trusted him and that her lack of faith had surely sentenced him to more terrible punishment.

As Chrissie and Saab approached Deborah, Chrissie let go of Saab's hand and dropped her long fingers loosely onto Saab's shoulder. Saab patted them and they both giggled and pushed their heads together in friendship.

Chrissie stroked back her long, black hair and leant against Saab.

"Deborah, what an entertainment you have been. Theron is so considerate to us. He always tries to fulfil our wishes." She laughed and kissed Saab fully on the lips. Saab reached up and wound her fingers into Chrissie's hair as she drew her closer.

Deborah remembered the woman with Saab on the dockside: the same dark hair, the same embrace. Then her dream came flooding back into her confused mind. As she watched Chrissie pressing her full lips against Saab's she remembered how she had dreamed of being with Chrissie in the back of the car. She recalled the warm feeling she had of their friendship and then the terrible realisation of treachery and the horror of being taunted as she had been flung out into the gutter. The image faded but, as Chrissie released Saab and they both turned back to Deborah, she felt the same anxiety in her stomach as she heard again the mocking laughter of her cruel tormentors.

Saab pointed at her.

"Oh my dear Chrissie, I think she is surprised. What a stupid little bitch she is."

Deborah looked down ashamed and embarrassed as Chrissie broke away from Saab and turned back to Deborah.

"We have both so much enjoyed watching you suffer and cry out and we have laughed at how you have unwittingly given me all the pleasure I have wanted. Yes, what a stupid bitch you are."

Deborah looked up meekly, hoping that it was not true.

"Chrissie, what are you saying?"

"I'm saying you're a stupid bitch. A really stupid

bitch. Did you honestly think I was interested in you for any other reason than my own pleasure?"

"Chrissie, oh Chrissie, I thought - "

Chrissie swung around to Theron. "Oh, Theron! Darling master Theron. Please can we have another one? Please can we have a new one to play with?"

Theron smiled as he walked around Deborah.

"Of course my dear, but be patient, we have not finished with this one yet. But yes, when you have had enough of her we will send her to join the others and you can have a new one."

Chrissie laughed loudly and ran up to him delighted.

"Oh Theron, you are so good to us. But I think I am bored with her now."

Deborah could hardly believe what was happening but, as Saab glanced across to her and smirked and, as Chrissie clutched her arm around Theron's neck and kissed him on the cheek, she realised that she had been cruelly deceived. All her suffering had been just a game to them. Chrissie was not her friend but one of her tormentors. There was no escape for her now. The cage would be her only time to rest and she knew that her desire for punishment and humiliation would never allow her to stay inside it for too long. All that lay ahead of her was more pain and suffering.

"Oh, don't disappoint her my dear Chrissie. Give her some final lashes before you finish with her. It's up to you how many of course, but make them count, I want to hear how much she enjoys them." Chrissie smirked and stepped forward but Theron suddenly held her back. He bent his face to Deborah's ear.

"What a foolish little slave you have been. And how you treated poor Gross. What trouble you have got him into."

Deborah shuddered as he mentioned Gross's name. She felt ashamed of how she had not trusted him. But he would come to her again. She knew that. He would come to her again when she was locked in her cage and then, she thought, she

228

could still make it up to him no matter how much he had suffered on her behalf. At least she had Gross. Yes, faithful Gross, her secret lover, would seek her out and satisfy her.

"And, my little slave, don't expect to see your poor friend Gross again. No, poor Gross has been bad, of course you know that. Yes, very bad. How naughty you were to try and get him to help you escape. Of course I punished him for that, and he was sorry, but when I found out he had been visiting you. Oh dear, that was too much. It was very bad of you to lead him on like that. Poor Gross. No, I'm afraid he's had to leave. Oh dear, does that make you sad? You think he will be back? No, I'm afraid not. No, this time poor Gross will never come back. Never."

Deborah's heart sank and tears welled up into her eyes.

Saab laughed loudly as Chrissie lifted a short leather whip and held it above Deborah. Deborah felt giddy and confused and started shivering. Perhaps this was just a trick or a game? Of course, Theron must be forcing Chrissie to play this part before he punished her? She could not be so cruel. And he was lying about Gross. It could not be true that he would never come back. No, it was all a lie, a terrible lie ... But, as Deborah looked up at Chrissie appealingly, she could see straight away that it was no trick, no game, no lie.

"I thought you were my friend, I thought - "

Her bleating was silenced as the whip fell across her back and her words were replaced with the piercing screams of her exquisite agony as her mind filled with terrifying and delightful images of what lay ahead at the hands of her cruel tormentors.

As she screamed loudly, and Chrissie drew the whip back and flicked it in her hand before bringing it down again, Deborah was unaware of the commotion outside Theron's stronghold. When the whip fell again and she screeched with renewed agony, she could not imagine that Jabari, free from Theron's clutches and with his own band of greedy followers, was already outside the city gates determined to crush the empire of the avaricious Theron.

And here is the opening of next month's title "BUSH SLAVE 2, Lisa's Torment" by Lia Anderssen.

Chapter 1

The interior of the long, low limousine was cool, the efficient airconditioning keeping at bay the sultry heat of the African night. The expensive-looking car purred smoothly through the streets, the driver doing his best to dodge the numerous potholes.

Every now and again the black livery would be illuminated by one of the few street lights that still functioned in the neglected streets, and occasionally a pedestrian would appear, his or her dark skin illuminated by the powerful headlights of the vehicle. Each one of these walkers would shrink back immediately into the darkness at the sight of the vehicle, bowing deferentially as it passed.

The windows of the car were tinted a dark grey, so that, even with the soft lighting inside, it was almost impossible to distinguish its occupants. Anyone seeing them, though, would have almost certainly raised an eyebrow. They were, indeed, an unusual trio.

There were three of them, two men and a young girl. The men sat opposite one another in the spacious cabin, leaning back in their leather seats. Onewas white, a thin-faced individual with cruel lips and deep-set eyes. The African oppositehim was grossly fat, the buttons of his shirt straining to hold it together as he lolled back in his seat, sweat trickling down his face.

It was the third occupant of the vehicle, though, that was most likely to hold the attention of anyone seeing her. Small and slim, the lovely young white girl knelt on the floor between the men. In contrast to their lounge suits, the petite beauty wore only a thin, ragged T-shirt that came just as far as her waist, leaving the lower half of her body completely nude. The T-shirt itself was barely adequate to contain her beautifully shaped breasts These were perfectly rounded, and they pressed against the threadbare material, the erect nipples clearly outlined.

As the vehicle bumped along, the two men spoke in low tones to one another. The girl, however was otherwise occupied, and she seemed to pay scant attention to what was being said. This was hardly surprising, since her attention was concentrated on the massive black rod that jutted from the fat mans open fly. As the car bumped along she sucked hard at it, her long, dark hair spilling into his lap as she worked her head back and forth, allowing his penis to slip in and out of her mouth, her pretty, kissable lips pursed about its girth. Seemingly oblivious to her surroundings she fellated him energetically, one hand caressing his balls whilst the other gripped his shaft, masturbating him with firm strokes.

The man grunted his pleasure as the pretty twenty-year-old sucked him. His companion sat back in his seat, casting his eyes over the girls behind,the otherwise perfect white flesh of which bore an unusual mark, the shape of a leaping lion about an inch across. This was no tattoo or birthmark, though. Close inspection would reveal that it was a brand, burned permanently into the tight, firm skin of her behind, a permanent indicator of her previous experiences.

But the unusual nature of the young girls private parts did not end there. Crouching as she was, with her legs spread apart, an object could be clearly seen gleaming between her thighs. It was a ring, a thick, shiny brass ring, and it was attached to her through her pierced sex lips, the ring itself closed so that no join could be seen, making it as permanent a feature as the brand on her behind.

The beautiful young white girl was aware of nothing, however,but the thick black cock in her mouth. She moved her face back and forth with apparent enthusiasm, coating the shaft with a sheen of gleaming saliva, her tongue darting over the mans bulbous glans as she concentrated on bringing him pleasure. She looked neither right nor left, her fingers ma-

232

nipulating his heavy testicles as she sensed the tension in him increase.

All at once the man came, filling her mouth with hot, sticky semen, her pretty mouth struggling to contain the onslaught of fluid that gushed into her as she gulped his seed down, fearful of staining his suit by allowing even a drop to escape. For a few seconds it seemed that her efforts would be in vain as spurt after spurt of his sperm spat from him. Then the tide of spunk began to decrease and she seemed to regain control, swallowing hard as she continued to suck at him.

At last the flow ceased altogether, and she was able to let his rod slip from her lips. She licked it carefully, running her tongue up the length of the shaft, removing all vestiges of his orgasm. Only when he was completely clean did she begin tucking his now deflating organ back into his trousers and zipping them shut. Then she settled back in a kneeling position, sitting down on her ankles, her lovely green eyes cast to the floor.

"You see she is well-trained Mr Mbogu," said the white man.

The fat man smiled. "You were right about that, Bulcher. She certainly knows her place."

"But thats the whole point. She doesnt have a place."

"So what do you want me to do about it?"

"Very simple. You are the Minister for the Interior in Negorvia. That makes you an important man in the government here. You could help me get her registered."

"Ive already explained that such action is most unusual," said Mbogu, stretching back in his seat and placing his large, booted foot on the girls lap.

"I dont see why," replied Bulcher. "After all, the law in this country permits slavery as long as the slave is properly registered."

"And marked."

Bulcher inclined his head. "As you say, properly registered and marked."

The large man shook his head. "Those laws were passed because we are at war with Kombu, in the north. It permits us to enslave any captured Kombians and put them to work for our own war effort, or to sell them to other countries as labourers. It was never meant for the likes of this girl."

"Oh, come on Mr Mbogu," scoffed Bulcher. "Everyone knows the laws purpose is to side-step the Geneva Convention rules on prisoners of war."

Mbogus brow darkened. "You must understand you are in Africa now, Bulcher. We do not always have time for the laws of Europe here. Both the Negorvians and the Kombians have been enslaving their captives since long before the white colonialists came on the scene. We are merely following a tradition."

"Of course, Sir. All Im suggesting is that you follow the tradition in this case."

Mbogu eyed the beautiful youngster kneeling silently before him, his eyes taking in the pale creaminess of her breasts, visible through a large tear in the material of her T-shirt. His gaze dropped down to the thin patch of dark hair that covered her pubis.

"It is a nice idea," he concurred. "But shes not actually a prisoner of war."

"Does the law insist that she should be?"

"No. Not strictly. But all the others registered as slaves are."

"The law is the law," insisted Bulcher. "If it makes no discrimination, then surely neither should you."

"What about international opinion?" asked Mbogu. "You realise that we run the risk of losing our foreign aid?"

"Surely, sir, your government has circumvented such opinionbefore?" said Bulcher quietly. "After all, your country is rich with oil. Such things help. Look at the Middle East."

"Yes, but this case is different. Lets not forget that the girl is British."

A cold smile crossed Bulchers face. "She doesnt need to

234

remain British," he murmured. "She could become a nationalised citizen."

Mbogu raised his eyebrows. "What?" he exclaimed. "Make her Negorvian?"

"Possibly," replied Bulcher. "But why not a Kombian?"

"Are you serious? Make her a Kombian?"

"Certainly. After all, theres no record of how she entered the country."

"Even so, there is no evidence that she came in from Kombu."

"Surely a man in your position could arrange such evidence?"

Mbogu eyed Bulcher. "Hmm," he said thoughtfully. "Its an idea. But why should I?"

"Because I can sell you the weapons secrets from the Bellco corporation. Secrets that will allow you to construct the weapons you need to defeat the Kombians. You know that."

"You're right. We need that information," concurred Mbogu. "But what's your motive? Why are you so keen to have this slut enslaved?"

Bulcher lowered his eyes. "The reasons are personal. They are not important."

"All right. But do you really have the secrets?"

"You've seen the data I've already given you, Mr Mbogu."

"Yes I have. And I must admit that it seems genuine."

"Then the price of the girls official registration as a slave seems a small one."

Bulcher leaned forward in his seat. "Allow that, and I shall enter negotiations about the secrets."

"So if I agree to send her for registration, you'll name a price?"

"I assure you Minister that I shall make my offer during dinner if you give me your word. After all, she'd be just another slave as far as the law defines it."

Mbogu inclined his head. "You are right, I suppose." Once again he allowed his eyes to stray over the submissive young girls form. "It seems a shame to mark that body, though," he said.. "And the mark of a slave must be on view at all times, you know. Thats what the law says."

"I know," replied Bulcher, a sudden gleam appearing in his eyes. "And I have an idea about that. I shall tell you about it at the same time as we discuss the secrets. I think my idea might amuse you."

Mbogu chuckled. "Im sure it will. You are a very interesting man, Bulcher, and one whom I believe I can do business with."

"Then you agree?"

"I agree to discuss it with you. We are nearing the restaurant now, though. What should we do with this whore?"

"I thought we might lock her in the car, Mr Mbogu."

"No. She has no place in here."

For the first time, the beautiful youngster raised her head and gazed at the Minister, her eyes wide at his dismissive words. But there was no comfort in his expression.

"We shall put her out and collect her later," said Mbogu.

Bulcher's eyes narrowed. "Wait a minute..."

Mbogu raised a hand. "You want to make a deal, dont you?"

"Yes but..."

"Then she gets out here. You trust me, dont you Bulcher?"

Bulcher looked at him. "Of course."

"Good." Mbogu tapped on the window that separated them from the drivers compartment. "Stop here!" he ordered.

The limousine glided to a halt and the driver ran round to the rear door and opened it.

"Our passenger is disembarking here," said Mbogu. "We willcollect her later."

"Yes sir."

The driver turned to the girl, who was staring at Mbogu with wide eyes.

"Get out, you."

She opened her mouth as if to say something, then clearly

236

thought better of it. Slowly, she rose from her kneeling position and climbed through the door. The driver eyed her up and down, taking in the creamy whiteness of her bare behind. Then he closed the door.

As the car pulled away from the kerb, Bulcher turned to Mbogu.

"Was it wise to abandon her there?" he asked. "After all, this is a pretty rough part of the city."

"Dont worry," replied the big African. "My people control this area. She will not escape or be abducted. I have patrols of vigilantes who will ensure that she doesnt go far. Meanwhile, they will enjoy having a near-naked white girl to amuse them."

A grim smile spread across Bulcher's features.

"In that case, let's go to dinner," he said.

TITLES IN PRINT

UK £4.99 except *£5.99 --USA $8.95 except *$9.95